NEW S/M

DEATH BY ICE CREAM

A Pismawallops PTA Mystery

Rebecca M. Douglass

D1739016

S

This is a work of fiction. All of the characters, organizations, events and places portrayed in this novel are either products of the author's imagination or are used fictitiously.

ACKNOWLEDGEMENTS

No work of fact or fiction comes into being in a vacuum, and this book is no exception. I would like to thank the members of the long-ago book club who encouraged me to continue writing this book; Lisa Frieden, who has read it more than once and offered invaluable feedback along the way; and Laurie at the library for help with every step from idea to cover, with her unerring eye for good design and bad typos.

Thanks are due also to my editor, Inge Lamboo, without whom this would be a far weaker book. And thanks to the other readers who have offered feedback and encouragement: Jemima, Sue, and Emily.

- 1 -

EVERYBODY WANTS HER GONE

"Dad-blast it, Kitty, *do* something about that woman!"

To emphasize my point, I pounded my fist on the battered and scarred table between us, banging hard enough to make our cell phones jump. My hand stung from the blow, and Kitty Padgett flinched. Her chair scraped as she tried to shift a bit farther from me. Instead of apologizing, although I felt bad for startling her, I glared at our PTA President and waited.

"But—" She waved her hands vaguely. Kitty was my best friend, but I couldn't deny that sometimes she was more mouse than cat. Her lack of spine increased my irritation, so I pushed on.

"If she quits the Yearbook, fine, we'll manage. I'll do it myself it I have to." Everyone gasped, shocked by what I had just said. But it was too late to take it back.

A chance gripe session among friends had morphed into an emergency meeting of the Pismawallops Island High School PTA. We four—Kitty and me, Madeleine Takahira and Carlos Hernandez—had

1

gravitated to the teachers' room to plot damage control, and now I'd put my foot in it. I took a deep breath and stuck to my guns. I didn't like to back down, even from myself. "Letitia LeMoine is boorish, overbearing, and opinionated, and she's alienating everybody in the PTA. Heck, everyone on this Island!"

"She sure is." That was Carlos, our Secretary. We all looked at him and he shrugged. "She tells me I am not smart enough to run the Spring Faire. And that my English is not good enough to be Secretary." Carlos spoke with a slight accent, but his English was better than that of most people who posted opinions on the Internet. "I do not need that crap."

Carlos's complaint unleashed the feelings Maddy had been keeping politely bottled up. Before Kitty could offer Carlos reassurance that his English was quite good enough for us, Maddy was airing her own gripes.

"She thinks I'm no good! She says my bookkeeping is a total mess."

Kitty and I exchanged glances. We'd known Letitia LeMoine's opinion about Maddy's bookkeeping, but hadn't known she'd insulted our Treasurer to her face. Matters were even worse than I'd thought. It didn't matter that Letitia was right about Maddy's financial skills. If anything needed saying, it was Kitty, not Letitia, who should have brought it up. Kitty hadn't, because Maddy knew she had a problem. What on earth was she trying to do, anyway?

"She said she didn't see how anyone could be so incompetent!" Maddy sniffed and swallowed hard. I hoped she could keep her tears under control. Sloppy emotions made me cranky. "I can't help it if I have trouble with numbers," she half wailed. She didn't cry, but it was a close thing. I heard a few more sniffs.

I took a deep breath, tapped into some store of patience I didn't know I had, and reached out a hand. "Okay, Maddy. I'll help you straighten out the books. I just wish you'd come to me sooner." She pulled out a tissue and blew her nose, and pushed her long black hair behind her ears once more. For just a moment, I wondered if there was more bothering her than LeMoine's accusations of incompetence. I dismissed the idea as soon as I'd thought it. Mrs. Loudmouth's bullying was justification enough for tears, at least for someone as sensitive as Maddy Takahira.

"We were just fine until That Woman came along." Maddy's thoughts echoed my own.

"Yeah," Carlos agreed.

"Like I said, Kitty," I began.

Kitty sighed. She knew we were right. She just disliked conflict even more than I did tears. "Okay, okay. You guys are right. But I hate to do it." She eyed me. As her VP, I'm supposed to do whatever needs doing. "Can't you talk to her, JJ?"

"Do you really think that's a good plan?"

"No." She sighed again. Kitty had known me for seven years, ever since I came to Pismawallops Island. She knew tact wasn't one of my strengths. She might even have wondered if it was in my vocabulary. "Okay, I'll talk to her. She really does need to back off and let other people work in their own way."

"Truer words were never spoken," I encouraged. "You're the President. We do not need someone who makes everyone else want to leave."

I must've been a little firmer in tone than I'd realized, because Annette Waverly, the principal, stuck her head in the door just then, an incongruous wrinkle of concern creasing her carefully made-up face.

"Is everything quite all right? I thought I heard someone, ah, yelling?"

Nobody was yelling. I was just being . . . emphatic.

"Everything's fine," Kitty assured her before I

could say anything to further upset the principal's equanimity.

"Okay, then." Ms. Waverly's face reorganized itself into something like a smile. "I'll leave you to your work." She withdrew, closing the door gently, in exaggerated contrast to my banged fist and raised voice.

"Should I have told her about Letitia?" Kitty wanted to know.

We all shrugged. Ms. Waverly was new, and still, in April, something of an unknown quantity. Nor was the Vice Principal, Elvis Fingal, likely to be much use. If he were, it would be the first time.

"I think it would not be helpful," said Carlos. As the school custodian, he was in the best position to know how the principal would react. "It would just upset her. You talk to Ms. LeMoine, Kitty, and it will be okay. You are good with people, you know."

Kitty sighed, unconvinced by the compliment. "If only she'd at least learn to say 'please' and 'thank you.' But there you are. If she did, she'd be someone different, wouldn't she?" Kitty got to her feet. "The Orcaville PTA is not going to kowtow to Letitia LeMoine, even if she *is* from the City, and we're just Islanders." Out here in Puget Sound, Seattle was the Big City, even for those of us up closer to Bellingham.

From what I'd heard, Ms. L. was probably a bit more local than she let on, but I wasn't going to bring that up just now. It was enough that Kitty was ready to stand up and put the woman in her place before she could make a complete mess of our PTA. I just hoped she wouldn't get all huffy and quit the Yearbook, because I really, really did not want that job.

Most Friday afternoons found Kitty and me at the high school, puttering with PTA business and distracting the teachers during their prep periods. Most of the teachers liked us, so it worked out. We gave them the money they needed, and they put up with us.

Friday was also ice cream sale day at Orcaville High. As far as I'd ever been able to learn, Adam and Eve started it. We changed the variety from time to time, but we always sold ice cream. For one thing, we needed the money. For another, outside of football season, it was the most exciting thing happening on Fridays. Often, it was the only thing happening. During football season, the ice cream was usually tops, too. Schools of under 150 students don't field great teams, and ours was no exception. Sports just didn't seem to thrive on our little pile of glacial detritus surrounded by Puget Sound.

That Friday, Kitty and I were lying in wait for Letitia LeMoine, who was due any minute for the after-school ice cream sale, which she had insisted she would run this spring. Kitty had delayed all week, but today she meant to straighten the woman out about her tactlessness. She insisted that when she did, my place was by her side. To demonstrate her own grasp of tact, she did not add, "with your mouth closed." While we waited for the final bell we occupied ourselves with the little chores that never seemed to go away.

"Hand me the checkbook, will you?" I stuck out a hand without looking up from a pile of receipts.

Kitty passed the ledger across the teachers' room table and brushed back her mouse-brown hair. She needed a haircut again, or else to grow it out like Maddy and I were doing. "Well?"

"*Not* well," I sighed. "Letitia is right on this one, blast her. The records are a mess, and it's not clear what's what. We've missed a few bills, but we can still pay those. Assuming we can figure out how much, if anything, we have in the account."

5

"The bank will tell us, I suppose," Kitty consoled me. "Poor Maddy. What on earth possessed us to make her the Treasurer?"

"The fact that no one else would touch the job? I just wish she'd told us she was having so much trouble, before things got into such a mess."

"Letitia has plenty of suggestions about that," Kitty replied.

That didn't sound like her, and made me look up. "What do you mean? Is she accusing Maddy of cooking the books?"

"Well, she didn't come right out and say so. But if you sort through all her innuendos, that's what she meant."

"That must have been what was bothering Maddy so much on Tuesday. I thought she seemed more upset than was justified by hearing she wasn't capable of managing the books." I sighed again. It was becoming a habit, and I made a mental note to stop. Sighs age you, and I'd aged about enough. "But of course Letitia never actually *said* Maddy's stealing. She never *said* that Carlos wouldn't be able to handle the Spring Faire, either. She never does say things straight out."

"But she made herself perfectly clear, and now he doesn't think he can do it. I spent half an hour yesterday convincing him he owed it to himself to prove to her he can," Kitty said.

"I suppose she wants to run it." Part of me wanted to let her try, but reason prevailed. "Kitty, we can't let this go on. You promised to do something, and you really have to."

Now Kitty was sighing. "I know, JJ. But. . ."

"But me no buts, woman," I told her, my voice rising in panic at the thought that Kitty might back down. "You promised—"

My little pep talk was interrupted by the appearance of a head around the door of the teachers' room.

"Mom? Everything okay?" It was Kitty's oldest, Sarah, who shares Kitty's soft curls and pale brown eyes. Seeing it was just us, she went on. "Mom, school's out in ten minutes, and Ms. LeMoine's not here yet. Can I have the keys so we can get things set up for the ice cream?"

Kitty and I exchanged looks.

"See?" I said. "She's full of big ideas, but she can't even show up on time to sell ice cream. I do not want that woman running the Faire. And if we don't do something, she'll drive off everyone else, and we'll be stuck with her, and the whole PTA will collapse." It crossed my mind that she might even drive us away, but I banished the thought. I'd managed seven years as an outsider on Pismawallops Island, and I hadn't done it by giving up. Unfortunately, Letitia LeMoine also seemed to understand tenacity all too well.

While I meditated on the perennial difficulty of finding reliable volunteers, Kitty shrugged and dug in one of the two drawers allotted the PTA. "Where— oh, here is it. I suppose she couldn't be troubled to put it back in the right place." I heard a venomous emphasis on "she" and felt satisfied that Kitty was ready to confront the woman.

She fished a ring with two keys from the jumble in the bottom of the drawer and passed it to Sarah. "Get a couple of kids and pull the ice cream from the freezer. I'll be along as soon as I put this stuff away."

Sarah took the keys and trotted off down the hall. I put the checkbook away and followed, watching with an indulgent smile as the girl stuck her head into one of the classrooms. A moment later, three kids joined her in the hall. I recognized Brian among the faithful. Well, my son is loyal and hardworking, and his grades are good. I didn't have a problem with him missing class a little for a good cause. As for myself, I

7

went to make sure Carlos had set up the tables for the sale.

He had, of course. He was nowhere in sight, but the tables were ready. However much his feelings were hurt, Carlos wouldn't let us down—unlike that pseudo-urban viper who hadn't even bothered to show up.

I had turned to go back to the Teachers' Room when I heard a scream. It took an eternity for me to remember how to breathe. Then, as more shrieks followed, I broke into a run. I can run pretty well, even if I am pushing forty-five, though as a rule I don't move all that fast. But those screams came from the kitchen, where my son was. Where Kitty's daughter was. *Holy crap*, I prayed as I sprinted the length of the lunchroom. *Not the kids.*

I almost collided with Kitty as she burst through the other door. We steadied each other, pushed into the kitchen, and stopped.

Brian, Sarah, and their best friends Justin Green and Madison Takahira—daughter of our either incompetent or unethical Treasurer—pressed back from the open freezer, trying to keep away from whatever was in there, yet unable to tear their eyes from it. They were all yelling, the boys no less than the girls. That alone would have convinced me their horror was real. I stepped forward, curiosity overpowering good sense. My eyes followed the kids' frozen gaze into the chest freezer, which should have been full of boxes of ice cream bars.

There may have been ice cream in the freezer. I couldn't have said. All I saw were eyes and tongue bulging from a purple face. I wrenched my gaze away to survey the rest of the doubled-up corpse of Letitia LeMoine, a gaudy scarf knotted tidily—and tightly—around her throat. Her too-short skirt was rumpled, exposing a doughy thigh, a stain discoloring

8

the fabric. I could smell enough to know what the stain was.

Kitty looked over my shoulder and took in the face, so distorted in violent death as to be scarcely human, took a deep breath to calm herself, and caught the odor even freezing couldn't tame. A moment later she joined a general exodus through the outside door. I imagined them all puking, and cancelled my intention to follow them.

Instead, I took a deep breath, regretted it, stepped back, gulped once or twice, and reached for my cell phone. Then, catching another whiff of the odors of death, and remembering the ice cream, I stepped over to the sink and vomited until nothing more would come. I wiped my sweating face with a damp paper towel, ran water in the sink until the evidence was washed away, and looked around to make sure no one had noticed.

Then I phoned the police. I kept my back to the freezer while I dialed, but I knew what was in there. The image had burned itself into my brain.

Ron Karlson adjusted his hat—not a cop hat, but the marine fuel cap that on the Island fills the place occupied by John Deere caps in Washtucna where I grew up—and looked around the lunchroom, then back at me. I glanced up the few inches to meet his gaze. The face under the cap looked more grey than tan just now. Around the eyes, untouched by any hint of his usual smile, the crow's-feet seemed to have deepened since I last saw the Orcaville police chief.

We stood just outside the kitchen door, where neither of us could see into the freezer. Chief Karlson was a small-town officer, not a big-city cop, and he'd already seen more of the corpse than he wanted. He had confirmed she was dead, even taken crime scene photos with a camera I brought him from the Yearbook supplies. I tried to be helpful, without getting too close to the body. But someone had to do the initial investigation, and it was Ron's job. With just one deputy to help him, pretty much everything on Pismawallops Island was Ron's job.

I'd waited outside the kitchen door, making sure no one else saw the body until Ron got there, while Kitty took the kids somewhere to calm them down. Annette Waverly had tottered around the corner about the time I finished my call, Elvis Fingal trailing behind her. When I explained the situation Ms. Waverly seemed more angry than upset, as though I had deliberately disturbed the perfect operation of her school. I ignored her anger and sent her to announce that there would be no ice cream sale. Fingal had vanished, looking green.

So Chief Karlson and I were alone with the corpse, and I wasn't sure how I felt about that, given what I'd seen.

"Well?" I demanded.

"Well yourself, Ms. MacGregor." He took off his hat and scratched the thick dark hair underneath, then clapped the hat back on and pretended to be helpful. "She's dead. Someone strangled her and stuffed her in your freezer."

Not my freezer, I thought. "Tell me something I don't know."

"Can't." Maybe he was being cantankerous, but I thought he sounded more regretful. Like he wouldn't have minded my help except that it would be against the rules.

"So what do we do now?"

"*I* call the Mainland and see if they'll ship over the coroner and someone to see what the body can still tell us. *You* cancel your ice cream sale and go home."

I had the feeling he was telling me to butt out. Glaring at him, I pointed out, "I'm a bit short of ice

10

cream anyway. The murderer must have removed all thirty boxes to make room. Ninety-three dollars and sixty-four cents worth," I added with some bitterness. There was a good chance Kitty and I would have to pay for that out of our own pockets, given the state of the PTA finances. We'd probably have to toss the freezer, too. I couldn't imagine ever putting food in there again. I pulled myself together; the ice cream wasn't important now. "What I meant was, what do we do about finding the murderer?"

"That's my job. Your job is to explain to the student body why there is no ice cream sale, and then take your son home and hope he's not too traumatized."

I paused a moment at this suggestion that I should just focus on my son, like I needed reminding I was a parent. "Is that all? Just oops, and carry on?" I could feel annoyance turning my face an unbecoming shade of purple, just the shade Brian tells me it gets when I run uphill.

"And then," Ron added, "I start asking questions. Like, who might have wanted her dead?"

"Like who didn't," I retorted before realizing that might not be a tactful response.

He jumped on it. "What do you mean? I thought she was a mainstay of the PTA—and half the other organizations on the Island."

"Ron, do you know what the kids call—called—her?" I kept my attention on a colorful poster touting the virtues of veggies, unwilling to meet his eyes.

"No."

I could feel him looking at me. "'Mrs. Loudmouth.' And do you know where they got the name?"

"Well, now, I think I could guess. From you, maybe?" He crossed his arms, and I looked at him despite myself. He smiled, in a way I didn't much like.

11

"Me, and every other worker in every other enter-prise in this town."

"So you're saying she wasn't so well liked?"

I crossed my own arms. "I'm saying she came on like a Mack truck, bringing in what she called 'up-to-date methods' from the Big City."

The police chief made a face. I'd heard he detested the Bellingham officers who figured they knew more than he did, even if they were half his age and green as the mold in the back of the staffroom fridge. I could believe it. Just because he served on a dinky island in northern Puget Sound didn't mean he was an idiot. I'd always thought he was pretty bright, in fact.

"Huh." He adjusted his hat again. "Guess I'd bet-ter make those calls." He pulled out his cell phone and gazed at the tiny screen without enthusiasm.

"Ahem." A throat being cleared behind us an-nounced the return of Principal Waverly, buttoned up in her narrow skirt and not-too-high heels. She had been busy maintaining calm among the students, who had gotten out of class just in time to see the police arrive. I eyed her crisp, starched blouse and relent-lessly neat blonde hair, and had to stop myself from touching my own flyaway red tangles. I wouldn't even think about the clothes. Some women dress on purpose; those like me just grab the top t-shirt in the pile. I had thought that would change when I grew up, but as soon as I stopped going to an office, I re-verted. I'd begun to lose hope that I'd ever master adulthood.

"You may use my office to telephone," she told the Chief.

Ron nodded. "Good idea." He held out a hand for the key I had collected from Sarah, locked the kitchen, and followed the principal down the hall to the office. I tagged along just far enough behind to avoid notice.

When the two shut her office door I was left standing by the reception desk, feeling foolish and wondering why I didn't do what Ron had told me to: collect my son and go home. Maybe it was because of something else I knew and hadn't mentioned. Evelyn Peabody, the secretary, was giving me odd looks, so I stepped into the hall to do battle with my conscience. Conscience lost. Anyway, Chief Karlson didn't want my input, did he? He'd made that quite clear. So maybe I wouldn't volunteer anything.

I'd been trying to convince myself I was wrong, but I'd recognized that scarf around Letitia LeMoine's neck.

The scarf was mine.

That raised an interesting problem, as a police officer might be forgiven for thinking the murder weapon could belong to the murderer, which in this case it definitely did not. No, I wouldn't bring that up just yet.

When Ms. Waverly and Ron Karlson emerged from the office, I hurried to manufacture a justification for my continued presence in the hall. "Ms. Waverly, has anyone told Chantal?"

The principal looked confused. "Who?"

"Chantal LeMoine. The dead woman's daughter." I tried very hard to be patient. Ms. Waverly turned red and fluttered her hands. Maybe the woman was human after all.

"Dear God! I hadn't realized! You never said who was killed," she accused the Chief. "Oh, the poor girl!" Already she hastened off, wobbling a little despite her allegedly sensible heels—as though any kind of heels could be sensible.

Ron Karlson and I looked at each other. His face was like stone. I could see past his determined lack of expression to the distress he was hiding.

"The coroner is on his way. He should be on the

4:45 ferry, which means we'll have prompt service only three hours after the discovery of the body."

"Not much they can do about that," I commented, hoping to learn what had so upset him. We're on an Island. We don't expect prompt service from the Mainland. "Anyway, at least the body is in the freezer. That should preserve the evidence, right?"

"Maybe, but it's customary to send a crime scene investigator along, too. At least, it used to be. Part of the deal we have with the County. But now they tell me they can't send anyone. Remember the vote last fall? The one where we decided we couldn't afford to keep paying for on-call assistance from the Bellingham police?"

I nodded, knowing where this was going. I also recognized a certain irony: Letitia LeMoine had been one of the strongest voices behind the change. Keep taxes low, keep government out of our lives, and so on.

Ron ranted on. "So they reminded us that we are now on a case-by-case contract, which makes us low priority—to be served when they are not busy with cases in their own jurisdiction." He didn't need to add that any help would also cost money not budgeted by a tight-fisted Town Council.

"You mean we're on our own?" Now I shared his incredulity.

"I mean I am on my own," he corrected. "You, as I believe I mentioned, are just a parent who happened to be around when the body was found." He fixed me with a look that suggested that I might, just *might*, want to get out of his hair before he got to wondering if I had a sinister motive in hanging around the scene of the crime. So much for what I'd thought was a friendship. Apparently that didn't mean much to Ron Karlson when he had work to do.

I knew I was being unfair, but I also knew that I

was getting the bum's rush, and I seethed over it. Somebody murdered a member of my PTA—our PTA—and stuffed her in our freezer (stealing or destroying ninety-three dollars and sixty-four cents' worth of ice cream in the process), and I was supposed to sit back and wait for the local fuzz to do his thing? Not happening.

Oh, I knew there were no flies on Ron Karlson, but that deputy of his—! He had *moss*, he was so slow. The only thing he did quickly was jump to conclusions.

Take, for instance, the time he saw me in my neighbor's field, at eleven P.M., helping deliver a calf. This, I hasten to add, was not my idea. I do know which end of the cow the calf comes from, but I'd had all I wanted of such things as a kid in 4H. But the old man needed help, so I went. That's what you do in a place like the Island, just like back home.

When the deputy happened by, my neighbor had gone off after something or other, so I was alone with the laboring cow. Just as she deposited the slimy calf in my arms and I moved to wrap it in an old towel, up marched Homer Roller (his parents ought to be shot—that name is probably the root of his problems) and accused me of rustling.

I politely expressed my amazement at his conclusion, and he said that I must have wrapped up that calf so I could steal it. About that point old Cal came back and explained, in words of one syllable, that I was helping him. Even then, I'm not sure Homer got it. But he decided that if the cow's owner figured I was okay, it wasn't his business to interfere.

The point being, Homer was no one to have on your side in an investigation. Nor was he anyone I wanted handling traumatized teenaged witnesses, especially if one of those witnesses was my son. And I was heading Ron saying, "I believe Deputy Roller is with the children in the Music Room."

"Homer??!! You've left *Homer* with the kids?" I gave Ron a horrified glare and turned to go. I thought I caught a satisfied look on his face as I left, but I was in a hurry to rescue those poor kids from that certified idiot. Too much of a hurry to stop and consider what the sheriff was up to.

- 2 -

PUTTING THE DEPUTY IN HIS PLACE.

The scene in the music room was pretty much as I had imagined, except that it was all over by the time I got there.

Ready for battle, I practically ran to the free standing "portable" building that housed the band room. About halfway between the courtyard and the gym, it was where the kids had gone to try to recover from their shock. I assumed Homer would try to bully them into confessions, accusations, or whatever, thinking he was going to be some kind of by-glory hero and solve the case by roughing up some traumatized teenagers, and I was right. But I had to find that out later from Brian, because when I got there, Homer was sitting in a corner while across the room Patty Reilly, the music teacher, was serving the kids tea with lots of sugar. She had an electric kettle so she could have tea all winter, to keep from freezing in the uninsulated building, and it came in handy now to help the kids over their shock.

In the middle of the room stood Kitty, with steam billowing from her ears, more or less.

She turned when I came in, stopping me before I could go to Brian. "Glad you came, JJ. Could you

17

find the Police Chief and tell him that we need someone *intelligent*—" her italics were accompanied by a
withering look at Homer—"to talk to these kids before we take them home?"

I never had more respect for Kitty than at that
moment. I scarcely recognized my mousey friend.
Not only had she given Homer Roller holy heck and
made him sit down and shut up, she'd seen what Ron
and I had both missed. At least, I assumed he'd
missed it. Maybe he'd just been getting rid of me.

Anyway, he'd better get statements from the kids
before they went away and started talking and re-
inventing the whole thing. Not from malice, it's just
that once you start talking something over it gets hard
to tell what you actually remember and what someone else suggested. So far, they were still too shocked
and sick to compare notes.

I nodded my agreement to Kitty's suggestion and
turned right around, pausing mid-turn for an assessment of my son, who looked pale but calm. Then I
hurried out before I could be overwhelmed by the
urge to protect the hell out of him. Kitty was doing
just fine on that front. I'd be more useful chasing
down the police chief.

Ron was crossing the courtyard when I came out,
so it seemed he'd also remembered the kids were
witnesses. In fact, he was worried enough to ask me
if I thought Deputy Roller was ruining any chance of
getting usable statements from them.

"I don't know what he might have tried, but you
don't need to worry about him now. Kitty's in there,
and she's shut him down tighter than Scarlett
O'Hara's corset lacings." To my satisfaction, he stared
at me, his mouth falling open in astonishment.

"*Kitty* has? Kitty Padgett?" Ron had known Kitty
far longer than I had.

I nodded.

"Well I'll be damned." He smiled, and for the first time that day I remembered that Ron was a nice man. "I always knew Kitty had some fire in her. Somewhere," he qualified the statement, a bit unbelieving still.

I grinned back at him, but when he went into the music room, I stayed in the courtyard for a minute and my grin faded as my thoughts took their own turn. Just how far had Kitty gone in learning to push back? I knew it was a bit hysterical of me, but all of a sudden I remembered that Kitty had promised to "do something" about Letitia LeMoine. I hadn't thought she'd done anything yet, but what if I was wrong? And who was in a better position to get hold of my scarf?

I didn't care for my train of thought one bit. Kitty was my friend, just about the only one I had. How could I even for a moment think such a thing about her? I pushed the thought aside and went on to the music room. Brian was in there, and he needed his mother. Sure, he was fifteen years old and a long legged five-foot ten. He was still my boy, and when the world was falling apart around him I knew he'd want Mom handy, though I didn't suppose he'd ever say so.

Ron sent Homer out to direct traffic in the parking lot, with instructions to say nothing to anyone. The deputy hitched his paunch into place and strode to the door with an exaggerated swagger. Patty Reilly still presided over the tea, her expression as carefully neutral as the police chief's own. He asked her to wait outside as well, before turning to consider the kids. He knew better than to ask Kitty and me to leave.

The kids needed little urging to tell Ron everything that had happened, as if by turning it into a story they could make it less horrifying. I didn't think they told

19

him much he hadn't already guessed, or learned from me. They had unlocked the kitchen—yes, Sarah was sure the door had been locked—and the freezer, likewise secured. The lunch ladies didn't use that freezer. It occurred to me in passing that those ladies weren't going to be too happy when they learned about this. Letitia LeMoine's body had been in that freezer the whole time the women had been serving lunch. I hoped they wouldn't decide they couldn't bear to come back to work.

Sarah had handled the keys, but the boys had pulled open the freezer, since the lid tended to freeze shut between uses. Brian had said something along the lines of "What the hell?" and then they'd all seen the body, yelled like crazy, and backed away from the distorted and discolored face. Then they'd gone and puked, and that, as Justin said, was more than enough.

"So you only saw the body for a moment?" Ron asked.

"Well," Brian looked at the others. "I know I stared for a couple of seconds before I even got it. Before I knew what it was, you know. I was just, like, 'what the hell, this isn't ice cream'. Then it sort of clicked into place and I could see it was—I mean, you couldn't miss that."

They all nodded, pale-faced again at the memory. I hoped no one would puke again, because if they did, I would most likely join in. My own memory of that distorted face, and the smell, was a little too vivid.

"But it was like—I couldn't look away—" Brian fumbled for words, and again the others nodded, as did I. They'd still been staring into the freezer when Kitty and I arrived.

Ron seemed to understand. "Did you know who it was?"

The kids exchanged looks again. This time, it was

Madison who answered.

"The, the face was, it was. . ." She swallowed hard and started over. "But we all recognized that outfit." I recalled my own all-too-thorough view of the corpse and nodded. She'd been wearing a short pink skirt and tight electric-blue top, with four-inch heels, the sort of clothes most women in Orcaville wouldn't be caught dead in. Ugh. I wished I hadn't used that particular cliché, even in thought.

Madison was continuing, her voice thin. "It's Mrs. Loud—Chantal's mom, isn't it?" The much-detested Mrs. Loudmouth had become someone's mom. Someone's *dead* mom.

We all looked at Ron, who, after a moment, nodded. "It was Ms. LeMoine," he confirmed.

"I never thought I'd hear myself saying this," Sarah glanced at her mother, "but poor Chantal!" The kids all nodded again, no doubt imagining their own mothers in the freezer, and, I'm happy to say, not liking the image any more than I did.

After a few more questions, and no helpful answers, Ron sent Kitty out with the kids to wait for the other parents.

"I want to ask you a few questions, JJ, then I'll talk to Kitty. And, Kitty?" She turned back from the doorway, where she was ushering the kids out like a group of scared toddlers. Ron continued, "I want to talk to Ms. LeMoine's daughter. Could you get the principal and find out where she is?"

Kitty glanced at the kids, and said, "I'll have Mrs. Peabody page her. We'll all wait in the office." She had no intention of leaving the kids with anyone but their own parents.

When the door closed behind them, Ron Karlson turned and gave me a long, thoughtful look, as though he thought I might know more than I wanted to admit. I half expected him to open by asking why

I'd killed her. What scared me was how much sense the question would make, given her personality, my own temper, and what I'd already admitted about the troubles in the PTA. Not to mention my scarf. What in the name of all that was holy would I say if he asked about that?

"So, Ms. MacGregor. Who had access to the kitchen and the freezer?"

Distracted by his formal address, and not expecting that question, I had trouble thinking of an answer. Maybe he was just softening me up for the Big One. For some reason I still expected him to act like a TV cop. "Um. Anyone with keys to the school, or access to the teacher's room?"

"How so?"

I explained about the keys in the desk drawer, so neatly labeled 'Kitchen' and 'Ice Cream Freezer.' "And I think someone had been messing with them, because Kitty had trouble finding the keys when Sarah came for them just now. I remember her saying something about it." I wouldn't rat out her uncharacteristically uncharitable comment. Unbidden, the memory of her sending Homer about his business flashed into my mind. There were depths to Kitty I had never seen. I didn't like it. I thought I knew all there was to be known about Kitty Padgett, and I didn't like being wrong.

He sighed. "So that limits it to all the teachers, the staff, and at least half the students?"

"Well," I hedged. "Don't forget that pretty much any parent could go in to look for a teacher or leave a note in a mailbox. About the only people who couldn't have opened the freezer are the lunch ladies, because they don't have a key, and they don't have time to go to the teachers' room and get ours."

"You just leave all your keys in a drawer? Dammit, JJ, haven't you guys ever heard of security?"

"It's *ice cream*, not Fort Knox," I snapped, "And when was the last time you locked the cruiser?"

Now it was his turn to squirm. I'd have gloated if I weren't so upset about the whole thing. He didn't answer my question, but he didn't say anything more about security, either. I mean, no one on the Island worried about security, except in the summer when the dozen or so tourists were around. I knew people—a couple, anyway—who don't even have locks on their doors. They figured if anyone was desperate enough to walk off with their stuff, they must have needed it. A few kids got out of hand from time to time, but they'd soon find there was no market for hot goods, and someone would rat them out or straighten them out. I guess in some ways we on Pismawallops Island lagged a bit behind the times. Or we always had, anyway. It looked like the times had caught up with us at last.

"Well, then." Chief Karlson was thinking again. "But that's only true during school hours, when the building is open. After hours, someone would have to have a key to the building, right?"

I nodded. "I'm not sure—I don't know if it's hard to break in. Or what time it's locked up."

We couldn't get anywhere with that, since neither of us had the answers.

Instead, he asked, "When was the last time you opened the freezer?"

I was glad to have a clear answer for something. "Wednesday, when I brought the ice cream over from the store. We get it delivered to the Market," I explained. "The truck comes on Wednesday mornings. I have to pick it up right away, because they don't have enough freezer space to store it."

"So when you put the ice cream in on Wednesday everything was normal? Nothing strange about the freezer?"

23

"Well, I had to kick it to break loose the ice that froze the door shut, and use one of the big serving spoons to chip away enough to get it to close properly afterwards." He looked interested, so I added, "So, I guess I'd say everything was normal." I didn't know why I was being so contrary, unless it was guilt about the blasted scarf. I always did react badly to fear.

He was not amused. "Who wanted her dead, JJ?"

"You already asked me that."

"And you already avoided answering."

Blast! That was the trouble with hiring an intelligent police chief. He wasn't easily distracted. Not that I was trying to get away with anything. I just worried about who he might go after if I told him everything I was thinking. You can bet I had no intention of talking about the PTA Board. Yes, we had agreed things were out of hand, and yes, Kitty had promised to do something about Mrs. Loudmouth. No, I did not for one second believe she'd done anything so permanent. Except, I couldn't have imagined her telling Homer Roller to sit down and shut up, either. Kitty was *never* rude to people. So what did I really know about anyone? I pushed the thought aside. I had to say something, or he'd know I was thinking stuff I didn't want to say.

"Okay, Chief Karlson." He'd gone back to first names, but I wasn't quite so ready to get chummy. Not until I knew more of what he was thinking. "When I said everyone wanted her gone—not dead, mind you, but out of our hair—I wasn't kidding. Kitty and I wanted her out before she killed—er, broke up—the PTA by treating everyone like country hicks who couldn't do anything right. Carlos—that would be Carlos Hernandez, the school custodian and our Secretary—was upset because she constantly criticized his English and questioned his ability to run the Spring Faire. Oh, and she as good as accused

Maddy Takahira of cooking the PTA books."

"And did she?"

"Maddy? I doubt it. The books are certainly a mess, but she never was any good at math."

"Oh?"

"Yeah. Even Kitty says we never should have made Maddy Treasurer, which is true."

"So why did you?"

"Because no one else would have the job on a silver platter." I was amazed he needed to ask. "Same reason most people help with the PTA. We mostly have to beg and plead."

"Until Ms. LeMoine came along." He made it sound like a casual observation, but I knew better.

"Well, she never said she wanted any of our jobs."

"Don't play with me, JJ." He sounded like he meant it, so I tried my best to look earnest and helpful. He ignored my efforts. "She came on like a house afire, and all your reluctant volunteers felt threatened."

"That's pretty much it," I admitted. "I mean, maybe people don't want to volunteer for stuff, but no one wants to be told they don't know how to do their job, either. Even if it's true," I added, thinking of Maddy.

"Still," he said, rather to my relief, "none of this sounds like cause for murder. Cat-fights in the school parking lot, maybe, but not murder. So what else do you know?"

I wasn't so sure I liked his dismissive tone. Not that I wanted him to think we would kill someone, but he needn't sound like we were third graders having little playground spats. Instead of saying what I was thinking, I told him about the ladies who ran the Library, who were being steamrolled much the way we were. I wasn't sure how many other organizations she had moved in on. Church groups? "Letitia LeMoine was determined to become a mover and shaker in Orcaville Society, with a capital S. As if."

"You mean 'as if' there were Society here, or 'as if' she could be a mover and shaker?"

I hadn't thought about it that way and had to laugh. "Either one, I suppose. Look, I'm not denying her ability as an organizer. What she lacks—lacked—was any sense of, well, empathy. She figured she knew better than anyone else how to do just about everything, and she didn't even have sense enough to keep that feeling to herself."

He nodded. "No tact."

"And no understanding that any was needed."

"A subtle but important distinction," he agreed, and I had an uncomfortable moment of wondering where he thought I fit on that point. Why did I even care? There was something going on here I didn't understand, and it made me even more cranky.

"So." The police chief seemed to be having trouble saying something. He studied his notebook as though inspiration might lurk among the pale blue lines. "It sounds like she was a real hazard to your PTA." He looked at me for a moment. "Just how desperate were you and Kitty to get rid of the woman?"

I saw red. I thought he'd already dismissed that idea. When I could speak, even I felt chilled by the ice in my tone. "Are you accusing me—us—of murder?"

Instead of denying any such thought, he just studied me some more. That was when I got really mad.

"Look here, Ron Karlson, Kitty and I are normal, civilized people. We don't go around killing people. Nor do we consider murder a solution to personality conflicts. You can stick that in your pipe and smoke it. What's more, neither of us is an idiot. If I'd killed Mrs. Loudmouth, I would not have been fool enough to stuff her in what you erroneously refer to as 'my' ice cream freezer. I'm certain that, had I given it, say, two milliseconds of thought, I could have come up with something a little less calculated to point the finger at me." Nor would I have used my own scarf to strangle the witch, though even in my anger I remembered not to mention that.

He grinned at me, so impudently that if he hadn't been in a position to throw me in jail I'd have slapped his face.

"Thanks. That's what I wanted to hear."

I glared some more. "Are you telling me you as good as accused me of murder for the fun of hearing me tell you what you could have figured out for yourself if you'd thought about it?"

"Just checking my instincts, that's all. You *do* tend to fly off the handle," he added.

"Well, you can take your instincts back to the station and stuff them." I stormed out the door.

Absorbed in my annoyance, I barely noticed Ms. Waverly leading a distraught Chantal across the courtyard. I started paying attention when I heard her say, "You can stay with me for a bit if you need somewhere to go. You mustn't go home alone, child."

Chantal jerked away from the principal's comforting arm. "No! Oh, no." She added a belated but unconvincing, "Thank you. I—I have an aunt I can call."

"Can I take you somewhere, then?"

"Oh. No, she'll come for me, I'm sure. Please, I'll just wait in the office. Mrs. Peabody will take care of me, I know." Her words fell over each other in her eagerness to avoid the offer.

At that point they went in the back door to the Principal's office. I didn't hear any more as I went through the lunchroom to the main office to collect Brian. *Poor girl*, I thought, before returning to my irritation with Ron Karlson.

I alternately fumed and felt sick all the way home, trying to hide it in case Brian was still feeling traumatized, as I assumed he must. Had Ron Karlson accused me of murder? Or was he just asking necessary questions?

My ruminations failed to distract me from my real worries. The problem was, I had walked out in a huff, and now the police chief was talking to Kitty, and I had no idea if she would see through his manipulations. On the other hand, since we hadn't killed the woman, we had nothing to worry about, right? I trusted him—I really did, the man was no dummy—but I still worried. It bugged me, too, that I couldn't remember where I'd left my scarf. How had the killer gotten hold of it? Surely not from my house! If someone did break in, that's scarcely the first thing they'd steal. My mind wouldn't even consider that Brian could have taken it. Kitty could have picked it up, but why? A hundred thoughts raced through my head, visions of different people who might have killed the woman, and how they might have gotten the scarf.

By the time we were home, though, I had decided to concentrate on worrying about Brian. He didn't speak on the whole drive. I made a few openings, but he didn't respond, and I didn't push.

As soon as we got home, Brian retreated to his room and went on not speaking. I fixed dinner and pretended everything was normal. I heard music from upstairs, and I thought maybe he was calling his father. Allen was out of town—well, he didn't even live with us, if I was honest. Me being for all practical purposes a single mother was part of why we had moved to the Island, a place far away from big-city problems. Until now.

The thing is, about seven years earlier Allen had

taken a new job for the sake of a bigger salary, a job that had him on the road about three weeks out of four. So we bought this place and he settled Brian and me here on the Island, exclaimed about how nice it would be to have it to retreat to when he returned from his trips, and took off. Everyone got used to him being more of a concept than a person, except maybe Brian. He missed his dad, especially at first. Now, while I fixed dinner with little attention to what I did, I thought about what had happened. Maybe I thought it would have been nice if I'd had a husband to make me feel less vulnerable.

Instead, I'd carved out a life of my own on Pismawallops Island, and done it so well that I failed to notice when Allen started taking longer and longer trips. I didn't think about it until now, when it felt like a man might be nice to have around. I pushed that thought aside. It wasn't going to happen. When Brian was in the eighth grade, Allen had phoned from Dallas to say he had a new job, and we should sell the house and move down there. He hadn't asked how we felt about it, just issued his order and expected compliance. I had fumed for a day and a half while trying for Brian's sake to pretend it was okay. Then Brian came and told me that he didn't want to move. That he'd rather live here with just me than in Dallas with both parents.

I was stunned. I asked if he meant that he was willing to leave his father just to live where he wanted, because I didn't think Allen would change his mind no matter what we said. Brian's answer had shocked me even more.

"Mom, Dad left us a long time ago. Don't you remember? He was going to travel for just a year, and then we'd all be together again." His voice rising in anger, he'd gone on. "Didn't you even *notice* he stopped coming back much?"

And I hadn't. My husband had walked out on me a little bit at a time, and I hadn't even realized it. It had taken a teenager to point out the obvious: that although Allen sent money, he'd left, and our lives had closed around the gap.

We hadn't gotten a divorce. Allen had never suggested it, and I'd never brought it up. I had never stopped using my maiden name, but Allen was still Brian's dad—Brian is a Davis, like Allen— and I didn't have any ideas about other men. We'd just gone on living parallel lives. Allen bought a house in Dallas, and we stayed on the Island. He came for the holidays, and once or twice a year Brian and I went south, usually when the winter here got too dark and grim. It was like having our own desert resort. Or maybe aversion therapy. We never loved our cool, damp, vegetated home here on the Island so much as when we'd just come back from Dallas with its heat, Republicans, and oil.

So it made sense, in a way, that in a crisis like this, Brian would call his dad—and that I wouldn't. It did cross my mind to call my Mom. Unlike Allen, she can be a comfort, but it would take time, and energy, to tell her about it all. I glanced at the clock and put it off.

- 3 -

I MARRIED A JERK AND DIDN'T EVEN NOTICE

Nothing in my ruminations prepared me for what happened when Brian came back downstairs that night. He slouched into the kitchen in a way that reminded me he's a teenager, and stared moodily at the veggies I was chopping. It looked like a full-on adolescent funk. Well, he had every right to be upset about finding a corpse where his ice cream should have been. Who wouldn't be? I figured I understood pretty well what was going on, and offered a hug. He shrugged me off.

"I just talked to Dad."

"Uh huh." I'd been right. When the going gets weird, a boy wants his father.

"When did he become such a jerk?"

"Huh? Ouch!" Startled by his tone as much as by the question, I sliced my finger instead of the carrot. I ran the injured digit under the faucet, grabbing a paper towel to sop up the blood.

"Oh, geez, I'm sorry, Mom." Brian sounded more exasperated than sorry, but he raced off for a bandage while I sat down hard at the kitchen table, clutching

31

the paper towel around my right forefinger.

Was Allen a jerk? I had a hunch Brian was right. More to the point, why hadn't I noticed?

Brian came back and began fussing with my finger, which wasn't cut all that badly. I let him fuss.

"Geez, Mom, I'm sorry," he repeated while smearing antibiotic ointment on the wound and wrapping it in a bandage. "I didn't mean to upset you. I thought—" He broke off, still looking so worried I almost laughed.

"I'm okay, Brian. I was just. . . surprised."

"Sorry," he said again. He looked away, though not quickly enough to keep me from seeing his distress.

"But look at it from my perspective," I said, beginning to feel a giggle building in me despite my concern. "I expected some kind of comment on what happened today." I wasn't bringing up corpses unless he did. "Or maybe a demand for food."

He managed a little grin of his own. "And I asked about Dad. But seriously, Mom, when did he become a jerk? I'm pretty sure he was okay when we all lived together. He even used to be funny, sometimes. It's almost like he's a different person. A self-absorbed jerk," he repeated, growing angrier.

"Well," I began, and stopped. Brian's pain deserved a real response, not the flip retort I'd been about to toss off. "I don't know. . . I'm not sure I'd actually. . ." I stopped and looked at him, at last grasping the heart of the matter. "What did he say to you?"

Now Brian laughed, if a little bitterly. "There you are, the mama lion ready to defend her cub." He reached out and patted my arm. "Don't worry. Nothing horrible. It's just, well, I called and told him about finding Ms. LeMoine, and he just said he hoped I'd stay out of the papers, and how were my grades this term. Like it never even occurred to him that I might be upset or anything. Which I'm not," he added, but I gave him a look, and he backed down. "Well, I guess I am, a little."

"I should hope so," I said. "Do you want to talk about that, or do you want to talk about Dad?"

He didn't say anything for a minute, just pushed carrot bits around on the cutting board until the little disks resembled a mad checkers game.

"I want to talk about Dad. I want to understand what's going on." He took up the knife I'd dropped. "What's *with* you two, anyway?" he demanded, and started slicing the remaining carrot with fast, angry strokes.

"I don't know," I said. Brian looked up, and saw I was serious. "I remember when I met him. I'd been out of college for a couple of years, but had only just started my first real job. I was new in Seattle, and pretty lonely and scared."

"Not much like Washtucna?" he asked with a grin. He's been to my old home to visit his grandma. There's not much there now, though the town was still alive when I was growing up. I wished Mom would move down to Walla Walla.

"Not even much like Pullman." I pulled my mind back to the point at hand. "So I'd just come from Eastern Washington and started work, and I met Allen, and he was funny and fun and kind of glamorous too. Not to mention Norse-god handsome. And he made me feel funny and fun and glamorous."

"And then what happened? Me?"

"You know better than that. You said yourself you remember when he was still fun. I don't know. He's ambitious. I didn't see that at first. And I don't know, maybe he didn't completely like it when I became a stay-at-home mom."

"Let me guess." Brian spoke with more bitterness

33

than I liked to hear, but I had to let him talk it out. "Dad wanted someone to help hoist him up the corporate ladder. A hostess, or maybe a businesswoman just a little less successful than he is."

I'd never thought of it that way, but as soon as he said it I knew Brian had hit the nail on the head. Allen was accessorizing when he married me. All of a sudden I resented it like crazy. For one thing, it looked like I'd been desperate, and he'd decided I didn't measure up after all. Was Brian thinking the same thing?

"But, uh, Mom, you don't really seem like the type, you know?"

I couldn't read his tone at all. Was he as disgusted with me as he was with his dad? I tried not to sound as defensive as I felt. "Well, we met when I was in my executive phase. You might find it hard to believe, but for a little while I thought I could put on heels and suits and enter that world. Like I say, he made me feel glamorous. I thought I liked it."

His eyes ran over my jeans and sweatshirt, and I knew what he was thinking.

"Yeah, I know." I laughed, trying not to sound bitter. "In retrospect, I was trying my darnedest to be something I wasn't. He thought he'd found the right accessory, and I thought I wanted that life. Then I quit work and the jeans and tees came back out. I was ecstatic when I found I was pregnant, and I swear half of it was because I'd never have to put on pantyhose again."

Brian nodded, though he couldn't have understood half of what I meant. "But what were you looking for, Mom? I mean, were you really caught up in that whole scene?"

I didn't answer for a minute. I wasn't sure what the answer was. Memories were bubbling up in me, memories that I had ignored for years. I could remember the sense of validation I'd felt when Allen proposed to me, sort of a confirmation of my 'grown up' status. To have a man so good-looking and successful after me. Me! And he did make me laugh, back then. But did that explain it? I looked across the table at my fifteen-year-old son with his gangly arms and legs, his occasional pimples. He was a rather good-looking specimen of the adolescent male, having inherited blond hair and blue eyes, as well as height, from his father. And he was nice, genuinely nice. I felt the smile before I knew why I was smiling.

"I was looking for you."

It seemed like a beautiful thought, but Brian looked at me in disbelief. "You mean you got married because you wanted a baby?"

I felt like an idiot. "I guess that sounds stupid, doesn't it?" He didn't have to nod so enthusiastically. "And it's not completely true. After all, I didn't get pregnant for several years after we were married. But by then I was nearing thirty and I wanted a family, and so, well, I guess I became a stereotype. Biological clock and all that." I watched him as he struggled with this idea. "I don't regret it, Brian," I added. "Even if Allen is a jerk. Which, now that you point it out, I suppose he is. Sorta self-centered, I guess."

For a moment he was distracted from his original train of thought. "You mean you hadn't noticed?" Disbelief made his newly-baritone voice crack.

"I guess not. I suppose I haven't seen enough of him to notice."

"That might've been your first clue," he said, and we both burst out laughing.

"Do you *think*?!" we chorused, and laughed some more. But I wondered what had happened to the man I'd married. Had he ever existed?

One reason I hadn't noticed how Allen had

changed was that I'd never gotten in the habit of talking about him with my girlfriends, the way most do. Kitty and I talked a lot about parenting, but I'd never talked about Allen. You'd think it was because it was a sore spot, but it was more like how you don't talk about a distant cousin you seldom see. I had nothing to say about him. I supposed Kitty didn't ask because she assumed I didn't want to talk about something she must have imagined was painful. Had I even told her when Allen bought the Dallas house?

Well, I suppose everyone figured it out. You don't keep secrets in a town this size. Everyone knows what everyone else is doing almost before they do it. Maybe I hadn't talked about this stuff was because the only thing a person could keep private on Pismawallops Island was her feelings.

What I was feeling that evening after dinner was sick. I wasn't sure which was more upsetting: the murder, or Brian's unexpected insight, not to mention his anger. At his father, or at me? I hadn't expected to get lectures in interpersonal relations from a fifteen-year-old boy. Maybe the time had come to have one of those girlfriend talks all the chicks in books and movies seemed to thrive on. I could call up Kitty. There was no reason not to talk to her about Allen. I could ask her if I should worry because Brian was more upset about his father than about the corpse. That would be easier than calling Mom and explaining it all to her.

The problem right now was that Kitty was—was what? I stopped that train of thought. Kitty was my friend, and caught up in this nonsense just the way I was. I had no doubts of her innocence. But I didn't call her. I figured she had her own worries—and her own support network, since *her* husband was both helpful and present—and wouldn't want me adding my problems to her burden just then. I could cope. I always had. Nor could I shake the image of Kitty, breathing fire while she defended our children. How far would she go for something she cared about? I hated myself for even having the thought.

The clock read just past 8:30 when the phone rang the next morning. I was sitting in the kitchen wearing sweats and down booties, drinking my second cup of coffee and reading the paper. It was the Bellingham paper, since the local birdcage-liner only came out on Thursdays, and took about ten minutes to read.

I was wondering if there was anything in the paper about our murder, or if, as usual, the Island didn't exist, as it can't be seen from the Mainland. Brian wouldn't be up for a couple of hours, so I was pretending to enjoy the Saturday morning quiet, though I'd slept little the night before and could remember almost nothing of what I read.

On sunny days my kitchen was possibly the nicest place in the world. A big, old-fashioned room, we'd modernized the business end with new appliances and cabinets. At the other end, a sturdy wooden table was built into a bay window with a view. The view was of my neighbor's hay pasture, but it was still a view. On a bright winter day you could catch glimpses of Puget Sound past the bare trees that rimmed the pasture.

It wasn't a sunny day. The trees were bare enough, but the rain obscured pretty much everything beyond the end of the yard, and the morning was dusky at best. So I put on the lights, sat on the window seat with my back to the rain, and didn't look out. In my current mood, falling rain was just a little too evocative.

I picked up the phone on the first ring.

"JJ? It's Kitty. Can we talk?" I understood that she meant, could she come over and sit here in my kitchen and drink coffee and talk where none of her kids, or even her husband, Mike, would hear. What she meant was, she was worried sick and didn't want anyone to know. Anyone but me.

I didn't know whether to feel pleased or annoyed, but I knew how to respond. I had no great gift for friendship, but I did know some things.

"Come on over. I'll put the coffee on." Guilt over my doubts about her made my answer a little too bright, but she let it pass.

It was about time I started working on friendships. I had a hunch I'd need them. I also needed a clean Band-Aid, I observed. At least that was easy to take care of.

Kitty and I made full use of the rituals of settling in with our coffee, but eventually she came to the point.

"JJ, do you think Ron suspects us of killing Letitia?"

"Not really." *Not yet*, I amended silently. That might change when he found out about my scarf, of course. "Why? Did he ask you if we did?"

"Oh, of course not."

Why 'of course not'? He had asked me. I let it pass and she went on.

"He wanted to know who could have gotten into the freezer, who disliked her, that sort of thing. I told him I didn't think anyone actually liked her, but I can't imagine anyone killing her."

I nodded my understanding. This whole thing was extra upsetting because of the implication that someone we knew was a murderer. "It's awfully hard to convince myself it was a passing stranger though," I admitted. "It almost has to be someone affiliated with the school."

"I suppose so," she agreed.

I had another thought. "But why shouldn't it be

someone from the City? Someone from her life before the Island?"

Kitty didn't answer directly. "There's another thing." She gave me a sidelong glance over the coffee cup she held in front of her like a shield. "That scarf."

"What scarf?" I thought I faked innocence very well.

"You know." Kitty didn't even notice my effort. "The scarf around Let—the corpse—*Her* neck," she finished, searching the depths of her coffee for something.

"Oh. *That* scarf." I hunted for something intelligent to say. "What about it?" I couldn't tell if she was looking at me, because I was staring out the window so as not to look at her.

"It's yours."

"Kitty! How could you?" I put my cup down too hard, sloshing coffee onto the oak tabletop.

"Well, it is yours. I'm not accusing you, JJ," she added.

I tried to appear calm, occupying myself with cleaning up the spill. "I mean, how could you know whose scarf? You ran to puke almost as soon as you saw her." I worked up the courage to look at her.

Kitty shrugged. She didn't much like being reminded how she'd reacted. She had no way of knowing I'd done the same, and I intended to keep it that way. I might not have much control over my life, but at least I could pretend to boss my stomach. Kitty looked at me and sighed, as a much-tried parent sighs.

"I saw it. And, you know. . . ."

I sighed as well. I knew. My mother sent me that scarf. No one has a taste in color like Mom, which is just as well. "Well, I didn't put it around her neck. I can't even seem to remember when I had it last."

"I know that." Kitty was using the tone we employ

39

in comforting irrational children, and I considered knocking her flat. Then I wondered how she could be so sure. I hadn't managed to banish all my doubts of her, despite being quite certain they were absurd. At last I shut up and listened to what she had to say.

"I just wondered what you told the sheriff," she asked.

"Nothing. He didn't ask, and I didn't want to mention it."

"He'll find out."

"Yeah."

"Won't it look bad if you try to keep it secret?" Kitty took a deep breath, set down her cup, and occupied herself with lining it up with the grain of the tabletop. "The thing is," she said after a long silence, "I think I had it last."

Was she—no, it wasn't a confession of murder. But it explained why I hadn't been able to recall when I'd last worn it.

"Remember? I borrowed it, I don't know, three weeks ago, when I forgot my jacket, the day when it turned so cold?"

Now she mentioned it, I did remember. The scarf is the same shade of orange as a highway worker's safety vest, with lime green accents. I wear it because my mother made it, and because I don't like to waste things. Kitty wore it that day because she was freezing.

"I don't remember bringing it back to you," she said now.

"But how could it have gotten, well, to wherever it got so the killer could use it?"

Kitty just shrugged. "I don't know where it's been."

I made a decision. "Don't you think we'd better find out before we trouble the police about it?"

Kitty agreed. A shade too eagerly? I hated myself

for wondering. But if it had been at her house. . . there is more than one way of protecting your children. Could one of the girls have done it, any more than Brian could, or Kitty herself? On the other hand, why would she even mention it if . . . I gave a mental shrug.

"So, who do you think did it?" I stretched my legs out on the bench, my back in the window corner, and Kitty slumped a little in her seat so she could put her feet up next to mine.

"I don't like to say it, because I really like the idea of some stranger. But it seems like it has to be someone around the school. I mean, maybe we left the scarf lying around, but how would an outsider get hold of it?"

"That still doesn't leave out much of anyone on the Island," I pointed out.

She shook her head. "I suppose not. You know, though, I don't suppose she had to have been killed at the school."

"What do you mean?"

"Well, she couldn't have been killed *in* the freezer. So the killer had to move her. What's to stop him—"

"Or her," I said in a misplaced burst of feminism.

"Or her," she amended, "from bringing her from somewhere else altogether?"

"But why? Why bring her to the school, of all places? It's an awfully public spot."

"Maybe—oh, I don't know. I just don't want her to have been killed there," Kitty admitted.

I agreed. "What I'd like to know is when she died. I guess at night the school would be pretty private. But if it *was* night, we'd know it was someone with a key."

"And we could all prove we were elsewhere," Kitty agreed. "But the real problem we have now isn't her." She saw my shocked expression and shook her head. "Oh, dear, that does sound rather callous. But, you know, it's Ron's job to figure out what happened. You and I need to do something about the Yearbook."

The Yearbook. I'd managed to forget that the dead woman's one redeeming feature had been that she was doing the Yearbook.

"I checked before I left yesterday. JJ, the proofs have to be to the printer by noon Friday!"

"Good heavens!" I didn't know if I was more shocked at the time frame or the fact that Kitty had been calm enough yesterday to think of something like that. I gave her a thoughtful look, wondering again.

"Don't look like that! I'm not heartless. Ron asked about her PTA work, and that made me think about the Yearbook, so he wanted to know more. I told him that it was my proof I didn't kill her, because I'd have waited until she finished."

"Kitty! You devil!"

"Well, I was kind of annoyed with him," she admitted. "That's the other reason I didn't mention the scarf. I told him I could see where he was going with his questions, and I wasn't going to let him suspect my friends. I suggested he consider some of the people with real grudges against her."

I felt another wave of guilt about my lingering suspicions of Kitty. "Like who?" I didn't think anyone was that angry, though many were hurt or annoyed.

"How about Tina Ainsley, who was head cheerleader until Chantal showed up?"

"Yeah, but you'd think she'd have taken it out on Chantal, not her mom."

"Well, everyone can see that Chantal wouldn't go far if her mother didn't push and shove her way into everything," Kitty said.

"Okay, I'll grant you the cheerleader, for now.

Who else?"

"There's the whole thing about the play."

I knew Kat Padgett's best friend Callie Jenson had been a shoo-in for the lead, even though she was a ninth-grader. Then Chantal showed up, with her mother right behind her insinuating Callie was too young, and bragging about how Chantal had been taking acting lessons in Seattle. If she had, it didn't show. But by the time that was clear, it was too late. "But you wouldn't accuse Callie or her mom of murder, would you?" I was genuinely shocked.

"No. I was thinking more of Patty Reilly." The music teacher directed the annual school play along with her other duties. "She told me that the play was going badly, and as far as she was concerned, it was because of Chantal—and because her mother wouldn't stay away from rehearsals. It was driving her nuts, like having another director around running her own version of it all. The woman actually had the gall to try to override Patty's decisions."

"That might almost make a motive," I agreed. Patty Reilly took the arts seriously. I had a sudden, odd memory of her sitting in her room so calmly making tea for the kids. "So, did you tell all that to Ron?"

"Yeah, but I don't think he was impressed."

There didn't seem to be any good response to that. Our talk circled back to the scarf. We racked our brains, trying to remember where we'd seen it last.

I gave up first. "Oh, the hell with it. Kitty, what are we going to do about the damn Yearbook?"

"What we can," Kitty started to say. The buzz of the telephone cut her off, and I jumped to answer before it could wake up Brian, though I suspected the boy could sleep through the eruption of Mt. Baker, or the end of the world.

"Hello? Oh, hi, Allen." I glanced at Kitty, suddenly self-conscious about my odd marital arrangements,

43

and annoyed that a single conversation with my son had changed everything. Kitty pretended she couldn't hear. She gazed with great attention out at the rain, which was now falling sideways, driven by the wind that raced down from the Frozen North.

My contemplations on spring weather in Puget Sound dissolved as I took in what Allen was saying.

He wanted a divorce. Okay, I shouldn't have been shocked, but I was. Why now, after all this time? Had he found someone else? In light of what Brian and I had discussed last night, did I even care? About that point in my mental processes, the rest of what he was saying registered.

"And I want Brian. I don't know what you are up to on that island of yours—"

Wait a minute! *My* island? My memory said he'd picked it out and plopped us here. Though I'd not deny we took root. And that brought me to the important point. I kept my voice calm, for me.

"Brian is happy here. He does not want to live in Dallas, nor with you, as far as I can tell." Was that true? I went on. "I'm afraid it's a bit late to be asserting your rights to him."

My rational response did no good. He wanted Brian, and he wanted no fight from me. Brian was right. Allen *had* turned into a jerk. Then he went too far.

"You are a suspect in a murder," he accused, as though that would settle everything.

"I am not!" So much for mature discussion of our differences. "Who on earth told you that?" And why would he be so ready to believe it? He didn't give me an answer, and I rushed on. "It's completely untrue, and even if I were a suspect, which I'm not, I would soon enough be proven innocent, so there's no reason to think I can't take care of Brian."

"Okay, okay, calm down now, JJ." I remembered that Allen had always been least likable when pretending to be patient and rational. He backed off from the accusations, though, taking a new tack. "You know there's a murderer on the loose there somewhere. I just don't think it's a good idea to leave the boy in a place like that."

"A place like what? A place that's had one serious crime in the last seven years? How many murders has Dallas had?" He didn't answer, and I went on. "Furthermore, after the way you treated him last night, Brian has concluded you're a jerk, so I doubt you'll get much cooperation from him." I hoped.

"How dare you!" Allen exploded with a wrath I realized I was lucky to have avoided in person. Had he ever been like this before? "You set my son against me! Wait until the judge hears that!"

"Actually," I couldn't resist telling him, "Brian's the one who pointed it out to me. I had failed to notice your growing jerkiness, but he did. A boy notices things like that. Things like worrying more about your image than his feelings. You could have tried some empathy when he phoned last night." What could have changed Allen into this selfish, hostile creep? Could a woman have that much influence on a guy? Or was he on something? This was not the man I remembered marrying.

He ignored my comment, and had no way of knowing what I was thinking. What he said next was even weirder. Was it just meant to hurt, or was he completely crazy? "I want my boy. My heir. He needs to be trained for the position he will one day hold." His tone was somewhere between pompous ass and Darth Vader. I suppressed a shudder.

"I'm sure he'll appreciate being referred to in those terms." My voice had gone icy.

"I have the money and the lawyers, JJ. I think I can get what I want, over any protests you want to make. I have no intention of paying child support, because I will have my child." He was calm again, trying to sound as though Brian was the point, but he'd given himself away. The whole thing was about money—divorce me in a hurry when I might be too distracted to fight, and avoid a settlement. It wasn't beyond him. I might have missed his jerkiness, but I'd long ago seen his focus on money. With love long gone, what was left between us but money? Now it looked like money was, indeed, between us. And he had all the big guns.

My heart sank, but I wasn't giving in. "You know, Allen, until this minute I thought you were a jerk. Now I realize you're a greedy, vindictive bastard." I touched the button to end the call, set the phone in the charger, and sat down as my knees buckled. Kitty put my coffee cup in my hand and I drank. It took a minute before I could speak.

"That vindictive bastard!"

"You already said that." Kitty had given up pretending she didn't hear the discussion. No one could have ignored even the one-sided version of it. "I take it he wants a divorce? Funny, I assumed you guys got one a long time ago."

"No. We never bothered. I didn't even realize how dead the marriage was until Brian, of all people, pointed it out to me last night."

"Well, he's the one who knows you best."

"Meaning, I suppose, that the rest of you gave me undeserved credit for seeing things for myself."

I must have sounded hurt. Kitty reached across the table to touch my hand. "I'm sorry. I didn't mean it that way."

"It's not the divorce, Kitty. As you say, the marriage ended long ago. He wants Brian."

"Brian?" For a moment she seemed unable to process this. "He wants *Brian*?"

"Right."

"But he wouldn't stand a chance! He abandoned you guys years ago!"

"Well, he has maintained financial support. He owns this place," I gestured at the house, my heart sinking. Would I have to give up the home I loved, too?

"Yeah, but." Kitty didn't have any more answers, but she wasn't giving in.

"I think he wants to use this murder. Maybe to be able to say he's protecting Brain, taking him from a dangerous environment. Maybe he'll say I got us both dumped into the middle of it and so I'm not a competent parent or something. I don't know. I'm not sure he does; he's just looking for anything that will work. Anyway," I added, "we were the ones who wouldn't go join him in Dallas, so it's not clear who abandoned whom."

"In a real marriage, both of you get to have a vote about the big things," Kitty said quietly. "Anyway, this will be cleared up long before he can get anything before a judge, JJ. I don't think you have anything to worry about. Besides, I heard what Brian said about Allen."

"Every teenaged boy thinks his old man's a jerk from time to time. That's not going to cut any ice, Kitty. He also said he missed his dad, or at least the dad he used to have." I scowled into my coffee, unable to accept her comfort. If Allen took Brian, I didn't know if I could go on. Maybe that was what he wanted. Just to hurt me. If that were so, he really had changed.

Kitty was talking. "Maybe every boy does say that sometimes. But unlike most teens, Brian has good reason to think it. Look, my cousin Anne is a lawyer, and she has a part-time office here on the Island. I'll go with you Monday to talk to her, and she'll figure it all out. She's good. But in the meantime," she paused and checked my reaction from the corner of her eye before continuing, "meantime, we have a Yearbook to produce."

"Right." There wasn't a thing I could do about Allen until Monday. I'd bet that's why he'd called on Saturday, so he could ruin my whole weekend. How had I ever failed to notice what kind of guy he was? Had I just ignored the obvious? I didn't think anyone could change that much in just a few years. I gave a mental shrug and directed my thoughts toward the Yearbook.

"We need to get permission from Ron to get back into the school and see what we have," Kitty said. "I don't know how much she got done. It's all on the computer."

"That should make it easier than sorting piles of prints."

Kitty gave me a pitying look. "Unless she made a good start on editing, I can tell you one thing: there'll be zillions of pictures. There's nothing to stop kids with digital cameras from taking about a million shots of everything, so they do."

Most of them bad, I supposed.

- 4 -

HOW BAD CAN IT BE?

I poured us each another coffee. Kitty reached into her voluminous shoulder bag and pulled out a bag from the Have-A-Bite Bakery.

"Desperate measures for desperate situations," she explained, placing two chocolate croissants on plates and adding an espresso brownie to each before shoving one over to me. "Eat up, and then we're heading to the school."

I'm very careful about my diet. I run at least four days a week (even if Brian does like to remind me that what I do is more of a jog than a run, and more of a slog than a jog) and I never eat sweets before noon.

I pulled the plate toward me and took a big bite of brownie. Coffee and chocolate together worked their magic, and my brain came to life.

My black mood stood no chance against the triple assault of sugar, caffeine, and chocolate. I took another worshipful bite of brownie, then turned to attack my croissant. Pastry crumbs gathered on my sweatshirt like some sort of gluttonous dandruff, but I didn't care. When I finished, I stood up, showering the floor with evidence of our dietary indiscretions. "Okay. I'm calling Ron. Though I don't suppose he's at the station. It's Saturday."

Ron was at the station. No one else was—Deputy Roller was on patrol, for whatever that was worth, and the dispatcher was the only other employee. Ron answered the phone himself. I couldn't tell if he was glad to hear from me, and didn't waste time trying to find out. I figured a brisk, all-business approach was the best way to avoid conversations I didn't want to have.

"JJ MacGregor here. Kitty and I need to get into the school and start working on the Yearbook stuff. Can we? I mean, you haven't closed it as crime scene or anything, have you?"

"You can go in. Just stay out of the freezer."

"That isn't funny!"

"It wasn't meant to be," he answered in a mild tone. "I just meant that's the one place you need to stay out of—the whole kitchen, actually—because I'm not done with my investigation."

"Oh." I felt myself blushing. I'd been sure he was making some kind of bad joke about not getting ourselves killed. Then I processed what he'd said. "So she was killed in the kitchen?"

"Well, I never said that. I just need to go over it more thoroughly."

"So she wasn't." I was in no mood for games, partly because I was afraid he'd pick up on my own evasions if we talked too long.

He sighed. "Look, JJ, we don't know where she was killed, okay? We don't know anything yet."

Well. We were back to first names. That must be good for something. But I was more interested in his pronouns.

"'We?' Did they send over a detective after all?"

"Well, no," he admitted. I could hear his regret. "They're still too busy. At this point, 'we' is me."

"Well, what do you know? Do you at least know

when she died?"

"Planning your alibi?" His tone gave nothing away. If we'd been face to face, I might have been able to tell if he was joking.

I turned so red he'd have arrested me on the spot if he'd seen, and Kitty gave me a funny look. Well, of course I wanted to know if Kitty and I had alibis! "I just wanted to know. If you don't know where, maybe at least we can know when! Anything to help it make sense."

"I'm sorry, JJ. I'm worried about the kids too. But I don't have any answers. The coroner did come take the body last night, but I won't have her report for another twenty-four hours at best. Probably not until Monday."

I felt a little guilty that he'd assumed I was worrying about the students, but wasn't ready to explain why I needed answers so badly. I wanted this thing cleared up, closed, and packed away, preferably before Allen even had time to call a lawyer. "Well, if there's anything Kitty and I can do to help out, let us know, okay? It's in our best interests to get this all cleared up, the sooner the better. If you want us, we'll be in the computer lab working on the Yearbook." I thought of something else. "What about the ice cream?"

"What?"

He could hardly be blamed for not following the gyrations of my mind. "Have you found any sign of where the ice cream went? The stuff that was in the freezer," I clarified.

"Hmm. Haven't looked, to tell the truth. I imagine it's in the dumpster, wouldn't you think?"

"I suppose so," I admitted. "I just had a thought that it might be important, though I don't know why. Mind if I take a look when we get to the school?" Not that I cared if he minded. He couldn't stop me, even if he wanted to.

"Help yourself," he said, leaving me full of fight with no opponent.

I hung up and turned back to Kitty. "Okay, we're good to go." I scribbled a note to Brian and we left.

Kitty talked out her stress while she drove us to the school. "I haven't any idea how to deal with all those pictures. I know that the Yearbook people sent a template so that we can just paste pictures in where we want them. We have to do the special pages—events, sports, clubs, all that."

I felt the cold hand of doom at the thought, but tried to put a bright face on it. "Well, that shouldn't be too bad. How many teams do we have, anyway? Six? Eight?"

"Ten, if you count boys and girls everything, which of course we do. Then there are about a million clubs."

"Geez." I whistled. "I only know about Chess club, Spanish club, and Honor Society."

She rattled off a long list of activities.

"Hey," I interrupted, "Band and Choir are classes, not clubs."

"I know. But they've always gotten coverage in the Yearbook along with the clubs. Where was I? Oh, yeah, Jazz Band, and the *Clam* staff."

"The *Clam*? They haven't published a paper all year!"

"Yeah, but they meet, and they filled out all the paperwork to be a club. So they get their pictures in the Yearbook."

"Good Lord."

"Well, the only advisor they could get was Elvis Fingal," she said by way of explanation.

I nodded. The Vice Principal was no fan of hard work, and didn't like people who rocked the boat.

The perfect advisor for the student paper, at least from Principal Waverly's perspective. She, too, preferred to avoid anything that might make waves. Fingal had probably just kept the kids talking about what the paper should do, rather than taking the risk of publishing one. As long as they didn't do anything, Fingal would like being *Clam* advisor. He seemed to be one of those adults who wanted to be "one of the gang" with the kids.

"Is that all?" Maybe we could do this.

"Well, we'll also need pages for student government and Homecoming. Likewise the Fall Formal and the Senior Clambake." That last was an Island tradition. Long ago, the seniors had gathered each year on the last Saturday of September to dig clams and roast them over a beach fire. Nowadays they mostly roasted hotdogs, since not many of the kids liked clams. Even fewer were willing to get gritty in the pursuit of the little guys. But it was a tradition, so it was still called the Clambake.

"Okay, okay," I protested, laughing. "Stop already. I think we're doomed."

I was relieved to see Kitty brighten. A discouraged Kitty Padgett was enough to make me despair—it just wasn't right.

"Well, Letitia was working on it for months. She must have gotten something done," she said with a smile and a shrug.

When we got to the school, I detoured to where a battered dumpster collected the off-scourings of the school day. I had no idea why I thought it mattered where the ice cream had gone—even if we'd thought of it yesterday, we couldn't have salvaged any, and it was certainly trash by now. But my gut said to find out, so I pried up the lid and peered in.

"Pfew!" The aroma of dumpster struck my incautious nose, a noxious blend of mildew and decaying food from the lunchroom. I had to turn aside and get my breath before I could open the lid more and peer in. My gut was saying something else now, but I went ahead and looked.

A number of black plastic bags covered the bottom of the dumpster, all displaying the irregular lumpy outlines expected of bags filled with lunchroom trash and the leavings of wastebaskets. None suggested the geometrical regularity of thirty boxes of ice cream bars.

I let the lid drop back into place and considered what I'd seen—or, rather, not seen. This must be why I felt the ice cream was important—because it wasn't there. Maybe if we could find where it had gone, we'd know who killed Letitia LeMoine.

I considered the possibilities while I walked around to the door Kitty held open for me, and down the hall to the computer lab. What we found there drove all thoughts of ice cream from my mind.

What had Kitty said? "She must have gotten something done"? Nowhere could we find the least evidence that she had. In fact, we found no files at all on our PTA computer. None. Nada. Zilch. Not a photo, not a single file. It was as though someone had deleted everything.

"Or as though someone hadn't done a bit of work on it," Kitty muttered.

"Still," I pointed out. "The kids *have* been taking pictures. I've seen them. So have you. They must be somewhere." Except that someone had completely reformatted the computer and erased all the data. I tried not to think about that. Later we could think about the amount of work we'd lost and would have to redo. Right now, we had to hope there were photos elsewhere, like on the other computers.

We ran around turning on all the machines in the

little lab, and began a frantic search through the myriad files and folders on each. After a few minutes, little triumphant noises started coming from Kitty, then from me. We found folders here and there full of photos, and figured they were created by the kids who did the actual photography. But there was no sign that there had been any effort made to sort, edit, or organize the pictures. I didn't know why the students had downloaded to any computers but ours, but thanked the stars they had. Then I thought about what remained to be done.

"That rotten bit of flotsam didn't even *start* work, Kitty! She set us up for failure, that's what!"

"But," Kitty tried to be reasonable. "She couldn't have intended to end up dead, so it would have been her failure, and she wouldn't want that. She must have done *something*!"

"My guess is, she planned to come to us on Monday and say she just *couldn't* do it, and could we please finish up, because—because of something." I imitated Letitia's pseudo-cultured voice, and we giggled, but not much. The woman was dead, and we were stuck with her mess.

Kitty sighed.

"Don't do that, Kitty. Don't you know that every time you sigh it ages you a month? I read it on the Internet."

She sighed again. "I really don't like this, JJ. What was she playing at? This close to the deadline, even if she turned it over to us, everyone would know she'd blown it. And all this Island needs is something like that to hold against her."

Kitty had a point. A closed society like Orcaville's could freeze a person out in no time. Odds were it would have happened to Letitia LeMoine soon anyway—the same pushiness that got her in would soon enough have gotten her cut off. I frowned, even though I've been resolving not to frown. Makes a nasty wrinkle between the eyes, worse than sighs even. "Maybe she accidentally wiped out the files," I suggested. "She was too embarrassed to confess, so she was trying to think of a way to blame it on someone else."

"So she went and strangled herself?" Once again Kitty's thinking was clearer than I'd ever given her credit for. I really needed to stop thinking that nice equals slow.

"I think we need to call Ron," she said.

"Stuff happens to computers all the time," Ron shrugged. "They crash. Doesn't mean anyone made it happen."

He'd come to the school when Kitty called, mostly because he was headed there anyway. He seemed less impressed by our new clue than I was. Still, he didn't completely dismiss us. Maybe the blank hard drive was a coincidence, maybe it wasn't. Maybe Letitia LeMoine had accused someone of destroying months of her work, and he or she had taken umbrage. Maybe she'd even caught someone in the act. Maybe a student had been mad because his rival had gotten more space than he—or she—had. Our police chief listened to me ramble on for a bit, running a hand through his hair in a gesture I was beginning to associate with fatigue or impatience. Maybe both, in this case. I shut up.

If the hair he was rumpling was graying a bit at the temples, it was still thick and curly, and mostly a rich brown that—I pulled myself together. What was *wrong* with me?

"I don't know about any of that," he was saying. "But I'll agree that coincidences raise questions. Was there anything on this computer that isn't somewhere on one of the others? It's not just the pictures that are gone, after all. What about your financial records? Did you keep them on the computer?"

I gave him a blank look. "I don't know," I realized. Maddy brought a printed budget report to PTA meetings, but I'd always assumed she just typed it up from the ancient account book.

"We should find out," Ron said, and I suddenly understood. Did he think Maddy had—I couldn't even finish the thought.

"It would be a motive," he pointed out. "Getting caught in the act of sabotaging the Yearbook doesn't seem worth killing over. But covering up evidence of theft—that might be."

I could see that. I just didn't have to admit it aloud.

Kitty looked as shaken as I felt. "I don't think we had any important files on here—just flyers and newsletters and stuff we probably should have deleted anyway. The pictures were the only thing that was, well, different."

"And now we'll never know if there were any of those on this computer and nowhere else," I said. "When Ms. Loud—uh, Letitia—offered to do the Yearbook, Kitty and I were more than happy to leave her alone with it, and we never looked at anything, or even asked how it was going."

He looked at me with those blue-grey eyes that made suspects squirm, and I—what was going on with me? I'd known Ron—Chief Karlson—for years, and never given his eyes, or his hair, a thought. Now all of a sudden I was seeing him in a way that ought to make me blush. Was about to make me blush, because I suddenly knew what had changed, and it wasn't him. It was Allen. Or, rather, no Allen.

I hurried to cover my confusion with words. "I guess we didn't dislike her as much as we dislike the Yearbook." Heat crept up my face. Sometimes the pale complexion that goes with my light red hair is a curse.

Ron turned to the computer again, apparently unaware of my discomfort. No doubt he was being polite, as it would be hard to miss my flaming face. "I don't know as much as I should about these things, but you say the whole hard drive has been erased?"

"As far as I can tell. I'm no expert either," I said.

"Which pretty much proves Letitia didn't just not do anything," Kitty pointed out. "Because I don't think Maddy kept records on here, and I simply cannot believe she would either steal or kill."

I had to agree. As long as I clung to my belief that Maddy was honest, the computer proved that Letitia LeMoine had done something, if only to ruin it all— our files as well as hers. I tried to remember when I'd last used the computer. It had to have been at least a week. "She could have been incompetent, and she wouldn't want to admit she'd destroyed everything. Maybe she hit the wrong key and, you know." I suspected it wasn't that easy to reformat a hard drive, but I was torn between a desire to blame Letitia for everything, and my need to find something that would lead to her killer, as long as it wasn't one of us.

The Chief looked like he understood me all too well, so I looked at Kitty. She didn't look convinced either, so I tried again.

"So maybe Letitia came in and caught someone messing with the computer, and they killed her so she couldn't stop them. But it doesn't have to be Maddy. Maybe someone else was taking advantage of her lousy bookkeeping." They nodded. It was possible.

After a moment, Kitty asked, "Do you suppose she kept a back-up?"

I snorted. "I doubt it. Worth checking, I suppose." I didn't bother to point out that we hadn't kept a back-up either.

"She must have put the disc from the Yearbook people somewhere." Kitty wanted to get to work. "It would help if we could at least find that. It has all the templates and instructions. And I suppose we'll have to audit the accounts, just to be sure," she added. "Later."

"Do you have someplace you keep stuff like that?" It wasn't clear if Ron meant the account book or the disc, but the answer was the same either way.

"Bottom drawer of the desk in the teachers' room. I'll go take a look," I offered, happy to give myself a minute away from this man who was doing such strange things to me.

To my dismay, he followed me. Kitty stayed put. I shot her a look, but she appeared innocent, sitting at another computer and calling up photo files. Had she noticed my blush? Or was she giving me a chance to tell him about Allen's call? Either way, I wished she'd come along to lend moral support—or defuse a situation I wasn't ready to face.

I led the way down the hall and through the office to the teachers' room. Ron looked around with mild interest. When he saw me use a key to open the desk drawer, he asked, "You keep it locked?"

"Just this drawer. We keep the money box and financial files in here, Chief Karlson."

"You used to call me Ron," he said, then before I could respond, added with more interest, "You keep your computer discs locked in here too?"

"Just because that's where there's space. Not," I assured him, "because we have anything on disc that requires actual security. Just archives of meeting minutes, useless free software, and occasionally some flyer one of us made at home. I guess that's all we have left now. If we'd been more up-to-date I guess it would all be on the Cloud or something."

"Hmm." I could tell he was looking for something

of interest in the PTA, and I might have told him he wasn't going to find it. We just limp along, trying to fill in some of the smaller financial gaps. Even the accusations about Madeleine's bookkeeping were pretty pathetic, because though you could siphon off a few dollars here and there, no one was going to get rich cheating the Pismawallops High School PTA. The account book was right where it belonged. Killing over our money would be absurd.

I flipped through the discs in the drawer and pulled one out. "Here's the stuff from the Yearbook people. Kitty'll be glad to see that."

"But it's not Ms. LeMoine's work, right? Just stuff the company sent?"

Ron had moved to peer into the drawer, and I wished he'd stand a little farther away from me. I shifted a bit, but instead of getting more distance between us, somehow I bumped into him. He moved then, all right, like he'd been burned. He jumped away so fast I didn't have time to do the same. I didn't like this chemistry I was feeling with a man who might at any moment arrest me, or one of my friends, for murder. And what did his reaction mean, anyway? Had he felt it too? Or was he just reacting to my reaction?

I answered his question as though it were the only thing on my mind. "No, it's just the templates and instructions. Maybe she kept a disc at home, though. We could ask Chantal if she knows."

"The daughter?" He shook his head. "She's a piece of work, I'll tell you."

"Oh?" I kept my voice innocent. I was pretty sure what kind of girl Chantal LeMoine was, but I was interested to hear his view. I wondered what in particular had led him to make the comment.

"Girl comes across as either an innocent playing at being a tart—or vice versa."

"And the verdict?" I asked, trying to make it a joke.

He shrugged, too smart to commit himself. "It doesn't matter. She says she was home all evening Thursday, and that her mother was, too. Says she didn't hear her mom go out, but she—Ms. LeMoine—wasn't there when she—Chantal—got up for school."

I tried for a non-committal noise.

"I asked her if that was unusual," Ron continued.

"And?"

"She just shrugged, in that annoying teenaged way."

"I think I've seen that," I admitted.

"So I concluded that the LeMoine women, mother and daughter, did not keep tabs on each other."

"What time did Chantal get up?"

"She says six?"

I nodded. "Sounds reasonable. Girls take a long time to get ready for school. A lot of the boys, too, these days."

"But not yours?"

"Nope, not mine. Seldom more than forty-five minutes, bed to breakfast table," I added with a laugh. "But, about Chantal. Do you think we could ask her about the Yearbook?"

He shook his head. "She's gone off-Island to stay with an aunt. She couldn't very well go on living in that house by herself."

"Oh." I recalled the conversation I'd overheard, when Chantal told the principal that she had a place to go. Of course the aunt would be on the mainland. We all knew Letitia LeMoine didn't have any relatives on the Island. She'd made sure we knew she was from the Big City.

"But we have warrants for the house, and I'll keep an eye out for your pictures. CDs, I suppose?"

"Or a thumb drive, or even those little tiny camera disk thingies. But you don't think the computers have

61

anything to do with her death." It was a statement, not a question.

He shook his head. "It's odd, that happening just now. I just can't imagine how Yearbook photos from the high school could cause a murder. Or why someone would kill over being caught messing with your computer, unless it had something to do with money, and this makes that unlikely." He touched the account book.

"But she is dead, and someone did wipe out our computer. Well, we'll be looking at every photo we can find, so we'll keep an eye out for the clue that breaks open your case."

"You do that," he said. I couldn't read his expression. He stood aside and waved for me to precede him out of the room. I noticed he took care to stand well clear, so that I didn't brush against him as I went through the narrow doorway. I'd have to ask Kitty about that. For the first time in years I was remembering what girlfriends were for, besides an excuse to eat chocolate. I was wracking my brain to figure if he'd ever been like this before. I wondered if he'd noticed I'd managed to avoid calling him anything since his reminder that we were on a first-name basis. Well, he'd changed that first, with his formality at the murder scene.

I wondered, too, what his wife had been like. I knew, vaguely, that Ron had been married once. She had died before I'd moved to the Island. I thought she must have been very special, for him to stay single so long. Though maybe he'd just been too busy to do anything about it. His was a more than full-time job.

When we got to the library he stuck his head in just long enough to ask Kitty if she'd found anything.

"Lots of photos. We've got plenty of those," she answered. "But if she did any sorting, it's gone now. These are just the kids' rough files—every shot they took, untouched. Come Monday I'll round up the Yearbook crew and put them to work—and ask if there were any pictures on her computer that aren't anywhere else."

I sat down at a computer.

"He doesn't seem very concerned about the pictures," Kitty commented, when Ron had gone.

"Why should he be? Compared to a dead body, or even the unlikely possibility of someone monkeying with our money, the Yearbook is unimportant."

"Not to the kids, it isn't," she said. Then she took a closer look at me. "Say, what happened in there?"

"I found the Yearbook templates," I offered, handing her the disc.

"And that makes you look like you're sitting on an ant hill?"

"Huh?"

"Do you think he really thinks Maddy did it? Or one of us?"

I wasn't sure how to answer. "I don't know. I'll take the account book and make sure our money's all here, just to be safe. But Ron's acting weird. Strange." I could feel myself blushing again, and Kitty wouldn't pretend she didn't see.

"I don't think that has to do with the murder," was her assessment. "He's had his eye on you for a while. When you started scoping him just now, I thought maybe he'd decided to do a little investigating." She winked in case I missed the point.

I was stunned. How on earth did Kitty reach these conclusions? "His eye on me is professional. He wonders if I'm a killer, remember?" I'd hoped to divert her, but Kitty wouldn't be diverted.

"I don't think that's the way he was studying you."

I told her what had happened—and how fast he'd distanced himself when it did.

There. If you're so good at this stuff, analyze that. I

hadn't given much thought to male-female relationships for years and wouldn't even pretend to know if what had happened in the teachers' room had been chance or deliberate.

"Hmm." Kitty considered the matter. "I'd say he's attracted to you, but he's a professional. He's not going to act now, and especially not if he thinks you're still married. I do think you ought to let him know you're getting a divorce, JJ. Just casual-like," she hastened to add. "Maybe as if you're just letting him know because it connects to the case."

"Maybe he thought I was coming on to him and it scared him off," I suggested. "Especially if he thinks I might have killed her. He's a cop, Kitty. He's not going to flirt with a suspect!"

"I don't believe he could really think for a minute that you did it. But you do need to fill him in on Allen's call and his threats, anyway. Encourage him to keep your name out of things. Then maybe he can see what he can do to help you."

I could see how that would appeal to Ron's sense of chivalry. I just wasn't sure I liked the idea. I wasn't even free of one dysfunctional relationship. No way should I be thinking about another. And, to be honest, I don't think I was thinking about a relationship. I was thinking about sex. I realized I'd been thinking about sex for quite a while.

- 5 -

YOU CAN'T PROTECT A TEENAGER FROM LIFE (OR LIFE FROM A TEENAGER)

We would have to get Brian and Justin, the best computer geeks we knew, to try to restore the PTA computer. In addition to whatever the dead woman had done on the Yearbook, if anything, and the big question about the accounts, we'd lost the files for all the fliers and things we used on a regular basis. Things like the template for our newsletter.

We didn't have time to think about that now. We opened the Yearbook instructions on one of the student computers and took a look. I was pleasantly surprised: they made sense the first time through. What they couldn't cure was the necessity of sorting through all the pictures, probably several times. We had the added problem of having photos scattered randomly about on six different computers.

"Okay," I suggested after thinking it over. "Let's do it this way: we'll each pick a computer and delete all the hopelessly awful pictures. The rest we dump into one file and upload to my thumb drive. When we get our computer up and running, we can copy all the files onto it." I rooted in my purse.

"And then we can sort them by events and what-not," Kitty finished. "Good idea."

I rummaged deeper into my purse. "Uh, I don't think I have a drive with me. Do we have any discs?"

Kitty winked. "I know where Evelyn keeps hers." Mrs. Peabody, the school's secretary, could fix anything, even when she wasn't there.

"Good enough."

We worked until about half past one, when my stomach declared independence and threatened to walk to the deli by itself. I was starting to worry about Brian, too.

"I've had it, Kitty," I announced. "I want to go home and have lunch and see if Brian's okay. He had a bit of a shock last night, and there's a worse one in store," I added, thinking of the phone call from Allen. My cut finger throbbed, and I had a headache. What I really wanted was to go someplace where someone would just hand me a plate of food. But I'd better stop counting on the gravy train and start paying attention to my spending.

She glanced at her watch. "Good Lord! I've got to take Mikey to his swim lesson." Mikey's her youngest, still in grade school. He seems to have a lot more activities than Brian ever did. Kitty says it's because he's trying to get away from his sisters. I like the girls, but she may be right.

Kitty started shutting down computers. To save time, instead of hauling the six discs we'd burned back to the teachers' room and putting them away, she just dumped them in her purse. "Well, that's a start, anyway. I'm sure I saved a lot of poor photos, but at least we've done something." More than Mrs. Loudmouth had managed in several months, but neither of us said it aloud. For me, that was progress.

I turned off the lights and she locked up. We almost ran to the car, and she dropped me at the end of my driveway, the sooner to go get Mikey ready, if he hadn't gotten himself ready.

"Which he won't have," Kitty predicted. "If no one tells him it's time, he'll never notice. And Mike's at the shop," she added, referring to her husband, who ran the Island's only service station.

"Good luck," I called as I jumped out. She sprayed gravel into the bushes as she pulled back onto the road.

I proceeded at a more relaxed pace down my lane and around to the kitchen door. Brian was sitting at the table eating a sandwich that made my mouth water. I resisted the urge to snatch it from him. Instead, I ruffled his hair and opened the fridge, hoping something delectable would appear, and wondering how to broach the subject of divorce. He shrugged away from me and smoothed his hair.

Some rooting around on the bottom shelf turned up a carton of leftovers that didn't appear to be growing anything. While they were in the microwave, I leaned against the counter and watched Brian. He'd grown a lot over the past year, and was a little taller than me. Okay, a lot taller than me. Better looking, too. After a bit, I stopped admiring his adolescent good looks and noticed that he lacked some of his usual energy and cheer. In fact, he looked downright glum. My heart sank. I hated to add to his troubles.

"What's up, Brian?" That direct approach isn't supposed to work with teens, but Brian and I had always been up front with each other. If we wanted to know something, we asked. Then we could decide what we wanted to tell. No picking and prying and trying to trick information out of each other. It had worked well for us, though his adolescent moods had strained my self-control a bit, and now all bets were off.

He didn't answer for a bit, just went on chewing his sandwich. The microwave dinged and I pulled out my bowl, carried it to the table, and sat down opposite him, looking out the window at the pasture, where rain was not actually falling. At last he finished chewing—and thinking—and answered my question.

"I heard your conversation with Da—with Allen this morning." The way he stopped himself from saying "Dad" told me everything, but he went on. "I'm sorry. I know I shouldn't have listened. But the phone woke me, and I checked the caller ID so I knew it was him. I wanted to tell him I was mad about the way he reacted yesterday."

"So you picked up in time to hear him saying he wants you to live with him?" I tried to make it sound good. So I didn't have to tell him, but I was hours too late to spin it, too.

He scowled. "You mean, threatening to take me whether I want to go or not. You could have come and talked to me!"

I felt a stab of guilt as his anger made me realize I'd left him to brood about this all morning, while I thought he was asleep. Before I could apologize or explain, Brian added, "Do you think he can?"

"I doubt it."

"But you don't know for sure."

I really, really wished I could promise him, but I couldn't. I had to be honest. "I know very few things for sure, Brian, and most of those are wrong." That was truer than I liked, but he at least smiled a little. "Kitty and I talked about it, and we'll get a lawyer and make sure you get what you want. That does mean staying here doesn't it?"

He shrugged. "I don't want to live in Texas." The way he said it, you'd have thought Texas was next door to hell. He may have gotten that attitude from me. "But—" he broke off with another shrug.

"But what about your father? Do you want to live with him? I mean, aside from the whole Texas thing?"

"I don't know. I don't think he cares that much about me. So I don't see why he can't just leave us the hell alone now." His voice took on that harsh edge that told me he was fighting off tears.

What did I want to hear? That Brian believed Allen had decided to be a dad after all these years? I knew I should encourage him to maintain his ties with his father. All the same, I couldn't help hoping that he'd want to stay with me.

"Maybe he figures I'm more interesting now. You know, the way you said he married you as, as an accessory? But I think he just wants to get out of paying child support." His anger faded as quickly as it had flared, leaving only the misery, and the tears that made his blue eyes glisten, though they didn't overflow.

My heart sank. So he'd heard that part, too. I thought he was correct on both counts, but what a horrid thing for a boy to know about his father!

"Your father loves you, Brian. You know that."

"Do I?" He gave me the kind of look that reminds me there's a very intelligent near-adult in there, and I can't get away with the little lies that made life easier when he was small. "Actually, I don't know that at all. I don't think you believe it, either. So don't lie to me."

I concentrated on eating, collecting my thoughts. I would have been happier if he'd said that in an angry way, but his tone was dull, as if he was in too much pain to bother getting mad.

As usual with Brian, it looked like complete honesty was the only way to go. "Okay, you're right. I don't know what your father feels about you, but I think that if he really loved either one of us he wouldn't have walked away without even trying. So I guess I think your assessment is correct."

"Thanks, Mom." He gave me a wan smile. "It's nice of you to admit I'm right, even if I'd rather be wrong." He took another giant bite of his sandwich. He had to chew for a minute or so before he could speak, and when he did it was a change of subject, sort of. "What about Ms. LeMoine? Does Chief Karlson know anything more about that?"

"And am I really a suspect?" I laughed. "Remember the rule: no pussyfooting around what you want to know."

"Fine. Are you?"

"No, I don't think so." I mentally crossed my fingers, thinking about that scarf. Sooner or later Ron would get around to asking. "Chief Karlson has to check out everyone who was there, and everyone who might have had access to the freezer, but I don't think he takes me very seriously as a suspect. We don't know just when she was killed, but when the coroner's report gets here, I suspect we'll find I was right here making your breakfast or something."

"She was probably killed during the night," Brian pointed out. The kid refused to be comforted.

"Well, that does seem likely. According to Chantal, her mom must've gone out sometime after eleven, and she hadn't come home when Chantal got up at six. I guess it must have happened before then. And I was here all night, so we're just fine. No sudden urges that took me out driving alone or anything. Just asleep in the room next to yours, right where I belonged."

"And right where no one can prove you were, since Dad's not here," he muttered, so quietly I almost didn't hear him. Was the boy actually afraid I'd done it, or just worried that any crack in my defense might buy him a one-way ticket to Dallas? Or was he simply angry because life had gotten weird?

"I didn't kill her. And I trust Ron Karlson to find the right person."

Brian put his plate in the sink. I'm still trying to train him to take it all the way to the dishwasher.

"I have to do some homework," he announced, not responding to my comment. "But could we go over and run on the Old Loop later?"

The Old Loop was a bit of abandoned road that ran along the West Side of the Island a little too close to the edge of the bluffs overlooking the Sound. With the pavement gradually returning to the woods, where it hadn't fallen into the water, it was a good place for running. And thinking, and maybe even talking.

"Sure." He had something on his mind, I could see that. It would come out later, whatever it was, if it was anything more than being upset about his dad. That, and finding a body, and wondering if his mother would be arrested for murder—Brian had reasons enough to be cranky.

After Brian went upstairs, I sat at the table and fretted. What on earth was I going to do about Allen and his threats? How could I hire a lawyer to fight him when pretty much all the money I had came from Allen in the first place? When he'd moved to Dallas, I'd opened a bank account here in my own name. Allen had arranged for an automatic deposit to it every month. A deposit that was due in just a few days. I wondered if it would come. It also occurred to me to wonder how much his salary had increased over the years. Our allowance hadn't changed.

I didn't have any real income of my own. We'd agreed that I should stay at home and be a parent to Brian. I'd never regretted that, but the thought of divorce made me sorry not to have a career of my own. I'd done a little writing, an article here and there for quirky little industry journals or obscure magazines, but nothing that amounted to much. I was going to have to come up with some real work, and I wasn't going to be able to return to the life and career I'd had when I met Allen. Nor was I willing to remain dependent on him, no matter what a judge decided.

I sighed. I couldn't do much about that mess until Monday. Not to worry, I had plenty of other things to fret over. For one thing, I needed to call Mom and tell her I was getting a divorce. Although I wanted to tell her about Letitia LeMoine, I hated to tell her about the divorce. "I told you so" would be the least of the things she'd say. Mom never much liked Allen, though I had to give her credit for keeping her mouth shut about his shortcomings. But with this news, all restraints would be off. She'd think it would make me feel better, but I didn't feel up to the drama. That was one aggravation I could—and would—put off.

Meanwhile, how on earth were Kitty and I going to get a Yearbook assembled in a week? Especially since we had to start over from scratch, thanks to Mrs. Loudmouth's incompetence, or negligence, or whatever it was. From there I shifted to wondering if Ron had found anything helpful. I also wondered about the Bellingham police not sending a detective. I couldn't decide if they were proving a point about our need to pay for the services we demanded, or showing respect for Ron's ability. Maybe they really didn't have anyone to send.

Of course, that led to thinking about Ron himself, unnerving territory. I'd met Chief Ron Karlson soon after moving to Pismawallops Island, and for years saw him around from time to time, often at special events. I'd joined several Island guilds and committees early on, things like the PTA as a matter of course, and others—the library guild and later a planning commission—because I was interested in how things were run. Allen encouraged that sort of thing, and I won't deny that influenced me. Back then I was still trying to be the wife he thought he'd bought. Married. I hadn't yet realized I'd never please him, but I did discover that I liked being a person who didn't just gripe about stuff, but made things happen. And I admit I liked being in charge, or at least in the know.

I'd never really gotten to know Ron, though, until homecoming last year. That was Brian's first year at the high school, and I hadn't known any better than to volunteer for parking patrol during the homecoming game and dance. I'd figured it was a way to get out of watching the game. I didn't like football, and thanked whatever gods there might be that Brian was a runner, not a footballer. Directing traffic kept me out of the dance, too, which was part of my plan. I had no desire to numb my eardrums for good.

But there'd been a huge traffic jam after the game, which everyone but me had expected. So I found myself there with Ron, trying to sort it out, and by the time we were done I had developed a profound respect for his skills, and he seemed impressed by my vocabulary, if not my traffic management. The next time I saw him in the grocery store, he'd addressed me as "JJ" instead of "Ms. MacGregor." It had felt good to be called by my first name, a feeling I had never stopped to analyze.

The memory made me realize how much it had hurt when he'd gone back to the formal form of address yesterday. I was glad it hadn't lasted, but I'd gotten his message loud and clear: he wouldn't cut me any slack just because we were friends. If we were friends. I sat there a long time, until Brian came to insist we go run.

I started our workout pumped on adrenaline: Brian drove us to the trail, an experience guaranteed to turn my hair grey and ramp up my heart rate. He's not bad for a beginner, I just tend to get a little tense when other people are driving, especially since I still thought of Brian as a little kid, and he'd only had his learner's permit for a few months.

The silence between us on the drive wasn't good. We spoke only once, when Brian asked, "Any word about Ms. LeMoine?" and I said, "Nope." Then we both went back to concentrating on the road.

We made it to the trail in one piece, and Brian tucked the keys into the little pocket in his running shorts. He was taking no chances about who'd drive home. We stretched for about a minute and hit the trail together. Brian didn't stay with me long, accelerating away from me as soon as he had warmed up. I kept plodding and tried not to envy his youth and energy.

We were just finishing when Ron found us. Brian had gone out about twice as far as I had, and had caught me a quarter mile from the car on the way back. That forced me to pick up the pace to stay with him, leaving me drenched in sweat and gasping for breath, but a little pleased with myself, too, for having done it.

Ron was leaning on my car watching our arrival, a hint of a smile creeping past his best efforts to suppress it. I wanted to turn around and run away, but scotched that cowardly notion, mostly because I couldn't run another step. I knew I looked ghastly, because my hair pretty much gives up and dies when the real sweating begins. The day was warm and humid enough to make me sweat a lot. And what with my uniboob bra squashing me in all the wrong places and a certain aroma wafting about me, I didn't want to go any closer.

A few days ago I wouldn't have cared how Ron Karlson saw me. He was just a friend—an acquaintance, really. But a lot had changed in the last two days, even if he didn't know it.

I wiped my face on my shirt and grabbed my hat out of the back waistband of my shorts, where I'd stuffed it when I got too hot, and jammed it on my head. If you can't fix the hair, hide the hair.

"Hi Ron. Were you looking for me?" Did I hope he was, or fear he was? Either way, I was dying from trying to keep my breathing calm when I wanted to bend over and draw in great gasping gulps of air.

"I was checking the lot and saw your car, so I thought I'd stop and let you know I haven't found anything for you at Ms. LeMoine's house."

"Blast!"

Brian looked from one of us to the other. "What? What were you looking for?"

I glanced at Ron and saw nothing to indicate I shouldn't answer. I managed to explain, gasping for breath every couple of words. "Something for the Yearbook. She seems to have managed to wipe the hard drive on our computer. We'd hoped she'd saved her work somewhere."

"No kidding?" Brian sounded impressed. "Destroying a computer's *hard*. She must've been really something." Fortunately, he gave me no chance to elaborate. "You should talk to Justin, he's really good with computers. Maybe he can recover some of the files."

Ron and I exchanged looks again. I could see he was trying to decide if Brian was boasting, unreasonably optimistic, or onto something. I knew Justin; Brian was probably right.

"If he managed to restore the thing, it would be a

huge help," I managed to say without excessive panting.

"That it would," Ron conceded. "Especially if there turned out to be financial records on there." That's a cop for you—always chasing the money angle.

"I can tell you that Maddy doesn't work that way," I grumbled, meaning either on the computer or illicitly. "And I've made a good start on an audit and I think you're barking up the wrong fire hydrant." "Started the audit" was an exaggeration, but I had made a start at balancing the checkbook.

Brian looked from me to his watch. "Justin'll be at work now, but maybe we can go over tomorrow and try to recover stuff."

Justin Green, having turned sixteen a couple of months ahead of Brian, had entered the workforce with flair. He was creating a web site for Island Arts, so they could join the Internet world and sell to more than the straggle of tourists who made it to Pismawallops Island and into the Orca Café and the attached gallery. I suspect Justin talked them into it in order to get himself a job that didn't involve bagging groceries or serving food. Not that I held it against him. I hoped Brian could do as well when his turn came. It looked like he'd need a good job.

"I'll take the boys over tomorrow and see what they can do," I told Ron. "Probably not too early."

Brian rolled his eyes, but refrained from voicing the "No, duh!" he telegraphed.

Ron nodded. "Good enough. Call me if you find anything."

I wanted to think of something else to keep him there, talking to us, and was shocked at myself when I realized it. This was completely demoralizing. The last thing I needed was for Brian to tumble to the fact that I was getting the hots for the police chief. He'd either freak out about it or he would try to help things along, figuring an old lady like me couldn't handle a romance on my own. Given my track record he might have been right, but I still didn't want help.

"I've got to cool down," Brian said, starting to jog off up the road. "You should too, Mom."

"Right." I tried not to sound as incredulous as I felt. Move more? I was ready to sink to the hood of my car, but Ron—or was he the Chief today?—took my arm. I cringed, aware how damp my skin must feel. A trickle of sweat ran down my cleavage and I desperately wanted to wipe it out of there, but some things you just can't do in front of witnesses. I tried to ignore the tickle and pay attention to where we were going.

Ron was propelling me up the old road. "I'll walk with you for a few minutes. There's something I want to ask you."

This was the cop, not the friend. I tried to sound casual, but worry over what he would ask, and an excessive awareness of his hand on my arm, made it an uphill battle. "Oh? Have you learned something new?"

"You might say that." He dropped my arm and turned to face me. He didn't look happy, and I had a sinking feeling it had nothing to do with my personal hygiene. "Why didn't you tell me that was your scarf wrapped around Ms. LeMoine's neck?"

All hope of an intelligent response abandoned me. "Umm. . . maybe I wasn't anxious to lay claim to the murder weapon?" Great answer, JJ. That not only sounded guilty, but stupid.

"Try again."

I gave the matter some thought. "Well, I didn't want to claim the murder weapon. But I also—well, I don't even know when I last wore that thing." Last was right. I certainly would never put that scarf

77

around my own neck again. "I could have lost it anywhere and anyone could have picked it up."

"I'm not even sure she died at the school." He started walking again and I followed along. My sweat was drying, leaving me cold. Or was it the implications of our conversation that had chilled me? I knew I ought to tell him what Kitty had said, that she might have had the scarf.

I couldn't do it. I just couldn't point the finger at my best friend, or her family. I guessed that meant I'd resolved my doubts about Kitty. I gave up and concentrated on my cooling muscles, keeping moving so they wouldn't stiffen too badly.

Brian had turned and was coming back down the road, walking now, so we had a minute or two more.

I finally decided to ignore all the questions about the scarf and focus on the other issue Ron had raised. "Where was she killed, then?"

"I don't know. I don't know much of anything, but something feels off. JJ?" He turned his head to look at me, making me painfully aware how close he was standing. "Keep all this to yourself, will you? I shouldn't even be telling you. Hell, I must be getting old, running off at the mouth this way."

"I'll keep quiet. And thanks for telling me." And for believing I didn't do it, I wanted to add, but wasn't quite brave enough. Nor did I dare point out that he wasn't old, still on the sunny side of fifty, if the rumor mill could be trusted. Only a little older than me.

"Just, for God's sake, JJ, don't keep any more secrets from me, please!"

Brian caught us before I could say anything regrettable, and whatever had been on his mind all day, he was ready to talk now. Just not to me.

"Chief Karlson? There's something you ought to know."

78

"Oh?"

Brian shifted from one foot to the other like a little kid who needs to pee. "It might be nothing, really, sir. But, well, when we all left after practice on Thursday, the girls were there too. The cheerleaders," he clarified. "And Justin heard Chantal saying her mom was late."

"And?" Ron prompted him.

"Well, about an hour after he got home, Justin saw Chantal drive by. She goes past his house to get home, you know."

"So her mom finally got her and they went home," I shrugged it off.

Brian gave me a reproachful look. "Justin says Chantal was alone."

"Alone? Was she driving her own car, then?" Ron had his notebook out now.

"No, sir. I think they just have the one car."

"So how is Justin sure that it was Chantal and not her mom?"

I stood aside, watching the two of them play ping-pong with the questions and answers. Brian was a little pale in his earnest desire to get things right. Ron did nothing to rush or intimidate my son, and I warmed to him again.

"Well, he's sure it was their car. It's that hot pink Bug," Brian added. "Kind of hard to miss, you know? But I'm not sure about the driver, if he could swear it was her and not her mom."

Ron nodded. "Chantal and Ms. LeMoine look similar from a distance," he suggested.

Brian agreed. "Anyway," he blushed a little but stuck to his guns, "we wondered if Chantal was lying, if she maybe, well, you know," he finished lamely.

"You wondered if she killed her mom?" I could have bitten my tongue as soon as I'd said it. Not for the words—he needed to say what he thought—but for the tone. All horrified-Mom, like nice boys wouldn't think that.

"Well, yeah, Mom. I mean, maybe Chantal just dropped her off in town or something." He glanced at Ron for encouragement, and got a nod. "But she didn't say anything about that, did she?"

"Well, no. She didn't. I didn't ask about the afternoon, though. Just when she'd last seen her mother, which was when she went to bed Thursday night."

"But she might have been lying," Brian insisted.

I could see Ron agreed. "I'll talk to Justin, and then I'll have to have another talk with Chantal." He sighed. That would mean another trip to the mainland, nearly an entire day lost to unseating a lie. Didn't the girl want the killer caught? That was food for thought. Teens had been known to kill their parents, often for reasons that made little sense to the adult mind.

We reached the cars, and Ron fixed us both with his cop stare. "You two keep all this to yourselves, you hear? And Brian?"

"Yes, sir?" I'd never heard Brian use so many "sirs" before. He was feeling his way through unfamiliar territory, taking no chances.

"Don't talk to anyone else about this, okay? I don't want any rumors started."

Brian started to speak, but Ron raised a hand. "I'll talk to Justin, and find out whatever he can tell me— and tell him to keep quiet." He glanced at me for the first time in the whole exchange with Brian. "You two go on home now, and good luck with your computer tomorrow."

I'd almost forgotten. We'd be seeing Justin tomorrow to try to fix the computer. It looked like we were all in this together, like it or not.

- 6 -

PRAYING AND PRYING

By the time I got up Sunday morning I had figured out one thing I could do. I couldn't chase down Chantal and make her talk. I couldn't slap some action out of the mainland cops. I couldn't even get Brian out of bed until lunchtime. But I could go to church.

I wasn't getting religion, nor planning to go dump it all on God to figure out. As a rule, I was more inclined to sleep in on Sunday morning than go to church. But church had something thing my bed didn't: other people. In particular, many of the people who had interacted with Letitia LeMoine would be there. Two of the library ladies attended the Methodist church, while the third was Presbyterian. Maybe I could find out what had upset them. It was a place to start, anyway.

Over a quick breakfast I worked it out. I knew Ms. Day, the PE teacher and cheerleading coach, was a Methodist. Maddy too. Add in a couple of library ladies, and that seemed like the place to concentrate my efforts. Patty Reilly was Episcopalian, where according to the listing in the local paper, services started a half hour later than the Methodists. If I timed it right, I could attend church with the Methodists, chat with people at the coffee hour, and then show up among the Episcopalians just in time for the benediction, and buttonhole Patty Reilly during their coffee hour.

I put some thought into dressing for the occasion. In the end, I selected my only decent dark slacks and layered a cardigan sweater over a blouse, so I could adjust for varying temperatures. As I recalled, the Methodist sanctuary was cold. But Fellowship Halls could get warm when everyone crowded in to drink coffee and share gossip.

I left a note for Brian just in case he woke up before I returned, and headed to town. We call the cluster of homes, businesses, and churches huddled near the ferry dock "town," and the mapmakers even give it the name of Orcaville.

A glance at my watch as I left the house told me I was cutting it a bit close. I didn't want to get pulled over for speeding on my way to church. Given how seldom I attended, I didn't think the Big Guy would get me out of it, and it would strain relations with Ron even more. So I made it just in time to slip into a back pew as the first lines of the opening hymn rang out. I happily joined in with the best part of any church service, taking my seat with the rest of the congregation when the song ended.

As I sat looking over the congregation—an advantage of the rear pew, though it's not always easy to identify the backs of heads—I wondered why I'd come for the service. I could have slipped in for coffee hour, the same as I planned for the Episcopalians. Maybe it just seemed wrong, somehow. Or maybe I'd come for the music.

I wasn't there for the sermon, I decided half an hour later. Since nothing the pastor had to say was holding my attention, I gave up and jotted a list on the back of the pew bulletin. After listing the people I wanted to talk to—I included Carlos, and Mrs. Ainsley, the mother of Tina-the-Cheerleader, as well as Maddy and the other women I expected to find at the churches today—I added a note: *where's the ice cream?* Those missing ice cream bars bothered me, though I couldn't say why. Surely the killer wouldn't be dumb enough to dump them anywhere they could be traced back to him. Or her. But why weren't they in the school dumpster? Did our killer have an ice cream obsession? Would we find a heap of empty boxes in someone's trash, and a ten-pound weight gain, if we just knew where to look?

I stood for the final hymn, and made my escape to the Fellowship Hall, first in line for a cup of coffee. Despite my sweater I'd gotten chilled during the service, and realized too late why, in defiance of church tradition, the back pew had been unoccupied. Closest to the drafty doors and farthest from the heat source, it served to distinguish the regulars from the rest of us too ignorant to avoid it.

I thought I was in luck when I realized that the library ladies were serving the refreshments, but had no chance for more than a quick greeting as the line moved me on and away. I'd have to come back to them, a decision made all the easier when I realized I had no idea what to ask, short of whether they'd decided to solve their conflict with Letitia LeMoine in a permanent way. I didn't think that was the kind of reference question the librarians would rush to answer. I took a couple of chocolate chip cookies and moved along.

I had better luck with Ms. Day. As I stood nursing the warm coffee cup to thaw my fingers, she came through the line, spotted me, and headed right over with her coffee and cookie. I smiled a little to see she wore her gray-streaked hair in the same long braid she did in gym class.

"Why, Ms. MacGregor! How nice to see you here." Her smile felt genuine, and I didn't even detect the irony she might have put into it, given how seldom I attended.

"Yes, somehow it seemed right to come today," I answered in perfect truth, though with every intention to deceive.

"Oh, that was dreadful, wasn't it? So upsetting, the poor woman."

"And her poor daughter," I put in. "She's one of your cheerleaders, isn't she?"

Ms. Day's pleasant expression took a turn toward the sour, but before she could answer we both saw something that surprised me and turned her even sourer. Elvis Fingal descended the stairs and headed straight for the coffee. As usual, he was dressed like a man twenty years younger, and the effect was, in my opinion, unfortunate.

"That man." Ms. Day's lips were tight. "Since when does he come to our church?"

I felt a frown furrowing my own brow. "I don't know. I thought he was a Baptist."

Ms. Day gave an unladylike snort, which I took to mean she didn't think much of Fingal's religion, wherever he might go to church.

That was interesting. "Do you know something I should know?"

She shrugged. "I don't think it's any secret that he likes to watch the cheerleaders. Well, that's what the men do, and don't think I don't know it. But most of them are, well, a little bit discreet. Fingal is always hanging around practices. To check on progress, he says."

I decided to play devil's advocate. "It's his job to make sure they are doing okay, isn't it?"

She didn't look any happier. "It's his job to be sure

that they do nothing indecent. But in making me cheerleading coach, he has delegated that responsibility. Seeing that in all the years I have been coaching the girls there has never been a scandal, he could show a little trust."

"True enough. Plus," I added, "it's not like he handles his own work that well. If he has time to hang out and watch the cheerleaders, he should have his work done. So why does Annette have to cover for him so often?"

Ms. Day gave me an appraising look. "So you noticed that, did you? I can't imagine why the school keeps him on."

"I'm surprised at you, Ms. Day."

"I call them as I see them."

"I'm surprised you didn't know his uncle's on the School Board."

"Oh, Lord." She shook her head. "How could I have forgotten that? He's been there since the Flood, more or less." She shook her head again. "I suppose that's how Fingal got to be hired back here. He never was much good as a teacher, yet when he moved back last year, they promoted him to where he couldn't cause trouble, rather than fight with Old Fingal. At least, that's the rumor."

"So now he works hard holding up the pillars in the lunchroom," I commented, and we both laughed, with a guilty look around to make sure we weren't being overheard. "I hadn't realized he was so new, or that he'd worked here before. I didn't pay much attention to the High School until Brian started last year."

"He taught here a couple of years right out of college, then moved on. I suppose they got tired of him wherever he was, so he came back. But if he doesn't leave my girls alone, he'll be one sorry Fingal, I can tell you that."

"Leave them alone?" I was startled. "Meaning what?"

"Oh, as far as I know all he does is look and leer. But that's more than they should have to put up with, I think."

I nodded, though part of me thought that any girl who went in for cheerleading was probably looking for some leers. I knew that wasn't fair. That was the teenaged JJ speaking, the one who had never run any risk of being labeled 'the one most likely to.' Even tarty teens didn't need to be leered at by a man nearly old enough to be their father, and one in charge of their school, to boot.

I said goodbye to Ms. Day, and tried once more to chat with the library ladies behind the coffee pot. I had to give up, unsure if they were deliberately avoiding me—with cheerful politeness—or were truly too busy to chat. Helen Arbuthnot smiled and peered over her glasses just as she did at the library desk, and spoke of the weather and the sermon until I had to move on. The other librarian—I thought her name was Finley—was even older, with a hint of a blue wash in her gray hair, and far fewer words. She also smiled, but as though she hoped a smile would be allowed to take the place of speech. Neither gave me any opening to ask leading questions before they turned to greet the person behind me.

In any case, they would have to wait. A look at my watch told me I had just enough time to walk down to the Episcopal Church and join the worshippers leaving their service for the social hour. I hadn't seen Maddy, who should have been present, but figured I could talk to her any time.

I waved greetings to several people as I left, but didn't stop to chat. Outside, I drew a deep breath, straightened my sweater, and strode off down the street, there being no fancy touches like sidewalks in

Orcaville. There also wasn't much traffic on a Sunday morning, though cars were starting to trickle out of the church lot.

Halfway down the block, I realized that Ms. Day had ignored my efforts to learn how she felt about Chantal and her mother. Had that been intentional?

I arrived at the Episcopal church in time to mingle with the people emerging from the sanctuary, and spotted Patty Reilly chatting with a couple I didn't know. I got a cup of coffee for protective coloration—though by this time I didn't really want any more of the stuff—and exchanged meaningless greetings with a few people while waiting for Patty to finish with her friends.

At last they moved apart and I darted to her side. "Good morning, Patty." My greeting sounded a little too bright and cheery to my ears, but she seemed to accept it.

"Why, hello, JJ. I didn't know you attended here."

"I just thought I'd try it out this morning." I hoped I wouldn't get struck by lightning for lying in a church.

"And what did you think of the service?"

I wondered if that was a pointed question. Did she know I'd snuck in just for the social hour? I managed not to blush or stammer. "Oh, it was pretty nice. I think I'll probably stay Methodist, though." I added a bit of honesty to offset my lies. "Well, actually I'll probably remain a backslider." She laughed, apparently without duplicity. Her next words gave me just the opening I needed.

"I suppose we all feel a bit of a need to touch base with our religion after what happened to Ms. LeMoine." She shook her head. "Those poor kids. Is Brian okay?"

"He seems to be handling it well. I won't say it didn't upset him, but he's recovering." I noticed she seemed more concerned about Brian than about Chantal, even though the girl was in her play. Was that just because I was Brian's mom? Or did she not like Chantal?

"Well, I'd be more worried if it didn't upset him," she said.

"Good point." We shared an understanding smile, and I dared to ask, "Who on earth do you suppose could have done such a thing, anyway?" I took a sip from my cup, and was pleased to find that the Episcopalians made good coffee. Maybe I should reconsider my allegiance to the Methodists, such as it was.

Patty considered my question. "Well, since I didn't—though I admit there have been times in the last few weeks I would have happily kicked her off the end of the ferry dock—I really can't say. She didn't exactly make herself popular, did she?"

"No," I agreed. "I know quite a lot of people who aren't sorry she's gone. But not one of them strikes me as a likely killer."

"I know what you mean," she agreed. "A normal adult does not kill someone for being an annoying know-it-all pain in the posterior."

I laughed. "Gee, Patty, don't hold your feelings in like that. I take it she really got in your way with the play?"

"Ugh. Constantly trying to direct. And I can't believe I let her persuade me to give Chantal the lead."

"Oh? I wondered how that came about."

"'Persuaded' might not be exactly the word I'm looking for. She dazzled me with offers of help and a great story about how she had her heart set on her daughter using those acting lessons she'd taken, blah, blah. If that girl ever took any acting lessons, they never got beyond how to act like an airheaded vamp."

I had a new thought. "You mean she isn't really one?"

Patty laughed. "Hard to say, you know." She gave the question some thought. "I don't think the girl is stupid. Not brilliant, not an academic type, but she understands the way the world works, you know? If she's a vamp, I think she knows exactly what she's doing and why." She gave me an assessing look. "Are you helping Chief Karlson with the investigation? Is that why you're here?"

I shook my head. "Ron Karlson wants none of my help. I just can't stop thinking about it, you know? Plus, Kitty and I are stuck now with the Yearbook, on which she did nothing at all. If she weren't already dead, I might be tempted to kill her for that." I decided not to mention the computer issues. The less said about that, the better. Maybe someone would say something that would show they knew more than they should.

We shared a guilty laugh over my tasteless joke, and I moved off to chat with another acquaintance. But I had a feeling that Patty Reilly wasn't one bit fooled. She knew I was investigating. I just hoped that my gut feelings about her were accurate, because if she was the killer, I was in trouble.

My thoughts gloomy, I turned to leave, and found myself face to face with a tall, perfectly made-up and well-endowed blonde. For the life of me I couldn't remember her first name, but I knew this was Tina's mother, and wasn't letting the opportunity slip.

"Good morning, Mrs. Ainsley! So good to see you."

She gave me a sour look. "Good enough, I suppose. And I suppose you're like all the others, eager to gossip about 'poor Ms. LeMoine.'"

"Er," I began, but she wasn't listening.

"That woman was a plague on our Island, pushy as anything, and whatever she got I'm willing to bet she deserved it." She finished up with a word I won't let

Brian use, and stalked off, leaving me breathless.

After a minute, I walked back up the street to my car, the only one left in the Methodist parking lot. What was that all about? There was a bitterness there that went deep. Deeper than resentments over cheer-leading jobs?

I glanced at my watch. Time to go home and schlep the boys to the school to fix—I hoped—our computer. But I couldn't shake that image of Mrs. Ainsley, perfectly dressed and coiffed and spewing venom over the corpse of Letitia LeMoine.

- 7 -

COMPUTERS AND COPS AND ACCOUNTING, OH MY!

The computer-recovery mission was a bust. I hauled the boys over to the school just after noon and turned them loose on the thing while I went to work on the PTA books. The boys knew I trusted them not to get into anything they shouldn't. Besides, nothing was as interesting to them as the problems with the computer itself, especially since the wifi was off for the weekend and the Internet unavailable. Kids today are weird.

While the boys worked, I went back to untangling the PTA accounts I'd started on the previous day. The longer I worked, the more convinced I was that we'd been idiots to make Maddy the Treasurer. I had no doubt that she was honest—Letitia LeMoine was either a fool or a troublemaker to have accused Maddy of cooking the books. Unfortunately, it was equally clear Maddy was no CPA. Furthermore, everything seemed to be in the account book, even if in a rather scrambled form, so the idea that she might have killed to cover something on the computer was absurd. I'd have to tell Ron so.

91

Had Ron talked to her? He'd made it clear she was a suspect, at least to the same degree Kitty and I were. I hoped she hadn't brought up the accusations about the books, but the odds were good she had. Maddy would never try to hide her reasons for disliking the murder victim. She didn't know how to be dishonest, and she was always polite. Which made it hard to imagine her killing someone and stuffing the body in the freezer, which was rude no matter how you looked at it. Still, Maddy was upset by the accusations, afraid someone would believe she'd stolen money, despite Kitty's assurances that we knew better.

I was deep in the numerical tangle she'd made of our ledger when Ron himself came in. I jumped when I looked up and saw him in the doorway.

"Geez, Ron, don't you ever knock? Or take a day off," I added, taking in his uniform and remembering it was Sunday.

"No to both of those." He raised one eyebrow, a trick I envied. "I stopped in at the computers, but the boys said you were in here. Those the PTA accounts?"

"Yeah."

"I thought Mrs. Takahira was the Treasurer."

"She is. But like I said, I'm doing an audit, trying to straighten out her mess." I hated it when he pretended not to know the obvious.

"Would that be the mess that led to Ms. LeMoine accusing her of theft?"

"Um, yeah."

"And what are you finding?" He wouldn't let me avoid the question.

"That Mrs. Loudmouth was wrong, as usual. Maddy's incompetent, not dishonest. And she kept the accounts on paper, not on the computer."

"You're sure?"

"Well, I'm sure it's all here, and I'm sure she flunked math. Ask Mr. Ammon. He taught her when she was in high school."

"He's been here long enough to be teaching the children of his old students?"

"Apparently." I wondered what he was up to, since I was certain he knew better than I how long Russ Ammon had been at Orcaville High. I decided not to let him get away with it.

"You grew up here, didn't you? You should know."

"Actually, I grew up down in Mt. Vernon. And I don't have any kids to have taken Algebra from him." He looked away, and I couldn't read his expression as he said it.

"You still know darned well how long Mr. Ammon's been teaching here."

"Twenty-three years this semester," he answered. "Does Mrs. Takahira need money?" He wasn't letting go of the real question.

"Doesn't everyone? Maddy is totally honest, and if she weren't, she couldn't have gotten enough out of the PTA to so much as make a single payment on their tractor." The Takahiras had the only working farm left on the Island and were getting rich about as fast as most small farmers. I figured Ron knew that, so there was no point in pretending Maddy couldn't have found a use for some extra cash. I just wanted to be sure he knew that she wasn't the sort to take it, and that she couldn't have gotten enough to be useful even if she were.

"What kind of money do you guys deal in, anyway?" he asked. If he was hoping for something impressive, he was out of luck.

"Oh, a few thousand a year, but we don't have more than a few hundred in our account at any time. We make most of it in the fall with the magazine sales, but it goes right back out to pay for the big stuff—mostly a couple of assemblies. We get a bit every week from the ice cream, which we pass out to the teachers for supplies and books."

"What's in your account right now?"

"According to the bank, three hundred seventy-two dollars and change. According to Maddy, about ten times that. I suspect the decimals got away from her again, but I haven't found the place yet. No pun intended."

He laughed. "I see what you mean. Not too likely she'd steal money and cover her tracks that way. Any chance she stole it and didn't cover her tracks at all?"

I shook my head. "I don't think so. We certainly never had thirty-three hundred in here, except for about ten minutes at the end of the magazine sale. I figure we should have somewhere around four hundred, so the bank statement looks pretty reasonable to me. We *do* use proper money-handling protocols, Ron."

"Okay. Mrs. Takahira isn't an embezzler. Now," he gave me a look as though wondering if he were a safe distance away, "I know you aren't going to like this next question, but I have to ask." He took a step backward before asking, "Could Ms. LeMoine have scared Mrs. Takahira enough that she would, well, fight back?"

I glared at him, just to let him know I hated the question. Then I gave it some serious thought, nibbling on the end of my pen to help the process. Could she? Maddy was mild-mannered, and lousy at math, but she was no weakling. Physically, she could have killed Letitia, though stuffing the body into the freezer would have been a challenge. But she wasn't stupid, either, and if she couldn't sort out the books, she knew that in the end they would get sorted out, and the money would all be accounted for. So I didn't see how she could have been that scared. Nor would Maddy have been stupid enough to leave the body in the freezer.

I explained my thinking, and Ron nodded. "Putting her in the freezer bugs me. It's sort of. . . crazy."

I had to agree. "Besides," I added, "I don't think Maddy has a clue how to reformat a computer, assuming that has something to do with it."

"Well, that's a lot less likely if you're right about the financial records all being on paper," he said, making no effort to hide his skepticism. "But I'll bear it in mind. I wonder," he added with a glance at me and another step backward, "what an accusation like that might have done to the family credit at the bank."

"Well," I pretended to consider the question. "I suppose it might be a problem, if everyone at the bank didn't know the Takahiras, and if the loan officer wasn't a close family friend."

He shook his head, disgusted with himself. "Geez, I should've known that. A person would think you were a local, the way you know this stuff."

That stung. How long did it take to become a local? Apparently more than seven years.

And, deep down, it bugged me that Ron, in particular, thought of me as an outsider. After all, he'd just admitted he wasn't born here either.

The police chief, however, had moved on to other matters. He was looking over his notes. To my delight, he kept them in the traditional little spiral-bound notebook. "I've got quite a list of people Ms. LeMoine annoyed or threatened in small ways. Mrs. Takahira, Mr. Hernandez—"

"Ah," I interrupted. "So someone told you about Carlos and the Spring Faire, too?"

"*He* did," he said with an emphasis intended, no doubt, to remind me I was not yet forgiven for the scarf. "Various people involved with the play where she thrust her daughter into the lead, the former head cheerleader, and I suppose, her mother."

I remembered Mrs. Ainsley's venom that morning, and nodded. "Definitely look at the mom. She's angry about something."

"Is she?" Ron asked. "I'll have a chat with her. But I know Mrs. Ainsley. She's usually angry about something, and has never so much as written a letter to the editor to try to do anything about it."

"That doesn't mean she didn't do something now."

"True. Also," he continued, dropping the Ainsley question, "the entire Library Guild is upset, including the staff. She tried to force her way in and insisted that they needed all sorts of modernizations."

"So that's what they were so agitated about."

"You know something about it?"

"I missed a couple of meetings, but at the last one, the ladies were all in a swivet about something that had been suggested. They refused to even discuss it. LeMoine wasn't there that night."

"A swivet?"

"Only word to use," I insisted. "You know those ladies." The Library Guild ladies, volunteers and staff alike, were an apparently fluttery bunch of seniors who somehow managed to keep our library running with wondrous efficiency. If they got upset, it was a swivet, not a snit or a rage.

"I know them," Ron conceded me the swivet. "But what's so terrible about modernizing the library? Seems like it ought to keep up."

"Mostly that libraries are supposed to be for books, I think. The ladies don't much like new-fangled technology." I didn't add that I rather sympathized, especially right now with all our new-fangled computer stuff lost in the ether.

"Why should they care what Ms. LeMoine said?"

"Because she came on awfully strong, claiming that

unless they moved with the times there wasn't much point in having a library at all."

"Ahh." He got it. The problem was Letitia LeMoine's idea of progress. "So. . . she threatened to convince the powers that be that the library isn't meeting the needs of today's patrons? Or did she try to get them all thrown off the board, so the little old ladies who run the place would lose their jobs?"

"Both, probably."

"Well, that's a better motive for murder than any I've seen so far."

I gulped, afraid he might really believe that. His next words set my mind at rest.

"But if the library ladies did it, I'd have expected to find a book embedded in her head, not your scarf knotted around her throat." He looked at me, one eyebrow raised.

I'd have preferred he didn't keep harping on it being my scarf. Maybe the best way to fix that was to talk about it.

"Um, about that scarf?"

"Yes?"

"I don't know just where I left it, so that someone got hold of it. But you know, I have to wonder if someone used it because it was handy, or," I hesitated and he finished for me.

"Or because it was yours?" He considered this. "Could be. JJ, I really do know that you didn't kill her. I just wish I knew what you think you're up to."

"I'm not 'up to' anything. I just want the killer found and the whole thing behind us."

Ron closed his notebook with a sigh. "Me too. I've got a list of people she irritated, annoyed, and threatened in minor ways, but nothing worth killing over. And I can't seem to find out anything about her life before coming here." He rubbed his head as though it hurt.

I had a thought. "I wonder if someone threatened to disrupt the little kingdom she seems to have been trying to build here, and if things got ugly—and, I don't know, they ended up killing her?"

"In self-defense? Blackmailers don't usually kill their victims. It's more apt to be the other way around."

"You don't need to laugh at me."

"I'm not." His brown eyes met mine and I felt an odd sensation in my gut. Like he was taking me way too seriously, but maybe not as a detective. "But I'm wondering what makes you think she had, well, something to hide?"

"Because she came here pretending to be something I'm pretty sure she wasn't."

"Meaning?"

"Meaning she came over all 'I'm the upper-crust lady from the City and I know how to do stuff,' but there are those around here who don't believe it. Who think she's not who she's pretending to be."

"You mean, those who think she's Lucy Lemmon?"

He'd clearly heard more than I had. Rats. Now I had to fish for information. "Lucy Lemmon?"

"She was before your time."

Blast! What was with this emphasis on my newcomer status?

"Lucy Lemmon grew up down at the South End with a dad who was drunk most of the time," Ron explained. "Her mom ran off when she was little, and Lucy disappeared when she was about sixteen. Her dad claimed she'd gone to the city to get a job, and maybe she did. I always wondered if he'd killed her, but I never found any evidence. Anyway, I wasn't chief then—just a deputy, and new here. Maybe seventeen or eighteen years ago. The dad fell off the ferry dock and drowned a few years later, so everyone just kind of forgot. Ms. LeMoine is about the right age."

"That sounds about like a match with what I've heard," I said, trying to pretend I'd known all that. In fact, I hadn't heard any more than a rumor that she had grown up around here and was poor as dirt back then. "Do you suppose she knew about the rumors?" Since Ron seemed in a mood to share information, I was going for anything I could learn.

"I don't see how she could have missed them."

I had to agree. None of us on the PTA had come right out and challenged her claims. But we'd all had a tendency to look polite but skeptical when she went on about her life in the Big City.

"The real question," Ron pointed out, "is if anyone had solid evidence they could have use to threaten her."

"Wouldn't people have recognized her? If she was Lucy Lemmon, I mean."

"Well, most of us had seen Lucy at one time or another. Some of her teachers are still here," he began.

That explained the question about Mr. Ammon. For that matter, Madeleine and Kitty must've gone to school with Lucy. Or not. They might have been enough older not to overlap. Counting on my fingers, I figured they'd be at least five years ahead. If Letitia was Lucy, she'd had her baby awfully young.

"Problem is," Ron went on, "Lucy didn't go to school much. Never made it into the Yearbook, and never made contact with anyone since she left. We didn't even have a photo. She had straight brown hair, is about all I can recall."

Letitia LeMoine had curly blonde hair, and every bit of the curl, as well as the color, was fake. But you could scarcely condemn a woman for coloring her hair.

"But it seems like Letitia was, well, older than that. Lucy would be what, thirty-three now?"

Ron shrugged. "About that. I can't guess women's ages."

I could. And that fake platinum hair, perfect make-up, and too-sexy clothing looked to me like a middle-aged woman trying to hang onto her youth. Or someone hiding from something. What had she left behind her when she came to Pismawallops?

"Anyway, Ms. LeMoine's license makes her the right age." He had another thought. "I wonder what she lived on? She doesn't seem to have held a job. And 'independently wealthy' doesn't sound like Lucy Lemmon, I don't think."

"I don't know. I had the impression she came off rather well in a divorce." That reminded me that I was looking at the same issue, and I grimaced.

Ron noticed, of course. "What's wrong?"

"Sore muscles," I lied. "Ran too far last night."

He didn't look like he believed me. I knew I should tell him about my divorce, but it didn't seem like the time. I pushed the conversation back to Lucy Lemmon.

"I can't see her background as worth killing her over, even if she was Lucy Lemmon."

He agreed. "Unless someone comes forward and says he or she was blackmailing the woman, it seems far-fetched." He thought for a minute. "Maybe she was blackmailing someone else. That would answer the income question, and make a more reasonable motive for murder. And in that case it seems more likely it was someone from the City. I don't think she'd been back here long enough to get anything that good on anyone, unless she got awfully lucky. What I don't understand," he confessed with male blindness, "is why she came back here at all, if she was Lucy Lemmon. Unless she was trying to hide, maybe?"

"Oh, I get that." I did. "She'd want to come back to where she'd been nobody and be a big fish, maybe even take over the little pond that didn't acknowledge her when she was a kid. Come back and show all those stuck-up snobs they don't know anything."

"Islanders aren't stuck up!"

I laughed. "Of course we aren't, Ron." If I emphasized the "we," it was only a tiny bit. "But she might have seen it that way if she was as much on the outside as it sounds."

He didn't agree or disagree with the implied criticism of Islanders, just grunted. "Huh. I don't think I'll ever understand women."

Probably not, I thought.

He was giving me that I-can-see-right-through-you look again. "JJ?"

"Hmm?" I pretended to be studying the ledger.

"What's bothering you and Brian?"

"Oh, murder, that sort of thing," I answered as lightly as I could. *Idiot!* I scolded myself. *Now's your chance. Tell him about the divorce!* Somehow, much as I wanted him to know I was about to be single, I couldn't bring myself to say it aloud. I didn't want to examine the reasons for that.

He leaned against the doorjamb and crossed his arms. "I'm sure it is. But what else is bugging you two, more than Kitty or Maddy or anyone else?"

"What makes you think anything is?" I was buying time, wishing Kitty were here to advise me.

"You've got worry written all over you. Both of you. Since I don't believe the two of you killed Ms. LeMoine, or whoever she turns out to be, I have to figure it's something else. Money trouble?"

"Not yet," I replied, the smart-aleck answer always ready to pop out before I engaged the brain.

"Meaning something's about to change?"

"Oh, hell!" I put down my pen. "I might as well tell you. Allen—my husband—is filing for divorce."

"Well, now." He seemed to be looking for a tactful

101

response, refusing to meet my eye. "I have to admit I thought maybe—I mean, I haven't seen much of him lately, seems like." He seemed to be mentally reviewing his behavior toward me for improprieties. If only!

"Oh, drop the slow-thinking local cop routine," I snapped to cover my own thoughts. "No, you haven't seen much of him. But we weren't divorced."

"And you two are upset because now he wants to be?"

"I'm upset because he wants to take Brian. Brain's upset because Allen doesn't act like he really wants him."

That got his full attention. "He what?"

"Allen says he's taking Brian, without even asking what either of us wants. And he's willing to use this murder or anything else he can think of as leverage. Bad environment for a growing boy, that sort of thing. If he weren't in Dallas," I added with malice, "I'd accuse him of doing the murder just to cause trouble for me."

"An understandably attractive theory." Ron might not understand women, but he understood human nature, which, come to think of it, ought to give him a pretty good start on women. "But someone here must be keeping him pretty well informed, if he already knows about this."

"Well, Brian called him Friday. Wanted to talk to his father about finding a dead body. He didn't get a very helpful response. But it must have been enough to make Allen think, because he called yesterday morning to say he was divorcing me and taking Brian."

"Brian doesn't want to go?"

"Not really, I think. He misses the Dad he used to have, but he pointed out to me just Friday that these days Allen's a jerk."

"You hadn't noticed?"

"Geez!" I exploded. "That's what Kitty said! No, I hadn't noticed. I hadn't paid any attention. I didn't care!"

"Okay, okay." He backed away a bit, but must have decided that was cowardly, because he came back, put a hand on my shoulder, and muttered something about "getting this whole thing cleared up." Then he was gone.

And I could still feel his hand on my shoulder.

This was getting totally out of control.

After a few minutes of trying to focus again on the accounts, I gave it up as hopeless and went in search of the boys. As expected, Brian and Justin were still in the library. Justin frowned at the computer monitor, and Brian wasn't offering any help. He turned when he heard my footsteps.

"Hi Mom. Did Chief Karlson find you?"

"Yeah. Thanks." I avoided his gaze and changed the subject before I could give anything away, I hoped. "Did you boys have any luck?"

"Not a bit." Justin sounded so mournful I almost laughed.

"Well, thanks for trying. Don't feel bad, Justin. I'll buy you guys lunch. Or breakfast, or whatever meal you're ready for."

He turned off the computer and swiveled in his chair, a frown struggling to make wrinkles on his teenaged face. "Ms. Mac, I just don't understand. When someone messes up and accidentally reformats the hard drive—which isn't very easy to do, but I figured that must've been what happened—there are always ways to retrieve at least some of the data. But if you really want to clean a computer—like if you're getting rid of it, and you don't want anyone to be able to access your personal information—you can do it. But you have to do that on purpose. You really can't do it by accident."

"So," I processed this information. "You're saying that Ms. LeMoine must have cleaned the hard drive on purpose?"

"Well, I don't know *who* did it, you understand. But I know it was done, and whoever did it dotted all the Ts and crossed all the Is."

"Dotted the Is and crossed the Ts," Brian corrected. Justin gave him a blank look.

"Someone wiped the computer clean," I repeated. "On purpose. Did you tell the Chief about this?"

"I wasn't sure yet when he was here. Do you think it's important?"

"What do you think?"

Justin grabbed his hair with both hands, standing it on end. "I don't know. But I suppose anything weird is important in a case like this, right?"

"I agree. Maybe it will help. How many people around here would know how to do that?"

The boys looked at each other and shrugged. They didn't know.

"Well, anyway, let's go find the Chief and get something to eat."

Computer geeks or not, they were normal teenaged boys with respect to food: pretty much always ready for a meal, regardless of when and what the last meal was. We locked up and went in search of enlightenment and calories—lots for them and very few for me. I had suddenly begun to feel self-conscious about my figure.

- 8 -

DINNER CONVERSATIONS CAN RUIN YOUR APPETITE

We stopped off at the police station en route to the Orca Diner. Ron just grunted when Justin told him about the hard drive. Like me, he wasn't sure what to make of it, and like me, he didn't want to say so in front of the boys.

"You guys go get your snack," he told us. "I'm headed over to interview Chantal again. Thanks to you," he nodded at Justin, "I know she's not telling me the whole truth about the day her mother died."

I had a sudden thought. "Where's their car?"

"Her driveway. Chantal apparently drove it to school the next morning, and she and her aunt parked it back at the house before leaving the Island."

"So her Mom must have come home, to have the car end up there. Chantal says she was home when she went to bed, and the car was still there—or was back—in the morning. Would Chantal lie about that? Could she have been killed at home, sometime during the night? Was Chantal really even there?" My mind raced through the possible implications, including that Chantal had killed her own mother. But how could she have gotten her into the freezer?

Brian has a more logical mind. "If the car was at the house in the morning, Ms. LeMoine didn't drive anywhere, at least not alone. So, either she was killed at the house, or Chantal dropped her somewhere, which would explain how Justin saw her driving by herself. Or someone picked her up to go somewhere. But Chantal said her mother was home all evening, but gone in the morning."

"Well, Ms. LeMoine might have met the killer after Chantal went to bed, and gone off somewhere with him to get killed," Justin suggested. "I mean, she didn't go to get killed, but, you know." His voice trailed off as we all followed his thought. If Letitia LeMoine didn't meet someone to be killed, it did look very much as though she'd met someone for something.

Ron nodded. "I think you have it, son. That's why I want to talk to the girl. I'm hoping she knows who her mother was meeting."

"'Whom.'" I corrected him automatically, a hazard of parenting. Then, feeling my face turn red, I rushed on. "So was it normal for Chantal to get up and take the car without talking to her mother?" I knew what would happen to Brian if he ever did that, and so did he. "And why would Chantal lie about being home, if she did?" Brian gave me the sort of look teens give clueless parents.

"Because she was up to something she shouldn't have been. Maybe she wasn't even home."

"Or," Justin again took Brian's idea one step further, "she's scared whoever it is will think she knows something and come after her."

"That's stupid," Brian argued. "Once she tells, she's safe enough, because everyone knows. It's keeping quiet that puts her in danger."

"Well," Justin defended his idea, "you see that, and

I see that, but Chantal is kind of a ditz, you know. Or maybe it's someone she knows. Her Dad, even. No one seems to know who he is."

Ron had listened to this exchange with interest, and his smile now was for Justin's bluntness, not his ideas. I admired his willingness to listen to the boys. Not just listen: to respect their insights. I remembered what Patty Reilly had said about Chantal not being dumb, or dumb like a fox, and wondered. Ditz or not, Chantal was hiding something, and Ron was going to have to find out what. I didn't envy him the job.

My phone burbled its absurd ringtone as the boys were finishing up their little snack at the Orca Diner an hour later.

"How about you and Brian come for dinner?" Kitty asked as soon as I picked up. "I think we all need a little distraction."

I looked at my watch. Four p.m. "Brian, how's your homework?"

He claimed he was done, so I promised to show up at Kitty's about six. We dropped Justin off on our way home. Before he got out, Justin whispered something to Brian, who turned bright red and punched him on the arm.

"Up yours, Green."

"In your dreams, Davis."

I looked at them, but got no inkling of their meaning. Whatever it was about, they weren't sharing it with me.

"C'mon, Mom," Brian urged before we were even in our own door. "We need to go run." Brian always claims he's looking out for my best interests when he makes me run. I think he's just sadistic. But he got me out, and we ran a couple of miles together at a decent pace—for me—in spite of the pile of food Brian had just consumed. Oh, for the digestion of a teen!

His little workout barely left us time to shower before leaving for Kitty and Mike's, and no time to talk. I wondered if that was his intention. If he wasn't ready to talk about his dad, I could give him time.

Of course, I had to let Brian drive, so I was sweating blood by the time he parked in the Padgett's driveway. I wanted another shower, or a stiff drink. Brian switched off the engine and pocketed the key, then twisted the mirror so he could check his hair before getting out. I raised my eyebrows. Maybe I wasn't the only one developing an interest in the opposite sex. Sarah? Kat? I had trouble imagining either, but the signs were there, including—I now realized—the exchange with Justin. Maybe this explained the way I'd been feeling. Were adolescent hormones contagious, like measles or the common cold?

Mike Padgett answered the door. He greeted me warmly, and I smiled to see him. Mike was the source of Kat's good looks, with dark hair and eyes, and a slightly crooked smile. He ran the lone service station on the Island, an old-style garage that offered repairs as well as gas. It wasn't glamorous, but he did well, since everyone had to buy gas. Most people also preferred to have at least minor car repairs done on the Island. Major ones, too, if otherwise they'd need a tow off the Island, an expensive proposition at best. Mike had a tow truck as well, and several employees. That made him a pillar of the community in my eyes. I wondered if he would give me a job.

Aware that I was staring, while my thoughts ran over what it would be like to be married to a guy like Mike, I mumbled some kind of greeting and followed him into the kitchen. Brian stopped long enough to be polite, before disappearing into the living room where the girls were watching TV. Mikey was annoying them by making sarcastic comments about the mushy parts. Give him another year or so to discover girls and hormones.

Kitty declined my offer of help, handing me a glass of wine instead. "Mike and I have it all under control."

I sat at the kitchen table, sipping the wine and watching them work. They did have it all under control, working together with the ease of long familiarity. An ease—and familiarity—I'd never achieved with Allen.

After a few minutes, no longer hearing the TV in the other room, I wandered off to see what the kids were up to. Sarah and Mikey were hunched over their electronics, but I didn't see Brian or Kat. I stood in the doorway, considering what that might mean. After a minute, Sarah looked up.

"Oh, hi, Ms. M. Looking for Brian?" She looked around as though she expected to see him somewhere, but Mikey spoke up.

"Him'n Kat went upstairs."

"I think she wanted help with her homework," Sarah explained a little too hastily.

Mikey just made loud kissing noises and smirked.

"Kat's going to kill you." Sarah didn't seem concerned at the prospect.

I sat down on the couch with a thump, weak-kneed and not at all sure what I thought of this development. Kitty had followed in time to hear just enough. She marched over to the foot of the stairs and hollered, "Kat! Come down and set the table! You two can help," she added to Sarah and Mikey. Then she looked at me and shook her head. I struggled to my feet and followed her back into the kitchen, where she asked, "Did I hear what I thought I heard?"

I nodded, still speechless. I was as poleaxed as if Brian were still ten and pulling Kat's hair for calling him names.

Kitty, on the other hand, seemed resigned. "That girl is too old for her own good." Seeing my face, she laughed. "Well, it's not that bad. I hope."

I found my voice. "Did you know about that?"

She shook her head. "I've noticed she's more than a little interested in boys. Well, what fourteen-year-old girl isn't? But Kat—I don't know."

Mike, Sr., was looking from one of us to the other. When he understood, his eyes opened wide. "You mean Kat and Brian?" I half expected him to be angry, but he just looked bewildered. "I'd have thought—huh." He broke off and shrugged. "Well, Brian and Kat." To my amazement, he started to chuckle. "Perfect."

We tried, but he wouldn't tell us what was so perfect about the pairing. I mean, given our own friendship, Kitty and I would be happy to have our kids get together someday. Like in twenty years. But something about the way Mike said it, I had a feeling it was more that he felt they somehow deserved each other. Well, maybe they did. Certainly they were different enough to make for some interesting moments in our future. Kat responded to Brian's careful deliberations with quick impulses and infectious enthusiasm.

"But they had better not do anything, and I mean *anything*, to get into trouble," Mike added.

Kitty called us all to the table before I could think too much more. Kat and Brian had appeared promptly at Kitty's command, giving no indication that they had been doing anything but homework. Maybe Mikey was jumping to conclusions. Still, I thought I detected a few of those special glances we exchange when we're in love—or think we are. They amused me almost as much as they scared me. It was difficult to take teen-aged love seriously.

But, maybe because I had relationships on my mind, I found myself watching Kitty and Mike, and felt a little depressed. They looked so contented. Like the cliché about comfortable old shoes, which would have sounded as dull as it was corny, if it weren't exactly what I'd never had.

Fortunately, I was distracted from my ruminations before I could become a whimpering wreck, lamenting the love I'd never had—or given. We were all making a deliberate effort to avoid discussing Letitia LeMoine or murder, but somehow the vice-principal had entered the conversation. In fact, Mike was soliciting my opinion.

"Fingal?" I asked. "I've never thought much about him. Or of him. Seems to spend most of his time leaning against the wall in the lunchroom. Maybe he's afraid it'll fall down if he doesn't hold it up."

The kids snickered, and Kitty admonished, "Now, there's no need to repeat that outside these walls, you kids hear?"

They all nodded, and I looked at Kitty, wide-eyed. "Shouldn't I have said that? Mike did ask what I thought."

"Oh, you know." She waved a hand at nothing. "I feel like I ought to insist the kids respect authority. And he's done a good job with the school web site this year," she added, groping for something positive to say about the man.

"Actually," Brian told her, "I think that was Ms. Waverly. I don't think Mr. Fingal knows how to do computer stuff, but she might. Or Mrs. Peabody."

"Anyway, Mom," Sarah put in, "I don't think I *can* respect Mr. Fingal. He flirts with the girls. I mean, gross!"

"And they let him?" I asked before I could stop myself.

Sarah shrugged. "I guess so. I think some of them like him. I've heard some say they think he's kind of cute." Mikey made a gagging noise, and for once I agreed with him.

"Well I think he's gross," Kat blurted. "I don't want to go anywhere near him."

Kitty transformed in a flash into a defensive mother. "What did he do? Did he touch you?"

"It wasn't anything like that, Mom. He just kind of, you know, just looked at me *that way*, and he tried to rest his hand on my shoulder the day Brian and I— oh!" She broke off with a quick glance at Brian. We all looked from one of them to the other, as they turned red in unison.

"I think you'd better finish that sentence, young lady," Mike put in. Out of the corner of my eye I could see Mikey looking gleeful at the prospect of seeing his sister get in trouble.

No one said anything for a minute, then Brian swallowed hard and said, "It wasn't anything much, really, Mr. Padgett," he promised. I couldn't see if his fingers were crossed, so I wasn't ready to relax as he continued. "Kat and I got sent to the office a couple of weeks ago for, for," he glanced at Kat. "For, um, well, for," he didn't seem to be able to finish the sentence.

"For *what*?" I demanded.

"Um, Inappropriate Behavior?"

"And what exactly does that mean?"

Mikey couldn't contain himself any longer. "You guys got caught snogging?" He giggled, but at his father's sharp look pulled himself together. Kat threatened to flatten him, while Kitty and Mike met each other's eyes and seemed to communicate everything they needed, but I sat there alone and lost. I had no idea how to respond, no idea if this was a serious problem or natural behavior. Well, okay, I knew it was natural behavior, I just didn't know if I should freak out about it happening between my fifteen-year-old and Kitty's fourteen-year-old.

"Okay, kids," Kitty said. "Tell us the whole thing.

Mikey, you will keep your mouth shut or you will leave the room."

Kat and Brian exchanged looks again, very like those through which Kitty and Mike were doing so much communicating. As a result of the consultation, Brian told us, "It was just a little hug and a kiss, honest Mom. Everyone does it. I think the thing Fin—er, Mr. Fingal didn't like was the way I used her scarf to pull her to me." He reached out his hands to mime a gentle tug on both ends of a scarf.

Kat nodded. "Yeah. Maybe he thought we were doing that choking thing."

"You stay away from that stuff," Mike commanded. "Kids die doing that."

"We *know* that," Kat said, rolling her eyes.

I didn't say anything because I was speechless again.

Kitty had picked up on something else. "What scarf was that, honey? You don't usually wear one."

Kat turned a bit redder. "I think it was Ms. Mac's scarf. That really bright orange one, with the green stripes? You left it on the hall table, and it was just right for tacky outfits day." That must have been part of Spring Spirit week. Brian wasn't taking part, so I hadn't paid much attention.

Kat realized what she'd said, covered her mouth, then started to apologize before realizing I wasn't offended. In fact, I'd already forgotten what she said. Kitty and I looked at each other, and shook our heads. If the kids hadn't realized what that scarf had done Thursday night, we didn't want to tell them. But though Kat didn't know, Brian and Sarah were putting it together fast. Both of them turned pale, and a moment's silence fell over the table. The topic was no longer the kids' behavior.

"What?" Kat asked, looking from one of us to another, bewildered.

"Kat," I asked, struggling to keep my voice calm, "where is that scarf now?"

"Gosh, Ms. Mac, I'm not sure. Oh, I hope I didn't lose it for you!"

"I hope you did," I muttered.

Brian had a very thoughtful look on his face. If he hadn't actually recognized the scarf around Letitia LeMoine's neck at the time, he was fast figuring out why we were asking. "Did you leave it in the office, Kat? Remember, Fingal made you take it off?" He looked at me. "He was trying to be all serious about the choking thing, but we were just having fun. Honest, Mom."

I wasn't ready to let it go. "A kind of fun we'll need to discuss later, I think." Besides, if we concentrated on their kisses, maybe we wouldn't have to think about what happened to the scarf.

"I've got it, Ms. Mac!" Kat interrupted. "I left the scarf in the office. Right on the front desk. Mrs. Peabody probably put it in the Lost and Found. So I'm sure you can get it back—what?" She broke off and looked at us again.

"Kat. Don't worry about it." Kitty sounded a little strangled herself.

Brian grabbed Kat's hand. "That was the scarf, Kat. The one around," he paused and swallowed hard. "Around Ms. LeMoine's neck. Wasn't it?" He looked at me and I nodded.

"Oh!" Kat stared at him for a moment, then collapsed back in her chair. "Oh." She swallowed too.

"So now we have evidence Mom didn't have it," Brian told her. "That's good."

"Yeah, but who did?" Sarah put in. "Mr. Fingal? I mean, he took the scarf, right?"

"No, we left it on the front counter, and he walked us to our next class," Brian said, with perhaps a touch of regret.

"And that was when he tried to get his arm around me," Kat put in.

"So pretty much anyone could have gotten that scarf, right?" That was Mike, speaking up for the first time. He'd been listening, a little slower to put it all together than Kitty and I. After all, he hadn't seen the body.

"Yeah," I mused. "If it sat in the Lost and Found from—what day was that, Brian?"

"Monday, I think."

Long enough for nearly anyone to have picked it up, but what with one thing and another I hadn't been into the office, so I hadn't seen and collected it. I wouldn't have thought of checking the Lost and Found, anyway, not knowing I was missing anything.

Mikey had been sitting there taking it all in, his jaw hanging open. Suddenly Kitty realized he was hearing what one would prefer one's twelve-year-old not hear. She started to send him away, but the damage was done, and she gave up.

Not that anyone had much of anything more to say. We finished dinner without further comment, but no one ate much, and we skipped dessert. Even Brian's appetite seemed subdued, though that might have been due to the late lunch.

When we got in the car, I told Brian, "There is so much I want to say to you, I don't even know where to start. But I'm not saying it while you're driving." All the way home I thought about exactly what I did want to say. I stopped him before he could disappear up the stairs and into his room.

"Hold it, Brian. I think we need to have a little conversation about what is going on with you and Kat."

"Not that much. Honest, Mom. I mean, I like her. We've been friends forever, you know. But we aren't doing anything stupid!"

"Up until now, I thought all you two did together was bicker. Not exactly sweetheart material." Even as I said it, I realized that bickering might have been their way of flirting. I tried to strengthen my point. "I didn't even think you liked her that much because she used to tease you about being a geek."

Maybe Kat's teasing wasn't all in the past, or maybe he didn't like being reminded, because Brian's temper flared.

"What do you know about it? We're friends now, and you'll just have to deal with it. She's fun to hang out with, but we're not doing anything wrong. Maybe you don't approve of kissing in the school hall. But, geez, Mom, everybody does it. Except you, I guess." The teenager-monster had reared its ugly head, and he added, "It's my life, Mom. It's not like you'd know anything about it, so just butt out!" He turned and stormed up the stairs to his room.

I stood there a minute, listening as the door slammed and the stereo came on. No headphones; tonight he wanted to drown out everything, especially me, and he wanted me to know it.

I blinked back sudden tears. Adolescence had been pretty easy up to now. I had a feeling the honeymoon was over. For one evil moment I thought about letting Allen take him. Then I realized Brian had probably over-reacted in part because he was upset about the divorce. If only he hadn't said that about me and love! *The truth hurts*, I told myself, and tried to smile.

When I picked up the phone to call Kitty, Brian was talking to Justin. At least it wasn't Kat. I hung up fast. I really didn't want to hear what they were saying.

After a prolonged rummage, I found my cell phone in the bottom of my purse. The battery was dead, so I spent another ten minutes finding the charger and cord. Great. Now I had a phone with the worst of all worlds: lousy reception, awkward handset, and a tether. "Ain't technology grand," I muttered as I punched in Kitty's number.

"Mine's sulking in his room with the stereo on high, and telling Justin what an awful Mom I am," I said when Kitty picked up. "What's yours doing?"

"Telling her diary what old fogeys we are, I imagine," Kitty answered. "She locked her door after telling me I was a nosy-parker and ought to be ashamed of myself. And telling Mikey that he is an insufferable brat, which in this case might be true."

I poured out everything Brian had said, and admitted I didn't know how to react, to that or to the kissing. I even told her Brian's cutting comment about my lack of love life, and she had the kindness not to make it worse by laughing.

We tossed around some ideas for responses to both kids, without reaching any conclusions. Neither of us had any objection on principal to them falling in love, but they were just too young. The fact remained that both kids obviously disagreed.

"Well," I pointed out, "we can refuse to allow them to date, but we can't really stop them from seeing each other. Maybe we should. . . ." My voice trailed off. Should what? Give them birth control and instructions and leave them alone? I didn't think either of us wanted that, though a refresher in responsible sex wouldn't go amiss. Maybe we should insist they be chaperoned by Sarah and the friend of her choice. Yeah, right.

"Well," Kitty brought me back from my wanderings, "Mike and I will talk it over, and I'll let you know what we decide for Kat."

"Good enough." I glanced at the clock. "I'd better clean up this kitchen and get to bed. See you in the morning?"

- 9 -

SELLING ICE CREAM BY THE BOX

Breakfast on Monday was a silent meal. I couldn't tell if Brian was still angry, or ashamed of his outburst, or too sleepy to care. I couldn't even tell if *I* was more angry or hurt, and that confused me. So we ate, and didn't talk, until Kitty came to pick us up. Sunday afternoon Ms. Waverly had sent out an automated call to all the students to say that school would be open, a counselor available, and that the cafeteria would be closed, so students should bring their own food. I made Brian three peanut butter sandwiches so he'd have some to share, since I knew from experience that some of the students wouldn't get the message.

Kitty and I dropped the kids off at school before going to see the Island's only attorney. By tacit agreement, we deferred discussion of Brian and Kat's love life until we'd addressed the shreds of mine. Kitty had insisted on coming along, "for moral support," and I didn't object. I'd take any kind of support I could get right then.

The attorney was Kitty's cousin, and had agreed to see me on short notice, and—miracles never cease—offered to represent me at a deep discount she called the "family rate." She didn't think Allen stood a chance of getting full custody of Brian, at least as long as I didn't actually get arrested and/or convicted for murdering Letitia LeMoine. I, in turn, was able to assure her I had not killed the woman, and managed not to add that it might have been a satisfaction to do so. I didn't think that kind of comment would amuse my attorney.

Just meeting Anne Kasper made me feel a lot better about the divorce, right up until she said I'd almost certainly have to settle for shared custody of Brian, barring a compelling reason not to. That hit hard, because I had to accept that things would never be just the same, even when this was over.

Then she gave me a succinct set of instructions, including a recommendation that I avoid romantic entanglements for the time being.

"There's no law against it, of course, but you'd be amazed how stuffy some of these judges can be about cohabitation and so forth. They seem to figure if you've a kid living with you, you should wear a chastity belt. Not all of them, but enough, so until this is settled, no love life."

I laughed. "That doesn't seem like much of an issue at this point."

Kitty gave me a look that reminded me I'd recently rediscovered myself as, not someone with a love life, but someone who might not mind becoming a person with a love life. Not someone ready to slip on a chastity belt and throw away the key. Ms. Kasper was still talking, and it was clear this particular issue really bugged her.

"I wouldn't mind that so much if so many of those same judges didn't seem totally okay with men having all the affairs they want."

"That's just not right!" Kitty exclaimed.

"Damned skippy it's not, Kitty," Anne told her. "If you think we women have achieved equality, you've been living under a rock."

119

From her expression, I guessed Kitty was re-evaluating her living quarters. So was I. I hadn't imagined my love life would have anything to with the matter. Of course, until yesterday I hadn't thought I had any love life. Which I didn't, I had to remind myself.

Anne Kasper finished up by recommending I direct any further calls or demands from Allen to her, go home, and stop worrying. It sounded like good advice, if only I could have taken it.

When we left Anne's office, we crossed the street to the Have-A-Bite Bakery. I needed a stiff drink to recover. At the Have-A-Bite, that meant skipping the sissy espresso drinks and heading straight for the pot of thick coffee simmering on the burner at the end of the counter. I poured myself a Large, diluted it with a generous serving of half-and-half, and followed Kitty to the pastry case. Espresso brownie. I'd be so wired I could finish the Yearbook single-handed. I'd also have to skip lunch to make up for the calories. Which was fine, because we'd be too busy to go out, and I had no intention of eating the alleged food that came out of the school cafeteria, even if it weren't closed.

I wondered if the lunch ladies would even want to come back, and hoped that Ron had hauled off our freezer. I never wanted to see it again.

Kitty took a less electrifying non-fat latte, but got her own brownie. "We're going to need it," she predicted as we munched away. "I called Annette this morning and asked her if the Yearbook students could help us this week. She told me that two of them are on academic probation and can't miss class. For the rest of them, she'll leave it up to their teachers."

The caffeine and sugar were already having their magical effect on me. "We'll just hope for the best, do what we can, and ship it out on Friday," I told her airily.

She gave me a sour look. "Sure, Pollyanna. What's with you, anyway, JJ?"

I shrugged. "I don't know. I guess I'm tired of being stressed, so I'm not going to be anymore." Even I noticed this didn't sound like me. "Too much chocolate?" I suggested.

"I bet I know what it is!" Kitty had a gleam in her eye I didn't like. "JJ's in love," she sang like a fourth grader on the playground.

"For God's sake, Kitty!" I looked around, relieved to see that Moira, the gossipy counter help (she refused to be called a "barista," and given the quality of her espressos, rightly so), wasn't close enough to have heard.

Kitty giggled. The sugar and caffeine were affecting her, too. "Come on, tell the truth. Don't you think Ron Karlson is wicked cute?"

"I think Ron is kind and, more to the point, is a competent officer," I told her with tremendous dignity. She just looked at me and raised one eyebrow. Geez. Could everyone on the Island do that but me? Was that how they pegged outsiders—by the inability to raise one eyebrow? I'd have to practice. "Kitty, you heard what Anne Kasper said. No romance until this is settled. Besides, I think it's enough to have the kids falling in love," I said, hoping to distract her.

It worked. Kitty rolled her eyes and sighed. "I know. Mike and I didn't come to any great conclusions last night. We ended up just telling Kat that she and Brian are too young to date except in groups. And that there'd better not be any more kissing in the school halls—or anywhere else. Then I gave her a packet of condoms and reminded her that actions have consequences."

"Good God!"

"I know. Shocking, isn't it?" She smiled, then sighed. "I told her I really, really hoped she'd have more sense than to need them, but that I'd hate even worse for her to need them and not have them."

I didn't think I could manage to say that to Brian. This was one time I wished he did live with his father. "What did she say?" How on earth was I going to manage to do this?

"She said she *knew* all that, and I should stop being *paranoid*, because they weren't *stupid*." Kitty's perfect imitation of Kat's italics made me laugh in spite of my worries.

"With all that, I can't believe you want me to fall in love, too. Anyway, isn't it a bit fast to be falling for someone two days after Allen files for divorce?"

Kitty wasn't letting me off the hook. "And how long since the last time you two, you know?"

Jeez. She would bring that up. I didn't answer, which told her everything she needed to know.

"I'd say that any marriage that hasn't involved either sharing a house or having sex for a period measured in years died a long time ago. I'm just amazed that you, well, never noticed."

"On reflection, so am I," I admitted.

A little while later we weren't laughing. I felt more like cursing, or maybe just running away. All the student computers had been relieved of their photo files. We called Brian and Justin out of their History class to tell us what happened, but they denied they'd even turned those computers on—all their attention had been on the PTA computer we'd asked them to try to fix. That left us with no way of knowing when the files had been deleted. Had we somehow damaged them when we copied the pictures onto the discs? Kitty and I fretted until Justin convinced us it wasn't possible.

"Well," Kitty brightened. "We have all the best pictures on our discs anyway."

"And losing the rest could be considered a blessing," I agreed. "Still, I think we'd better keep them that way. On discs, I mean." Too many things were happening to the computers. Someone was messing with them, and I didn't know why, but I'd bet it had something to do with Letitia LeMoine and her untimely death. But it didn't look like it was about our finances. Well, since LeMoine was doing the Yearbook, I'd have bet it was about that, but for heaven's sake, why? When all was said and done a Yearbook was a hokey collection of photos to be exclaimed over when it came out and looked at once every twenty years after that. We sent the boys back to class and I hauled out my cell phone.

I told Ron all about the computers, and he had to agree that there was something fishy going on. Since he couldn't imagine there was anything about a bunch of photos to inspire all this, he went back to his first idea and urged us to sort out our finances. When I told him I had, and they were fine, he changed his tune.

"Probably someone upset about the Yearbook, then." At least he didn't suggest we were going nuts.

"But that's still relevant. LeMoine was doing the Yearbook."

He couldn't argue with that. "Who's had access to the lab since you two finished up on Saturday, anyway?"

I gave it some thought. "The boys, of course, on Sunday, but they swear they never touched these computers. Teachers and staff could have come in. Maybe some of the parents—I think there are some keys floating around out there. I heard the old principal didn't keep a very tight grip on things like that."

"What about this morning?"

"Well, Carlos gets here about seven, and the school is unlocked after that. So anyone could have gotten to them between then and when we got here, which was just a few minutes ago." I looked at the clock. It was nearly ten. My marital difficulties had cost us most of the morning.

None of that got us anywhere, and we agreed there wasn't much point in him coming out. Kitty was disappointed in me for passing up an opportunity to see him, but even she had to admit that there was nothing he could do here—our problems with the Yearbook weren't police business, and there was no evidence for him to gather anyway. At least, the evidence was negative—the proof was what wasn't there.

"It would have been a great chance for you," Kitty complained. "I bet Letitia infected all the computers with some nasty virus," she added. I decided things must be getting to her, too. That was more the sort of comment I'd made than her usual attitude.

"That sounds like her, from what I hear," I said, more for the sake of a good snigger than because I believed it. In my mind, I was certain that there was something about the computers, or the photos, or the Yearbook, that mattered.

"Ms. Waverley came in while you were on the phone. She mentioned there'd been power outages Saturday night, so maybe that scrambled our files."

I didn't think so, but I nodded. "Could be, I guess. Oh, and Ron said he got the coroner's report this morning."

"And?"

"Well, I thought it would be tough to tell when she died, on account of the freezer. But since they knew, and assuming she was put in the freezer very soon after death—which everyone admits is only a guess—they can adjust for that."

"Ugh."

"Yeah. Anyway, they put the time of death between about five p.m. and midnight."

"That early?" Kitty asked.

"Yeah. I've been assuming it had happened in the middle of the night. Instead, she could have been murdered almost as soon as the school was clear of students."

"Scary," Kitty said. "Who could be certain they could do all those tricks with the freezer and not get caught at that hour?"

"I'm not sure it would be that hard. Anyway, it didn't have to be early. It might have been midnight for all we know." It felt less terrifying that way, but I had to ruin the comforting thought. "Maybe they didn't plan it. Maybe it just. . . happened. And then they needed someplace to hide the body fast, before someone did see them." We thought about that.

"Carlos gets off at four, because he starts so early," Kitty said, "and unless there was an evening meeting, all the teachers and everyone would be gone by six. Sports practices are all over at five and the kids scatter fast." Except, I remembered, girls who hadn't been picked up from practice on time. Girls like Chantal LeMoine. Well, she was Ron's concern.

"Who cleans up the locker-rooms after practice?" I asked.

"No one. Carlos does it first period. No PE classes then. The kids consider it inhumane."

I shuddered. "I would too. So no one was around once the kids and the coaches were gone." The high school is set back from the road just enough to keep passers-by from noticing a car in the lot, and the staff lot is behind the school out of sight. I frowned. "But they'd have to have keys." We were back to that. "I don't suppose it's that hard to get hold of keys?"

Kitty sighed. "I can think of at least three people with keys. People who aren't supposed to have them, I mean. Besides me. A lot of the teachers have them for various reasons. All the coaches, Patty Reilly, anyone who frequently needs to be here late."

We clung to the idea that anyone could have keys, but we both knew this cast more suspicion on Carlos, the one member of the PTA, besides Kitty, with official access to the school. Still, why one of us? Why not a teacher, or Annette Waverly, Elvis Fingal, or a random lunatic who snuck into the school? And what was Letitia LeMoine doing here, anyway? Meeting someone? Who?

While I ruminated, Kitty returned to the job at hand, stacking discs next to a couple of the computers. I started copying files. I knew we'd have trouble putting names to faces and all that, but we could start by picking our pictures, and worry about the rest later.

After a while the kids started drifting in. I knew most of them, and I knew that some—like Kat and Callie—weren't, or hadn't been, members of the Yearbook staff. I made a mental note to add their names to the list of staffers in the back of the book, if they stuck it out. Several of the kids who were supposed to be Yearbook staff were conspicuous by their absence. By noon I was grousing about it, and Kitty had to remind me that not all the kids could get away from class to come.

"Some kids actually have to work for their grades, you know."

I decided to take that as a compliment to Brian, who made high school look pretty easy. Where was my kid, anyway? Not that he was on the Yearbook staff, but I'd have thought he would lend a hand. Was he avoiding me? Or avoiding Kat? More likely avoiding Kat's mother. I decided that might be a valid reason to stay away, at least for a day or two. I wouldn't push the issue.

The kids came and went with each bell, checking in

with their teachers and returning or not depending on what was happening in class. The morning's caffeine jolt had worn off, leaving me cranky and irritable.

At some point in the afternoon, I was distracted from my single-minded pursuit of photos of the Wrestling team by someone talking about ice cream. I zeroed in on a girl sitting with Kat and Callie. I scowled, trying to remember her name so I could tell her to stop talking, especially about ice cream, the thought of which still made me queasy, and get back to work.

"So Joseph showed me how they've got three boxes of ice cream bars for the party, which is going to be fun, even if it is for his little brother."

I must have made a noise, because she looked at me and smiled.

"Oh, hi, Ms. MacGregor. I just think it is so brilliant, selling whole boxes of ice cream bars to people for parties. I bet the PTA can make a lot of money that way." Melissa. That was the girl's name.

"Why, yes, I suppose we can." I chipped a smile into my frozen face before turning back to my computer. "But let's get back to work, girls." The only Joseph I knew at this school was Joseph Hernandez. Carlos' son. I didn't like what this suggested, because we had never sold anyone any boxes of ice cream bars. But thirty boxes of the blasted things had gone missing between Wednesday and Friday, replaced with a corpse. And Carlos was mad at—and hurt by—Letitia LeMoine. The fact that he probably didn't know enough about computers to delete the files so thoroughly was small consolation.

Kitty hadn't heard the exchange. I made a mental note to ask her about the girl, Joseph, and the ice cream. I'd not ask her advice about telling Ron, because I knew what she'd say, and I wasn't ready to throw Carlos to the wolves, not even for a chance to

127

see Ron. But I wanted the murder cleared up, didn't I? Was I willing to pay any price for a chance at some answers? If I ratted out Carlos and he wasn't the killer, I'd still have cost him his job—and us our PTA Secretary.

There was one thing I could do. Carlos was just down the hall in the lunchroom. No kids would be in there at this hour, so we could have a nice, private talk.

I must not have believed Carlos did it, because it never occurred to me that confronting a possible murder suspect could be hazardous. I should have known better, but I didn't stop to think. I just upped and marched down the hall, walked into the lunch-room where he was mopping the floor, and took his arm.

"Carlos. I hear you have some of our ice cream in your freezer." Before I could continue my carefully phrased inquiry, he pulled away.

"No! I never took anything!"

"Carlos, they've been seen."

"Who's telling this about me? Maybe *she* started a rumor before—before—." He didn't finish.

"Before someone killed her?" I decided at the last minute not to point out where she'd been found. Carlos was scared, and he was lying. I had no reason to doubt Melissa.

"Yeah. I bet she did."

I shook my head. "Think it over, Carlos." I didn't want to threaten him, but he needed to realize how bad this looked. I thought he might talk to me, but he just snapped his mouth shut and turned away, swing-ing his mop with a vigor that told me I didn't want to push too hard, however much I thought we were friends.

"I must've misunderstood."

He relaxed. "Yes. I am not a thief."

I headed back to the computer lab, wondering just what I had learned, if anything. And I still didn't know what—or if—I should tell Ron about all this. Would he jump to conclusions and get Carlos in trouble? But the man was lying, I was sure of that. Was it just fear he could lose his job? I wanted to dump the whole thing into someone else's lap. But if I brought in the Chief, even if Carlos didn't end up accused of murder, he'd probably get fired. Then what would happen to Joseph and Johnny? The boys' mother died when Johnny was a baby. Since then, Carlos had worked hard to be both father and mother to his boys. I really, really didn't want to get him in trouble, even if he'd put himself there.

Besides, if I did tell Ron, would he think it was silly, that I was looking for ways to impress him? Or worse still, that I was making excuses to see him? I stifled a sigh and stopped off at the bathroom before heading back to my computer. Only about a million pictures to go.

- 10 -

RUNNING CAN BE HAZARDOUS TO YOUR HEALTH

We sat staring at those gawdawful photos until after five, when Brian and Justin came in from track practice. By then the only kids left were Kitty's girls and Kat's friend Callie—and they were only there because they had to wait for us to drive them home. Sarah didn't want to help at first. Instead, she sat at one of the tables doing her homework with a martyred air. But she's a nice kid, so she couldn't keep it up for long. When the homework got tedious, she asked if she could do the French Club page.

Given the shock she'd had on Friday, I was glad to see that Sarah could be her usual sixteen-year-old self, uncertain whether to be a human being or a drama queen. I put her to work, to keep her from brooding.

Brian and Justin, however, were not to be diverted from their quest for dinner, so when they showed up, we packed it in. We had assembled photos for nearly half the pages, thanks to the help of the students.

"I suppose we'll have to check over all the pages the kids do, just to be sure there's nothing inappropriate." Kitty spoke as one in the depths of gloom, which is what a long day hunched over a computer can do to even the sunniest personality. I felt the same, only more so, since I'm naturally about as sunny as November.

I rubbed the back of my neck, feeling as though something might snap if I moved too quickly. The morning's energy and optimism had long since evaporated, along with the caffeine that had powered them, and I was back to normal. Worse, because I'd had no lunch. "We're never going to finish in time," I moaned.

For some reason, it was the right thing to say.

Kitty laughed. "Sure we will. I'll just fill you with caffeine and sugar every morning, drag you in, and let you run like crazy."

"Run!" I groaned. "That's what I was supposed to do this afternoon. Run off that unspeakably caloric brownie!" I watched as Brian and Justin saved all the files to a thumb drive for me, with another one for Kitty. She thought I was paranoid, but even she was unwilling to leave a full day's work unprotected. I was determined to keep copies of everything we had, and to keep them someplace safe.

"Hey, Mom?" Brian asked as we went out. "Can I drive?"

"No, I came with Kitty. Plus, there're seven of us, which is more than we can legally seat."

His face fell. "Geez, Mom, when am I supposed to get the hours I need?"

"Sometime when we aren't breaking the law," Kitty answered, cutting off the complaint.

I gave her a grateful look as we followed the kids out, and said, quietly so Brian wouldn't hear, "Thanks, Kitty. I don't think I could handle that debate right now, and Brian's none too happy with me anyway."

"Well, that's no surprise, at least," she said.

We crossed the parking lot just in time to see Annette Waverly and Elvis Fingal locking the office and
heading to their cars. They parked in the staff lot, of
course, while we had been forced to park on the outer
fringes of the student lot, so they didn't come say
hello. They didn't even wave, in fact, just hurried to
their cars as though they couldn't get away from the
school—or each other—fast enough. Well, I could
imagine Annette wasn't thrilled about having to
spend so much time with a guy like Fingal. Especially
given what the kids had said about him last night.
Did he try to flirt with her, icy though she appeared?
Or was she too old for him, since she was probably
not more than five years his junior? Poor woman.
Ms. Waverly wasn't the world's greatest principal, but
no one deserved to have to work with a guy like Elvis
Fingal.

I did know she hadn't stayed just to lock up behind
us. She'd put her head in just before the boys arrived
to say she'd locked the doors, and would we please
just make sure they closed and latched behind us. I'd
be willing to bet her delay in leaving after that had
something to do with the useless Fingal.

There was no space for rumination in the car, with
five adolescents and two adults all talking at once, but
as soon as we got home I went back to thinking about
keys and boxes of ice cream. I couldn't decide whether or not to tell Ron what that Melissa had said about
it. I knew I should, but first I wanted to find out for
myself what Carlos was up to. I didn't—couldn't—
believe he had committed murder, but it certainly
looked like he'd stolen some ice cream. And he was
angry when he denied it. Frightened? No one on the
Island sold our kind of ice cream, and it was tough to
buy ice cream anywhere else and bring it home on the
ferry before it melted into a hopeless goo.

I pulled a lasagna dinner from the freezer, handed

it to Brian, and said I was going for my run after all.

"Good." He turned away and I sighed. He hadn't forgiven me. For what? For being the parent? All I really wanted was to eat, and to talk to my boy. Both would have to wait. My run was mostly an excuse to go see Ron Karlson. Whether or not I told him about Carlos, I wanted to take him a copy of our photos. I phoned, and he wasn't at the station. The night dispatcher said he'd gone home, which was good news, because he only lived two or three miles along the same road I lived on, and I could just about run that far. Then I'd get him to give me a ride home, on the grounds that it was getting dark. Kitty would have been proud of me. I phoned the house to make sure he was there, but when he picked up, I panicked and hung up, my face turning red. This was unbearable.

I plodded up the stairs to my room and pulled open the drawer with my running clothes. Saturday's stuff was still drying in the laundry room, so I pawed through the mess for my second-favorite shorts. They weren't as comfy as the other pair, but they were more stylish. Black jog-bra and a white T-shirt. I wanted to be visible if I was going to run along the road at dusk, and I looked pretty good in white. I was tying my shoes when it occurred to me what I was doing. Just when I'd been warned that any sign of, shall we say, impropriety, could be very bad for my custody fight, I was thinking about looking good for a man.

Never mind. No one could object to a nice, platonic friendship with the Island's head cop! I folded the thumb drive into the annoying little key pocket in my shorts, which was too small for keys but fit the little gizmo pretty well, and headed for the door.

"I'm off, Brian," I called toward the kitchen. Then, realizing I didn't want him to worry when I wasn't back in thirty minutes, I added as casually as I could,

"I'm going to stop in and see Chief Karlson for a minute."

He popped his head out of the kitchen. "Right, Mom. Don't get into trouble." His sarcasm cut the air, and I felt myself flush. Obviously, Brian wasn't blind to what was going on. And odds were he resented it, for a whole raft of reasons.

I walked to the edge of my rather weedy lawn, trying to convince myself I wanted to run. I didn't, of course. What I liked about running was the sense of being strong, fit, and virtuous, unlike the average American. Running itself was a necessary but often unpleasant stage along the way. In any case, I needed to see Ron, so after a minute I kicked myself into motion and started down the driveway at a slow shuffle, dodging the puddles left from Saturday's rain. The air was damp and a little chilly.

Our house is set back from the road about a quarter mile, and my goal was to be up to speed by the end of the driveway, lest someone mistake me for a staggering drunk rather than a fit woman out for a run. When I start off, I don't move so well. It could happen.

A few minutes later I was trotting along the shoulder of the road smoothly if not swiftly, surprised to find that a run was, in fact, a good antidote to the kind of work I'd been doing all day. I inhaled the aroma of damp forest and rotting leaf mold, and began to relax. The air that had felt chilly at first was a perfect temperature for running. I was, for a wonder, feeling good. Then I began to notice it was getting dark, and that I lived on a lonely road. The few houses were all set well back in the trees and out of sight, indicated only by mailboxes next to dirt drives. The road was lined with a wall of fir, madrona, and scrubby alder, with a tangle of blackberries, salal, and nettles rising to meet the bottom branches. In the growing dusk it felt like running through a narrow canyon.

Pretty soon I'd given myself a world-class case of the creeps, and no amount of trying to be sensible or laughing at myself could shake it. I kept glancing at my watch, gauging how far I had to go.

My jitters maybe saved my life. I was so jumpy that when a car did come by, approaching from behind in the opposite lane (I was, of course, facing traffic, just as I'd been taught at the age of six), I shied away. When that same car turned around at the first wide spot and headed back toward me, I paid attention. The headlights were on high—so many people don't think of dimming their lights for pedestrians. I couldn't see the driver.

I didn't recognize the car, which is to say that although it looked vaguely familiar I had no idea whose car it was or where I'd seen it before, if in fact I had. The light was by now too poor even to tell the color. I'm not great about cars. I divide them by color and then into basic groups: sedan, SUV, van, pickup, station wagon. Kitty drives a white sedan, Ron a cop car. It wasn't either of those.

By the time the car started to veer onto the shoulder, I was already across the ditch and pushing my way into the woods. A blackberry vine twined around my ankle and I kicked it loose, tearing sock and skin. I ducked behind a tree and tried to quiet my panting as the car slowed. Was the driver going to get out and come after me? If he did, could I get away by running deeper into the woods? Clad only in running shorts and t-shirt, the prospect of crashing through the dense and thorny undergrowth wasn't appealing. Nonetheless, I'd already turned to make my way deeper into the trees and brush when the driver changed his mind, stomped the gas, and sped off. Though it wasn't completely dark on the road, it was very dim under the trees. The car had no light over the license, so I couldn't make out the number. All I could say was that it was a sedan, and more new than old. At least, it had shiny paint. In the dusk it looked like some shade of grey, but in the dusk, all cars look grey. If Brian had been there, he could no doubt have identified make and model, if not year. A shuddering moment later I realized I was immensely glad he was not there, not if someone was after me.

I cowered in the woods for five minutes by my glowing sports watch, my foot falling asleep while dust, pollen, and God knew what else sifted into my hair and clothes. The rotting smell of wet Northwest forest filled my nostrils, and I had to pinch my nose to keep from sneezing. Sweat stung the long laceration the blackberry vine had left on my right ankle. Something, I felt sure, was crawling up my back. To keep from freaking out at the crawly sensations, I concentrated on thinking whose car it might have been. Carlos drove a truck, didn't he? So it couldn't have been him, however much I'd upset him. Right?

But Maddy had some kind of sedan. And what about Ms. Reilly, whose suspicions I had almost certainly aroused with my questions on Sunday? If she was the killer, she now knew I was investigating, and must have guessed I considered her a suspect. The same, I supposed, might be said of Ms. Day. I had no idea what kind of car either drove. Did either of them live along this road? No one could have known I'd be out running just now, so it must have been a matter of seizing an opportunity.

Eons later, with no further sign of the car, and my evaporating sweat chilling me to the bone, I unfolded as best I could and picked my way back to the road, limping until circulation returned to my left foot. I'd have stayed in the trees if I could, but that wall of brambles might have been designed on purpose to mortify the flesh while impeding progress. With good light and wearing sturdy jeans and boots I might have done it. In the gathering dusk—night, really, under the trees—there was no hope. I took to the road, every sense alert for the sound of a motor.

It was still most of a mile to the Chief's house, and I was pretty sure I set a personal record for the distance. Gasping for air, I ran up his porch steps and hammered on the door. I'd have yelled for him if I'd had any wind left to yell with.

The hall light was off, so when the door opened Ron was lit only by the fading dusk. I couldn't see much more than that he was—finally—out of uniform, but I noticed the service revolver in his right hand. In the normal course of things I don't much like guns, but just then it was a beautiful sight. I didn't even stop to wonder why he'd drawn it.

"JJ? What the hell?"

I pushed past him into the house and leaned over, hands on my knees, panting. He peered into the darkness outside before shutting the door. Pocketing the revolver, he tried again. "What is it, JJ? Just out for a run, or what?"

I had my breath back, a little. "Bringing you—computer back-ups. Someone—tried—run me—down." I wasn't at my most coherent, but he got the message.

"Tried to run you down? What? Where?"

"Mile back. Hid—woods. Then ran here." A sudden, unbearable thought struck. "Brian! The house!"

He didn't need anything more. Grabbing keys from the hall table, he opened the door again and ran out.

"You wait here!"

No way. I followed, surprised to find I could run a little more after all, and dove for the rear door of the cruiser just in time.

"Someone phoned a while back," Ron said. "Hung

up. Like they were checking if anyone was home." It served as an explanation for the gun.

I missed the opportunity to tell him that it was I who had called. Instead, I gave a slightly more coherent explanation of my experience on the road, and dug in my pocket for the thumb drive. I wanted to hand it to him, but couldn't, on account of the safety panel between us.

"Just hang onto that for now." He was driving fast; we'd already reached my driveway. He slowed down for the gravel ruts, while I admitted, "I don't even know if this is important. But someone does seem determined to destroy the files." *Or me*, I thought but did not say. This did *not* have anything to do with the ice cream. Carlos would never try to hurt me. I gave up that train of thought and turned my attention back to Ron.

"I was thinking," I began, and he made a noise that I chose to ignore. "I wondered if Letitia LeMoine interrupted someone messing with the computers— you know, trying to make her look like a flop with the Yearbook or something—and they had a fight. Or it could have been random vandalism, even. But she got killed and they panicked." I was talking to distract myself from fear for Brian. Ron played along.

"And they did it again over the weekend to divert suspicion? Seems more likely they still needed to cover up whatever they were hiding." I could see he was still thinking about Maddy. "Anyway, I was going to come see you and talk about it all." He stopped the car in front of my door. We both looked at the house. Everything seemed normal. There was no grey sedan in sight, no car at all but my faded red Toyota. "You stay here," he suggested. "I'll check it out."

"No way. If anything's happened to Brian—" I couldn't finish the sentence.

"All the more reason," he said, but he let me out of the back seat. "You can sure move fast when you want to," he added.

I wasn't interested. I had never been less aware of Ron Karlson as a man than I was at that moment. Right then, all I wanted was the cop. The guy with the badge and the gun, who would make everything all right.

He walked up to the porch, taking in the single light glowing in an upstairs room. Brian's room.

"You left it dark?"

"Probably, except the kitchen. Brian was heating something for dinner. He'd have turned off the light when he went upstairs."

He opened the front door and felt inside for the light switch. After a moment, he found it, and the empty hall lit up. We stepped inside, and, to my inexpressible relief, Brian called down the stairs.

"That you, Mom? How was your run?"

"I think I set a PR." Well, that much was true. My voice even sounded pretty normal. "Anybody call or stop by?"

"No. That Chief Karlson with you?"

God. The kid noticed everything. "Yeah. I got a bit carried away so he brought me home."

My son appeared at the top of the stairs, in sock feet and sweats. "Hi Chief. Mom give you the thumb drive?"

I stared at him. "Did I—how did you know what I went for?"

He shrugged. "Well, geez, Mom. What else? You've been guarding those pictures like gold, and you made sure you had a spare copy today. I figured you'd want to take them to the safest place you could think of. Mom," he added to Ron, "is feeling a bit paranoid about the Yearbook."

"And well she might," Ron told Brian with a little

'just between us guys' grin that said they were humoring me. I felt my face redden.

"I've got to finish my homework," Brian said, and disappeared back into his room.

I led Ron to the kitchen and flipped on the light. The dark windows reflected back our distorted images. I considered the empty pan in the sink. Brian must've been hungry. I'd thought there was enough lasagna for both of us. I ran water into the pan to start it soaking, a step Brian couldn't seem to grasp.

With no idea what I had to offer, I heard myself asking, "You had any dinner?"

"No." Ron gave me a look I couldn't interpret, and I felt suddenly self-conscious in my sweat-soaked running clothes. He pointed at my leg. "You're bleeding."

I looked down. Blood had oozed from the blackberry scratches to soak the top of my white sock.

"You should see the other guy."

He laughed. "You'd better clean it up. I'll wait."

For one fleeting moment I imagined Ron cleaning and bandaging my scratches, bent over my leg with tender care. I banished the image.

"I'll go change, then. I can fix us something to eat in a minute, if you want to stay." I actually blushed, and wondered why I'd made the offer.

'I'd love to. I'll take those photos now, too," he added, as I headed for the stairs.

"Oh, right." I handed over the little memory gizmo, and he looked at it a moment, then stuffed it in a pocket as I vanished up the stairs.

Five minutes later I was back in the kitchen. I'd done as fast a job as I could with the changing, not wanting to keep him waiting—or to let him think I was primping. I'd washed off the blood, sweat, and forest detritus in the fastest shower I've taken in years, and put my sock to soak in cold water. The scratch had pretty much stopped bleeding, so I smeared on some ointment and put on my best sweats, hoping to look attractive but sort of accidentally, as though I was just getting comfy. This whole business was starting to make me crazy. I thought I'd left it all behind in high school, yet there I was, getting giddy and trying to second-guess a man who probably had nothing on his mind but crime. In a manner of speaking.

Downstairs, Ron waited quietly in my usual place in the window seat, looking more relaxed than I'd ever seen him. I pulled a carton of stew from the freezer, popped it in the microwave, and suddenly I was shaking like a leaf. Delayed reaction. I sat down fast, trying to hide it.

Ron noticed anyway. I would have preferred him not to, but nobody's perfect. He reached out a hand to touch my arm. "Whoa. You okay?"

Dumb question. Someone had just tried to kill me, and I didn't even know why. Of course I wasn't okay! Embarrassment makes me cranky.

"I'll be just fine when you figure out who killed Mrs. Loudmouth, and why they just tried to run me over!"

He wouldn't rise to the bait. He just looked away for a minute. God knows what he was thinking. Probably making a note that I could turn in an instant into a total witch, which was, alas, true. Then he answered. "Me, too."

If I'd been trying to pick a fight, it all went out of me at the sight of his fatigue and discouragement. Now, instead of feeling bitchy, I felt like a worm. The emotional roller-coaster of romance was, well, on a roll. I didn't know what to say, so for once I didn't say anything, which may have been the most intelligent thing I'd done all evening. The microwave

141

dinged, and I broke the stew into two bowls and put them back to finish heating.

The atmosphere in the kitchen was less congenial than it had been, but I noticed that Ron wasn't giving up on his stew. How long had he been single, to put up with the likes of me for a bowl of leftover stew? Hadn't he ever learned to cook, for Pete's sake? You'd think in ten years or whatever it had been a guy would figure out the kitchen.

As soon as we'd eaten, he thanked me and headed for the cruiser. By this time I wanted to patch up the hurt I'd caused, but I didn't know how. So I just waved, and said, inanely, "Get some sleep. Things might come clear in the morning."

He looked back, opened his mouth, thought better of it, and got into the car and drove away.

That night I dreamed, the sort of dream I'd not had for a long time. Naturally, before I got to the good part, the dream changed and I woke up. I could still feel his hands on me, and my longing shocked me. It wasn't just the physical desire, but a craving to be cared for that no amount of fantasizing was going to satisfy. It took a long time to go back to sleep.

- 11 -

YOU CAN'T WALK WITH YOUR FOOT IN YOUR MOUTH

"Geez, JJ, you've got it bad!" Kitty crowed with unholy glee. We were back at the Have-a-Bite Tuesday morning, fueling ourselves for another round with the Yearbook. For some idiotic reason I'd told Kitty about my dream, as well as about the close call with the car. All I'd kept to myself was the dinner I'd fed Ron, mostly because I didn't want to admit I'd served leftovers to company.

"Come on," Kitty overrode my protests. "He's a great guy, and he's been single way too long. You know his wife was killed in a boating accident? It completely broke his heart. It's about time he looked up."

I didn't want to hear what she was saying, and I could feel my Inner Bitch stirring. "Oh, give it a rest, Kitty. More to the point, what are we going to do about finding out who killed LeMoine?"

"Are you crazy? *We* are going to put together a Yearbook. *Ron* is going to find the murderer."

"Kitty, someone tried to kill me! I can't just sit back and wait for someone else to figure it out."

"You don't really think they were trying to kill you, do you?" Kitty didn't believe me. "Someone passed you, turned around, came back and slowed, but you were gone so they took off. Maybe they wanted to ask directions." When Kitty put it that way, I thought she might have had a point, but my gut disagreed. That car had been swerving toward the shoulder, and accelerating, not braking.

"If it makes you more comfortable to think so, go ahead. I know what I know." My tone was arrogant, not to say snotty, and I meant it to be. We sat in silence for a minute, thinking about what I'd just said.

Kitty broke the silence, and her words had an edge. "We still have to do the Yearbook. Maybe you'll find inspiration in the forty-seventh picture of Chantal with a hunk from the football team."

"Maybe an asteroid will destroy the earth before I have to look at those girls again. But," I stuffed my Inner Bitch back into her cave, "I'm with you on the Yearbook. Don't worry."

"And with all those kids helping, we've got it in the bag," she said with all the optimism a mega-dose of espresso brownie could instill in a naturally cheer-ful woman who couldn't hold a grudge.

I snorted. We both knew we'd see fewer and fewer kids as the week went on. By Friday, we'd be lucky if Kat and Callie showed up, and they were not only dedicated to cutting class but also anxious to get Kitty free of the project so she could go back to being their personal chauffeur and chef.

I had intended to tell Kitty about Carlos and the boxes of ice cream, but the way she dismissed the attempt on my life changed my mind. I could handle it myself, without any snide comments from her.

We stopped talking, because a break in the steady flow of customers left Moira, the counter help, free, and she hovered nearby, hoping for gossip. I should have known this would happen sooner or later. Moira wasn't sensitive to the sort of "keep off" message Kitty and I projected. She brought the coffeepot to refill our cups.

"You two must know all about that poor dead woman at the school." She wore an expression of eager curiosity.

I didn't want to get drawn into any discussion of it, but Kitty's innate courtesy made her respond.

"Letitia LeMoine. Did you know her?"

"Oh, Lord, didn't everyone? She was in here every day, and something was always wrong. Coffee too hot, too cold, too weak, not enough foam, too much foam, you name it, she griped about it." Moira looked ready to bite the heads off nails. She sat down at the next table, sighing with relief at getting off her feet. I felt a momentary sympathy. Moira was at least ten years older than I, and working the counter had to be hard on the legs.

"So you didn't much like her?"

"Not just me. You ask any of the girls. She was a piece of work, that one," Moira went on. "I heard she was actually that nasty little Lemmon girl who disappeared way back when. I can believe it. Whoever she was, she was no better than she ought to be. But," she remembered what had happened and that one mustn't speak ill of the dead, "even so, I guess she didn't deserve to be murdered, poor thing." She leaned closer, eager to be horrified. I leaned back to avoid being poked in the eye by the mousse-stiffened waves of her home-colored hair. "Was she—you know?" She asked in a hoarse whisper.

Kitty and I exchanged glances. "No," I said, though I wasn't certain there had been no rape. Ron hadn't said anything, but he wouldn't, would he? I continued with spurious confidence, "she was just strangled and stuffed in the freezer." We needed to

145

get out of there.

Moira rattled on before I could get up. "I hear you've retained a lawyer. Are you a suspect?" Her hand flew to her mouth. "Oh, dear. That wasn't very tactful of me, was it?"

I cursed the efficacy of the Island grapevine, but didn't dignify either question with an answer. "Come on, Kitty. We've got to get to work."

We stood up together and left fast, Moira staring after us with, I was certain, no end of speeches left in her mouth. Speeches she would no doubt share with the next customer.

The morning went about as I'd expected. We hit the computers at half past eight, and by noon all of three kids were there, talking as much as they were working. By lunchtime I needed to get away for a while, and told Kitty I was taking a half hour off to eat. Too many mediocre pictures had left me unsure which were good enough, and, what was worse, indifferent to the whole question.

"Why don't you call Maddy?" Kitty suggested. "Ask if she can come. We need all the help we can get, and she is a PTA officer."

That fit my own plans well enough. With Ron unwilling to confide in me, I felt driven to find things out for myself. I wanted to know if Maddy was at home Thursday afternoon, and to confirm that she'd kept all the records in the account book, not on our computer. Just a couple of simple questions so I could set my mind at ease and concentrate on—well, the Yearbook.

I sat in my nice, quiet, photo-free car and ate a peanut butter and jelly sandwich I'd packed that morning, considering what I was going to do. My interviews with Ms. Reilly and Ms. Day hadn't told me much. Still, I'd learned that both women resented the thrusting ways of Letitia LeMoine and her daughter. Or was the daughter not pushy, but pushed? Could Chantal have resented her mother's approach as much as her other victims? I tossed the idea around a bit, but it seemed unlikely in light of what I knew of the girl. She'd been happy enough to make a splash on the cheer squad, and if she was less enthusiastic about the work involved in being the lead in a play, she liked being the center of attention. But what about the girls she'd pushed out?

None of which answered my questions about Maddy. Letitia LeMoine had made serious accusations against Madeleine Takahira, and someone had wiped out all our computer records. I had to know if there could be a connection, and just how much Maddy resented—or feared—the woman. I'd pooh-poohed the notion to Ron, but I couldn't shake my own doubts.

I swallowed the last bite of my sandwich and washed it down with the lukewarm dregs of my coffee. Then I spent another minute rummaging in my purse for my ever-elusive cell phone. After fishing up a notepad and my spare glasses, two used tissues, and a package of chewing gum, I found the phone. Flipping it open, I noted that I had plenty of battery power and a full three-bar signal. Such a constellation of unlikely developments had to be a sign.

Feeling encouraged, I looked up Maddy in my contact list and punched "call." She answered on the second ring, with a cheerful "good afternoon!"

The conversation went downhill from there. I knew what I wanted to ask, but I hadn't given any thought to how to lead up to the question. I couldn't just say, "I called to ask where you were when Letitia LeMoine was being murdered." For one thing, only the murderer knew when that was. For another, how offensive would that be? I could be tactless, but I wasn't a total idiot. I had to say something.

"Uh, hi Maddy. JJ here. Just, uh, checking that everything's okay."

"Sure. Madison was pretty upset over the weekend. You know. But she's doing better."

"Good. Yeah, Brian seems to be getting over it just fine. Still, I guess we'd better keep an eye on the kids, huh?"

We went on in that vein for another minute or two, while I wondered how to ask my question. I fell back on the Yearbook.

"Kitty and I wondered if you could give us any time to help with the Yearbook. I'm sure Madison told you we're really scrambling to get it finished by Friday. Any and all assistance appreciated, you know!"

"I'll see what I can manage," she agreed, though I could tell she didn't want to.

"Thanks. I know you're busy."

Her laugh sounded a little strained. "You must be about the only one. Most people think I'm just at home all day, eating chocolates and watching the soaps or something. They have no idea—"

I cut her off, not that I was unsympathetic. But I had to ask my question and get back to work. "Uh, Maddy? I've been working over the books—"

She cut me off. "I know. They're a mess, and you know as well as I do that Letitia used that as a reason to tell me I was no accountant, which is true, and to suggest that I was stealing, which I certainly never did."

Startled, I asked, "Did she really? Flat-out accuse you, I mean?"

"Yeah. The—never mind. Mustn't speak ill of the dead, you know." Her laughter this time was more than a little forced.

"And I suppose Ron Karlson has been all over you asking about it all, too."

A hint of frost marked her monosyllabic reply. "Yes."

I tried to make it sound like I was sympathizing over something we'd both been through, while I sought fruitlessly for a way to raise the question I needed answered. "Me too. He's probably asking everyone who knew her. I had to tell him where I was all Thursday and why everyone was annoyed with her."

I thought it was pretty smooth, but Maddy didn't agree.

"If you want to know what I told the police, you can ask Chief Karlson." The frost was more than a touch now, and I didn't know what to think. Maddy went on, and cleared that up for me. "If you think I killed Letitia, that's your business, JJ. But I'm not going to stand here and let you play sleuth with me. If Chief Karlson wants you to do his dirty work for him, he can think again. I hear *you* have retained a lawyer."

That again. I was going to have to publicize my impending divorce just to keep people from assuming I'd killed Letitia LeMoine and expected to be arrested. I hated the thought of the inevitable humiliation, given the reactions I'd gotten so far.

"Ron didn't ask me to do anything," I said. "And the lawyer's not—"

She cut me off before I could explain. "Then you're just prying for your own amusement?" Her words dripped ice now. "JJ, you need to butt out. I'll tell you once, and you can remember it: I didn't kill the woman. And I won't let you play at Miss Marple with me."

Miss Marple? That stung. I started to say, "The computer," but Maddy wasn't finished.

149

"So just go play with your Yearbook and leave me alone, please."

Even when giving someone the bum's rush, Maddy couldn't help saying "please." I took a breath to say something—maybe even an apology—but I heard a crash as she hung up her phone with vigor, a little-considered advantage of an old-style landline. The conversation was over, and I had a feeling we wouldn't be getting any Yearbook help from Maddy. Maybe I was an idiot after all.

I flipped my phone shut and closed my eyes. What on earth was I doing? I thought over the conversation and knew I had learned nothing. All I had done was offend Maddy, not an easy task. Why did she have to react like that? I realized she'd never let me get out my question about the records. Was that intentional? Did she want to avoid awkward questions?

I felt tears trying to push their way out past my eyelids. I never meant to hurt anyone's feelings. I just wanted this whole thing to be over. I wanted the murderer caught and our PTA to go back to having fun and trying to do a little good around the school. I wanted Brian to be safe with me, and happy with me, not angry and upset over his love life and mine. I wanted Allen to go back to sending checks and leaving us alone.

It didn't look like I'd get any of those wishes anytime soon.

I sat in the car and ached until I was sure I wouldn't cry. I had no intention of telling Kitty what I'd just done. Ron would be angry if he found out, and no doubt Kitty would be, too. She was already a bit put out with me over my bitchiness over coffee. I didn't want everyone I cared about mad at me.

It was a long walk back across the parking lot to the school.

A few more students trickled in during the afternoon—the class right after lunch was a good one for skipping because most students tended to doze through it anyway. At least, that's how I saw it. Fear, frustration, regret, and sexual repression conspired to make me an even bigger cynic than usual. Also, looking at so many pictures of the buxom Chantal and her equally over-endowed rival, Tina Ainsley, made me cranky. They seemed to be favorite subjects, presumably of the male photographers.

While considering what felt like the hundredth picture of Tina, I began to think. Tina was *the* babe on the cheerleading squad until Chantal showed up. Then Chantal took over the top spot and dumped Tina in the mud. Had Chantal taken her boyfriend, too?

I looked up. Kat and Callie were back, along with one or two other girls from the Freshman class, including Melissa, who'd mentioned Carlos' ice cream. I tried not to hold it against her. After all, she was helping. She'd even thought she was helping about the ice cream. It *was* helpful, just not in the way she meant. That I didn't like the implications didn't change the facts.

"It's okay, Mom," Kat was reassuring Kitty. "We have study hall now, and we got permission. Melissa and Carina, too."

"I just wanted to be sure, honey." Kitty couldn't help looking relieved. I wondered what the kids thought about this last-minute crisis. "I don't want you kids cutting any classes without permission," Kitty added.

"If we have permission, it's not cutting."

I considered the girls. They were all freshmen, and I didn't know how well they were tuned in to the issues of the Juniors and Seniors. Still, in a school with not quite a hundred and fifty students, I figured everyone would know whatever was to be known.

I waved a picture of the cheer squad in front of them. In it, Tina stood just a little apart from the rest, who were posed around Chantal. "Wasn't Tina supposed to be the Captain of the cheerleaders this year?"

Kat rolled her eyes. "Sure she was. But when Chantal showed up last fall, her mother insisted they hold new tryouts."

"Yeah," Carina chimed in. "She claimed it wasn't fair to choose the squad in the spring, because new students didn't have a chance to try out."

"Well, I suppose that's true," Melissa put in. She seemed like a nice girl, but a bit like Kitty: too inclined to see too many sides of an issue. "I guess Chantal deserved a chance to try out."

"Maybe so," Kat conceded. "But Tina was way bummed out. And her mom was even madder."

I exchanged looks with Kitty. *Texas Cheerleader Mom*, I mouthed, and she rolled her eyes. I suppose that's an occupational hazard when you have teen-aged daughters. You learn bad habits from your kids. What kind of bad habits was I learning from Brian? Obsession with sex, like any fifteen-year-old boy? I yanked my thoughts back to the matter at hand.

"What I can't figure out," Callie said, "is how she did it. I mean, the Captain is always a Senior, and Chantal is only a Junior. Plus, she's not any better than Tina. Really, she's not."

"I heard Mr. Fingal got the final say," Kat put in. "Maybe he just likes her better." The girls snickered in a not very nice way.

"I bet he just did it so he'd feel like he was in charge. Probably if Ms. Day had wanted Chantal, he'd have insisted it should be Tina," Carina said.

Callie wasn't done. "Old Fingal's an idiot. But, I mean, it's like Mrs. L. had some kind of hold over people at this school, she managed to get her own way about so many things."

Callie's bitter tone reminded me that she had been in line for the lead in the school play until Chantal showed up, backed by her mother.

"I mean, I swear she just walked in like the Queen of England, and whatever she asked for, she got, and she'd knock the peasants in the dirt if they got in the way," the girl concluded with dramatic bitterness.

"Hey, Callie," Kat reassured her, "with Chantal over on the Mainland, didn't Ms. Reilly ask you to take over the lead?"

Callie nodded and relaxed a little, and the girls settled down to working again, to my relief. At this point, the kids had taken on about half the clubs and sports, and Kitty and I had managed to knock off three or four more. That was just the layout, though. We still needed names, captions, all the rest of that stuff. With less than three days to go, we had to keep moving.

Something about the girls' discussion was tickling at the back of my mind, but I figured I'd better pay some attention to the Yearbook. In spite of my cranky-pants comments to Kitty, I did want to get the misbegotten thing done on time.

Of course, I also wanted to find out who had killed Mrs. Loudmouth and tried to run me down. Preferably before the whole mess cost me my son, my life, or my sanity. On the whole, I figured I had a better chance of success with the Yearbook.

By five o'clock we were trashed again, but we had most of the pages laid out. Brian and Justin dragged me home, and I realized that I had missed my workout. Plus, I had a headache that wouldn't quit and I still didn't know who had tried to kill me, what Maddy had told Ron, or if Carlos had stolen ice cream, let alone killed Mrs. Loudmouth. I didn't know how far Tina Ainsley or her mother would go to get revenge, or what Callie might do to get her lead role back, and if Patty Reilly would help her. I didn't know anything.

I tried to focus on the progress we'd made on the Yearbook, but my Inner Bitch was back in force, suggesting that only a loser would be thinking about that at a time like this. What I really wanted was to hear that Ron had arrested a passing tramp for breaking into the school and killing LeMoine. And that Carlos' ice cream was some other brand. And that when the woman was being killed, Maddy was at home surrounded by a dozen friends and relations. I was willing to sacrifice Tina's mom if I had to; she did have a streak of mean in her.

What I got, instead, was a call from Ron suggesting that he was still stymied, and implying—though of course he didn't say so—that he hoped I had come up with something useful. I wanted to have an answer for him. Not only was I desperate to have the case closed and the murderer caught, but I wanted to—what? To show Ron I was as smart as anyone and could solve murders as well as run the PTA? In order to have something to offer, and to keep myself from ratting on Carlos, I blurted out the first thing that came to mind.

"The kids were talking today, and Callie made an interesting point. About how Mrs. L. seemed to get her way everywhere, pushing Chantal forward, and herself, too."

"And?" I couldn't tell for sure, but suspected he was humoring me again. Well, I deserved it, didn't I? I knew I was trying too hard. But, having mentioned it, I figured I might as well pass on Callie's comment.

"She said it was like Mrs. L. had a hold over people."

To my surprise, he didn't scoff. "Like who?"

"Well, she was thinking about the school play—that would be Patty Reilly's department—because Chantal took the lead away from Callie, who has actual talent." I picked my next words with care, trying to make it sound as though this was old news, not something I'd ignored his instructions to learn on my own. "Patty blames herself for believing Letitia, who insisted the girl had too much experience to put her in a minor role, and bribed her with offers of help. But there's the whole cheerleading thing. I think Fingal has the final say on that, though the girls' PE teacher would have run the try-outs. I had the feeling she felt pressured." I didn't tell him about my Sunday morning conversation with her, either. I just gave him Ms. Day's name and remained vague about when I'd heard her gripes.

"Okay," Ron followed things to the logical next step, as he saw it. "What did Ms. LeMoine have on you and Kitty? I mean, you let her into the PTA and all."

I took a deep breath, fighting back the angry response that seemed to be my first reaction to everything he said. Did he still consider us suspects? Then I had to laugh. "Ron, we don't 'let' people into the PTA. We go around begging them to join. And, having coerced them into joining, we beg them to do stuff. She was unproven, but she was willing, even eager. We gave her the Yearbook because no one else wanted to touch it. When she agreed to do it, Kitty and I went and had a celebratory drink. By the November PTA meeting we knew we'd been had. She wasn't eager to work; she just wanted to be in charge. Since then, we've been fighting to keep her under control and stop her from offending all the other volunteers."

"So she didn't talk you into anything?" He was digging, and I suspected he sensed I was hiding

155

something.

All things considered, I shouldn't have resented that. In addition to my unauthorized snooping at church Sunday morning, Carlos weighed on my conscience.

"Well." Though I didn't like the implications of his question, I struggled to answer honestly. "She let us think we'd talked her into stuff. In retrospect, I guess she manipulated us." I let my chagrin color my voice. He ignored it.

"So she convinced Ms. Reilly that it was worth taking on Chantal in order to have help with the play, and—well, I don't know how she managed the cheerleading thing, though from what you say I should talk to Mr. Fingal. I'll have to see Ms. Day, too. Any chance Chantal really was the best cheerleader?" he asked.

I thought back to the one football game I'd attended. "Well," I considered, "I think she is good at it. I'm no judge of that stuff, but she didn't make a fool of herself. But the girls are right: it's unusual for a Junior, however good, to be captain of the squad. And a new girl—I mean, she wouldn't know our system, what cheers we're used to, whatever. So I guess if there was anything odd there, it was making her Captain. Holding new try-outs and letting Chantal onto the squad seems reasonable."

I thought about it all some more. "Maybe it was just girls' talk," I concluded reluctantly. "Callie was a shoo-in for the lead in the play until Chantal came along, and she was pretty upset."

"Callie Jenson? She was going to play the lead? A ninth-grader?" It appeared he knew the girl.

Since he couldn't see me, I made a "duh" face. "Talent isn't very thick on the ground here. As I mentioned, Callie has talent. Lots of it."

"More than Chantal, I take it."

I stifled something much like a snort. "Way more. Chantal might have made cheerleader on ability, but she did *not* get her part in the play that way, in spite of her alleged experience. Not according to the girls." Or to Patty Reilly, but I didn't mention that.

He thought about that for a moment. "JJ? Would you do me a favor?"

I was expecting him to tell me to stop imagining things. To my surprise, he said, "Keep those kids talking. And their parents too, if you get a chance. I want to know all the gossip you and Kitty can hear about Chantal, about Ms. LeMoine, whatever."

"Good Lord! You don't actually think there's anything in what Callie says?"

"I don't know. But if there is—well, you guys are a lot more likely to hear it than I am. I need any break I can get, and," he added almost plaintively, "no one talks gossip to a cop."

I thought about that. "I can see where that would be a problem. Kitty and I, on the other hand, seem to attract it." I told him what Moira had hinted that morning, leaving out the part about my lawyer. No doubt he'd hear about that soon enough, but I didn't want to talk about Allen right now.

Ron sighed. "I figured that sort of thing would start pretty soon. No, she wasn't raped. I'm sorry you have to listen to people like that. Still, maybe someone who actually knows something will talk to you. Just keep listening, and pass along anything that seems important, okay?"

"Well, sure." I crossed my fingers behind my back, promising myself I'd tell him about Carlos as soon as I'd had a chance to find out for myself about the ice cream. I thought about mentioning Maddy's odd over-reaction to my call, but then I'd have to admit I'd been prying.

"But," Ron added, as though he just remembered

what could happen, "be careful. You don't want anyone thinking you're nosy."

Too late. I thought about the car on that dusky road and shuddered. "Right." I let the sarcasm ring through to hide my fear. "Poke around, but keep a low profile."

He missed the irony. "Yeah. Take care of yourself. Call me if you come up with anything."

"I will. Oh, and Ron?"

"Yeah?"

"What did Chantal say to your new evidence?"

"Says she and her mom had gone home and she left her there. That she took the car and went out to see a friend."

"Who?"

"Won't say. Doesn't want to get 'her' in trouble."

"Lying through her teeth," I stated. "Dollars to donuts she was out with a guy."

"No doubt. Naturally, Chantal doesn't know just what time she did anything." He sounded tired, and I felt another flare of sympathy—or something—for him.

"Hard to believe, in a way. I mean, not being willing to be honest enough to help find out who murdered her own mother? Unless she did it herself."

"She could have," he conceded. "But, truth to tell, I think she's spooked about something."

I leapt on that. "What do you mean? You think she saw something?"

"I don't know." He spoke slowly, as though trying to sort out his impressions. "I could tell she was lying when she talked about the 'girlfriend' she went to see. But then, well, I asked if she knew any reason anyone would want to kill her mother." He stopped again.

"And what?" I tried to jump-start his slow progress towards the point.

"And she just about fell over herself swearing everyone loved her mom and she can't imagine unless someone was just jealous of her for being so pretty and smart." He sounded bewildered, and I almost smiled.

"Well, that seems reasonable. I mean, wouldn't you expect her to defend her mom?"

"I don't know." He brushed my point aside. "They don't seem to have been particularly close. But she looked downright terrified at the suggestion that someone might have hated her mom. Which made me think," he clarified in case I was slow, which I wasn't, "that there might be something in it, and she knows it."

I pointed out the obvious. "Well, you'll have to find out. Did she see something, or does she guess something, or," I got an inspiration that I really liked, "does she know of someone from their previous life who might have followed them here? Maybe that's why they came here—running from something."

"Just what I was wondering. But it'll take some digging. Chantal wouldn't say anything more, and her aunt—she wouldn't leave me alone with the girl—gave me the bum's rush when Chantal got upset."

"To protect the poor traumatized child, or to keep you from asking any more uncomfortable questions?"

"That's what I wondered. In any case, it kept me from finding out more about Ms. LeMoine's life before coming to the Island."

"So what are you going to do? I mean, how can we find out if she brought her murder with her, as it were?"

"I'll try the usual police channels. I've contacted the Seattle police, and they don't have any wants or warrants on either mother or daughter. But look," he got patient-sounding again, and I knew what was coming. "I know why you want to jump on that. I'd love it, too—some outsider committing the murder, and not someone we know. I hope SPD turns up something. But I still need to know everything that happened to her here in the days before she died."

"I know. Still. . . " I didn't bother finishing the sentence. He knew what I was thinking. If Letitia LeMoine hadn't been killed for something from her Seattle days, we were right back to a small pool of suspects, all of them known to us, most of them our friends, and many behaving strangely.

There didn't seem to be anything more to say about that, so I changed the subject. "Any luck with Yearbook stuff at her house? Was she working on her own computer?"

"I haven't seen any computer. I'm going back there today to see if I can learn anything more. I'll take another look. Maybe she had a laptop some-where."

I hung up, a little annoyed. As far as I could tell, he was asking me to help him out, but not really, and for Pete's sake don't let anyone know. Well, that part made sense anyway. But I didn't get the feeling he was trying very hard about the Yearbook thing. After a minute, I picked up the phone again.

"Well," Kitty pointed out when I'd finished my rant, "the Yearbook isn't his problem."

"But geez, Kitty, we're running out of time. If he doesn't find something soon, we'll have re-done the whole thing."

"Which might not be all bad."

"What do you mean?" I stopped ranting and start-ed paying attention.

"I mean, Kailey told me—she's the blond who came in with Sarah this morning? She's on the actual Yearbook staff, you know, unlike most of the kids helping now. Anyway, Mrs. L. had as good as told them not to bother taking pictures of unpopular kids.

That nobody wanted to see 'geeks and freaks' in their Yearbook." Except, presumably, the geeks and freaks. "The rotten snob," Kitty added.

"Good Lord! So are we going to find out we don't even have pictures of some of the kids?"

"Hard to say. Kailey says she and some of the others went on taking pictures of whoever they wanted. I mean, one of the rules Annette told them at the beginning of the year was that every kid gets at least one picture in the book, besides the formal portraits."

Annette Waverly was very into doing things properly. But would she have noticed if Letitia LeMoine had gotten the thing done her way?

"Maybe Annette killed Letitia for not following the rules," I joked. "You know how she hates anything that reflects badly on the school." We shared another guilty laugh.

"No one might even have noticed until it was too late." Kitty went quiet for a minute. "JJ," she said after a while, "every time I turn around I see another good reason to get rid of that woman. I even kind of want to punch her in the nose. But I still can't imagine killing her."

"I know what you mean. Still, Kitty?"

"What?"

"Can you imagine killing anyone over anything?"

A long silence. "Well, no. Unless they were hurting my kids."

"So we aren't dealing here with someone who thinks quite like us, are we?"

There didn't seem to be any good answer to that, because of course we always figured most everyone on the Island was like us in some basic way. Even the ones we thought were idiots, like Homer Roller and Elvis Fingal. Which, I suppose, was why I made my next bird-brained move.

- 12 -

WOULD YOU DIE FOR AN ICE CREAM BAR?

It was dark, and it was drizzling. As we crept up the long driveway to the Hernandez home, I was glad I'd changed my mind and talked Kitty into coming with me. She'd been pretty annoyed when I told her about Carlos, and she didn't want to go out. But I convinced her we owed it to him.

Neither of us believed that Carlos had killed Letitia, but we had to know, and the place to start seemed to be with those three boxes of ice cream bars Melissa claimed he had in his freezer. It seemed like the obvious thing to do was to go and have a look before we took any action. Well, I suppose we could've done like Kitty wanted, and told Ron. But if I told him, he'd either believe me or he wouldn't, and I'd end up feeling rotten either way. Even Kitty didn't want to get Carlos in trouble.

At my insistence Kitty had dressed for our covert operations in black jeans and sweatshirt. I could see she considered me a bit melodramatic, which I'm not. I just wanted to be discreet. In any case, we were both glad now to be camouflaged. Even though I weren't sure exactly what we intended to do, I was certain secrecy was a good thing.

"JJ?" A shaky whisper came from the darkness where Kitty walked next to me.

"Hmm?"

"What are we doing?"

"Finding out if Carlos has our ice cream." I spoke with confidence, hoping that would suffice.

"I know that." Kitty sounded exasperated. "*How*?"

"It'll come to me."

I couldn't see her, but a loud exhalation suggested she was sighing and rolling her eyes at me again.

Forging ahead up the driveway, I hoped inspiration would strike before we reached the back door. Moments later, we rounded a curve—after first continuing straight on and stumbling into the brush—and saw the house. At eleven p.m., there was one light still on, in what I took to be Carlos' bedroom. The kids, I trusted, were asleep. I didn't want to involve them in any of this.

I hesitated, wondering if we should wait until later, until he was asleep. To be honest, I'd expected him to be asleep already, given the hour he had to show up at the school. I looked at Kitty, but she shrugged, refusing all responsibility. The drizzle had soaked my cheap black windbreaker and dampness spread across my shoulders. I wanted to get this done and go home to a hot shower.

All we needed was one look in the freezer. How hard could that be? With luck, the kitchen door would be unlocked, the way many Islanders left them. Not me now, but I didn't think anyone had tried to kill Carlos lately. A tiny voice in my head tried to remind me that it wasn't his safety that was at issue here.

We crouched in the darkness and looked at the house. Then we looked at each other.

"This is insane," Kitty hissed.

"Shall we go away and call the Chief?" I whispered

back. We both knew what that would mean for Carlos. I hoped that we could get to the bottom of things and work it out without involving Ms. Waverly, let alone the police. What I would do if Carlos really had taken the ice cream, I didn't know. I hoped for a miracle—boxes of some other brand of ice cream being the best I could think of—and stood up. I took a moment to work the kinks out of my knees before reaching a hand to Kitty.

"You know, JJ, I think I'll wait out here," she suggested. "As a sort of back-up, you know."

"I think you're chicken," I snapped, but she didn't move, so I gave in. "You stay in the yard, then, where you can hear. If there is anything to hear, which there won't be, because I'm just going to sneak a look in the freezer and get out. It'll only take a minute and we'll be on our way."

"Right."

Really, Kitty was sounding more like me every day. Sarcastic. Nevertheless, she came into the yard with me, stopping to lean against the large pine that supported a homemade tire swing. Her black clothing blended with the trunk and left her nearly invisible.

I crept up the two steps to the kitchen door, grateful they were concrete rather than the creaky wood sort I have. My hand reached for the doorknob. It wasn't there.

Muttering curses in every language I knew and a couple I didn't, I scrambled about in search of it, then calmed down and stretched out the other hand, and at last touched cold metal. The knob twisted and the door swung open. I caught myself holding my breath and made an effort to relax. After all, what was the worst that could happen here? About then, my brain finally caught up with me, and I realized for the first time that the worst-case scenario included Carlos as the murderer, lying in wait and determined to put an end to my snooping. I had to stop and take several more deep breaths, reminding myself that the car the other night wasn't his.

The kitchen was dark as Letitia LeMoine's heart. I could almost hear Kitty's voice reprimanding me for thinking ill of the dead, but as far as I was concerned, being dead didn't change the facts. The woman had been a real pain in the horse's hind end, and was managing to cause us as much trouble dead as she had alive. More.

I couldn't see a thing in the dark kitchen, and moved in tiny, shuffling steps across the floor, hoping I wouldn't run into anything. I'd been in Carlos' house twice at most, and had only the vaguest notion of the layout. I touched the wall, figuring I could follow it around the room until I felt a fridge. Every move I made sounded to me like the thunder of a herd of restless wildebeests, but I kept moving, stopping every couple of shuffles to take two or three "cleansing breaths." They teach that breathing stuff in childbirth classes. During delivery I couldn't have taken a cleansing breath to save my life, but I was putting the knowledge to good use now. Shuffle, shuffle, breathe, breathe. It set up a pattern that did calm me down.

After a minute or two, I felt the cool, nubby surface of a refrigerator under my hand. Taking another deep breath, I felt for the freezer door, pulled it open, and was blinded by a painful flare of light.

A few blinks later, I realized it was the only the little light in the freezer, and that without it I'd never have been able to see what was in there, since I'd not though to bring a flashlight. I blinked once more, and found myself staring at three boxes of ice cream bars. Very familiar ice cream bars, the ones you could only get special order, the ones we sold on Fridays.

"Oh, Carlos," I whispered, and gently closed the door.

I'd thought the kitchen was dark before, but now, my night vision destroyed by the light in the freezer, I could see nothing but the after-glow on my retinas. I took one stumbling step, and crashed into the kitchen table, sending a chair clattering across the tile floor. Before I could recover my balance and bolt for the door, the light came on.

"*Que Diablo*?" Then, "what the hell?"

I stood in the glaring light, gaping like a beached flounder. Carlos blocked the doorway to the rest of the house, glaring at me. I couldn't help noticing the fireplace poker clutched in his right hand. I braced myself to dodge and run, suddenly certain I'd made a serious error of judgment. I wondered if I should yell for Kitty, and if she should run for help or charge in here to try to save me.

Before I could unfreeze and do anything stupid, Carlos relaxed, lowering his weapon.

"JJ?! What are you doing here?"

"I, ah," I tried to imagine an answer that wasn't idiotic. I failed.

His surprise shifted back to anger. He'd figured out what I was there for. "You didn't believe me. You thought you'd just sneak in here and find out for yourself." His face flushed. "Why did you have to go and do that?"

I thought his anger a bit much. After all, he had stolen the ice cream, even if he hadn't killed Letitia LeMoine. *Had* he killed her? He'd been waving that poker like he meant business. Maybe he'd thought I was a burglar, and maybe he hadn't. I eyed him warily as he stepped into the kitchen from his doorway, and took a step or two backwards, toward the door, I hoped.

Carlos didn't come after me with the poker. Instead, he bumped against the table and collapsed into a chair.

"Damn." We both said it at the same time, and the absurdity made us laugh, maybe just a teensy bit hysterically. It was a relief to know he wasn't going to beat me to death with a soot-blackened poker. When the back door flew open, we both went back to battle stations, laughter cut off.

It was Kitty, of course. I realized it a flash ahead of Carlos, but not as fast as you might have thought.

"What's happening?" she demanded, standing just inside. "Were you *laughing*?" Her gaze shifted from one to the other of us, taking in the poker with a lift of her eyebrows. I couldn't have explained the joke to save my life.

Carlos was looking at me. "Why did you say that? I swore because I'm sorry I got caught."

"Ditto, Carlos. At least, I'm sorry you needed to get caught, if you follow me."

Kitty looked at me. "So you found it?"

"Yup." I didn't know where to go, but Kitty seemed to.

"You stole some ice cream from our freezer, Carlos?"

"Yes." He didn't meet her gaze.

"Why?"

"John loves it. He wanted them for his birthday, and I didn't have the money."

They weren't that expensive. Did Carlos have expenses we didn't know about? Had Letitia been blackmailing him? I left my questions for later.

"When?" Kitty pursued.

"Wednesday night."

I looked up. "Wednesday? Can you prove it?"

"I don't think so," he admitted. "Who would know but the boys, and who would believe them?"

"I know who." I was getting excited again.

"Melissa. Joseph's, er, friend? When was she here last?"

"What does that matter?"

"She told me about the ice cream. But she didn't say when she saw it. Maybe. . . " I didn't finish the sentence. Carlos was thinking.

"I think she was here on Thursday, studying with Joseph."

"Not over the weekend?"

"No. On the weekend, I took the boys to Seattle to visit their grandparents."

"I'll talk to her." I realized we were all working together to prove Carlos hadn't taken the ice cream when he stuffed Letitia LeMoine into the freezer, but we still had a problem. He realized it, too.

"I know why you want to know when I took it. I didn't kill that woman." He stared at the floor. "But I'm not sorry she's dead." He looked up. "I don't think this helps. The ice cream, I mean."

"Well." I gave it some thought. "It tells me you didn't take the ice cream to make room for the body. And you didn't kill her on the spot because she caught you taking it. I guess that doesn't prove you didn't kill her later, but I don't believe you did. And we—" I glanced at Kitty for confirmation, and she nodded. "We're willing to settle the ice cream thing among ourselves, rather than turn it over to the police. I'd say, if you pay for the ice cream—when and as you can—we'll give you credit for coming up with a new fund-raiser, selling the stuff by the box. Nobody needs to know anything else."

His expression was unreadable. "Why?"

I didn't answer for a minute. Then, "because I like you, Carlos. Because you work hard for those boys, and you need your job, and you're good at it. You know the kids at the school and you make sure they know someone knows them. You're good for the

168

school and the PTA, and I don't believe this will ever happen again." A part of my brain screamed that we were dodging the main issue, but I ignored it. "Look, if this goes to the police, you might lose your job, and we'd have to let you go from the PTA board, and then I would have to do the Minutes and the Spring Faire. I don't think that is either necessary or good." He looked at Kitty. She nodded.

"It's breaking the law," he said.

I shrugged. "An internal PTA matter."

"Right," Kitty added, "it's no one's business but ours. As long as we get paid for the stuff," she added practically. "And Carlos?"

"What?"

"Next time you need help, come ask, okay?"

He stared at the floor. But after a moment he looked up, a hint of a smile warming his tired face. "Okay." He stood up. "Now I will see you out before you wake up my boys."

Kitty and I walked back up the driveway in silence. Carlos had lent us a flashlight, so we no longer had to stumble over the ruts or wander off the road on curves, leaving little to distract us from our thoughts. Mine were gloomier than they should have been. The problem was, none of this stuff about the ice cream was *proof*. Sure, maybe Carlos took the ice cream on Wednesday—and maybe Letitia found out, confronted him, and he killed her. I mean, I didn't believe it for a minute, but the evidence didn't preclude it. I wondered if Kitty had thought of that. And why was he so broke? Letitia LeMoine had gotten her money somewhere, and it sure wasn't from legitimate work. We'd already thought about blackmail. Was she bleeding Carlos for something we didn't know about?

"Kitty?"

"Hmm?"

"Tell me we proved something there."

"Well," she began, and stopped. "I have a nasty feeling all we proved was that Carlos did steal some ice cream."

"That's what I was afraid of." We walked on a few paces, contemplating the situation.

"So why am I so sure he's no murderer?" Kitty asked.

Unfortunately, I knew the answer to that, too. "Because we don't want him to be. Because he's our friend, for crying out loud!"

"And maybe," she ventured, "because he didn't seem to be as worried about that as about the ice cream?"

"You mean, like he doesn't truly grasp that he could be a serious suspect, because he knows he didn't do it?"

"Yeah. I guess that's not very good evidence, is it?"

"I'll take it," I admitted. "But why is he so broke? Do they really pay him so poorly?" Before Kitty could answer, I looked ahead and clutched her arm. "Kitty! There's someone at the car!" I switched off the flashlight, and we crouched next to a tree, hoping we hadn't been seen or heard.

She looked and clutched me back. A car had pulled up behind mine on the shoulder of the road, and a dark figure leaned on my hood. We halted and studied the situation. Who could it be, and why? He—I was sure it was male—waited without moving. We peered through the darkness, frozen with fear. Had he seen our light? Did he know we were coming?

I was about to turn back to get Carlos, when the man turned a flashlight on his car. It illuminated the reflective lettering that announced it as a police cruiser. I realized that he'd already seen our light, and we would look like fools if we kept trying to hide. I could see the waiting figure was tallish and lean, which assured me it was Ron Karlson rather than Homer Roller, so I stood up.

"It's Ron," Kitty announced, standing up as well.

We were too relieved to remember that we didn't want to talk to the police just then. By the time I remembered, it was too late. Kitty had already reached the car, and given Ron a bright greeting.

He didn't greet her brightly in return. Since I couldn't retreat, I bluffed.

"Ron! Nice to see you. You waiting for us?"

I couldn't see his expression, but his voice was hard. "What do you two think you're up to?"

"PTA business." I stole a glance at Kitty, who was trying very hard not to look at either of us.

"Kitty? What business are you doing at," Ron flashed the light on his watch, "a quarter to midnight?"

"What? Oh!" She took just a moment too long, and darted too obvious a look at me. "We, we were just talking to Carlos about the, the Spring Faire."

Smooth, Kitty. I rolled my eyes, confident the darkness would keep it my little secret.

Ron was having none of it. "Right. And left your car up here at the road instead of driving in, so you wouldn't disturb the children."

"Actually, it was to avoid the ruts. Carlos needs a load of gravel." I thought it was a good answer.

Ron stepped up and stood right in front of us, every inch a cop. Not a nice cop, either. A pissed-off, in your face cop. He shone his flashlight on each of us in turn, keeping it on my face just a little too long.

"Listen to me, and get this straight. There is a murderer on the loose. This is not a game, not a joke, and definitely not something for you two to mess with. Whatever you think you know about Carlos,

171

the right thing, the *only* thing for you to do would have been to come to me with it. Not go blundering around, messing up any chance I have to learn anything. And especially not to go putting yourselves at risk. Dammit to hell and back," he exploded, "don't you see that if he was the killer you could be dead right now!"

"You're over-reacting," I told him between clenched teeth. I did not like being chastised, not by anyone. Not even if he was right. Maybe especially not if he was right. "Kitty and I went to talk to Carlos about PTA business. That is all." I folded my arms across my chest, indicating I was done talking about it.

Ron wasn't. "I don't think so." He looked from Kitty to me, and back. "Come on, ladies. Before I haul you back to the station on suspicion of burglary."

Kitty was weakening, in spite of the obviously spurious nature of his threat. In a moment she'd tell him everything, and then Carlos would be toast. The best way out I could see was to negotiate a bit before talking, so I dove right in.

"Okay, you know and I know you've no reason to haul us in. But I'll tell you what we're up to." I had no intention of telling him everything. "Yes, there was something we needed to know, and yes, we took a chance finding out. But I was hanged if I'd get Carlos into unnecessary trouble, and I'm still hanged if I will."

"Just what are you saying?" His voice was calmer, but it didn't fool me a bit. I was going to be the one in trouble if I didn't pull this off. His flashlight lit my face again, though he lowered it a bit when I put up a hand to shield my eyes. The more he acted like a cop the more irritated I got.

"I'm saying that I'll tell you all about it, if you'll keep it off the record and let us deal with the problem ourselves." I tried to be calm, but I'm afraid my tone was more hostile than conciliatory.

"JJ, if it's relevant to the case, you know I can't close my eyes to it."

"I *know* that." I sounded impatient and unreasonable, even to myself. "I also know that—oh, hang it all, let me think." I reminded myself that just because Carlos didn't kill Letitia, that didn't mean the ice cream had nothing to do with the case. And we hadn't proven he hadn't killed her, except maybe by coming out of there alive ourselves. Maybe Ron did need to know about the theft. But he had to promise—I closed my eyes for a minute to collect my thoughts, ignoring Kitty's signs of growing distress. She'd start blabbing in a minute.

"Right," I started over. "Maybe you do need to know about this. But before I tell you anything I need a promise from you."

"And what would that be?" He didn't sound encouraging, but he didn't refuse outright.

"Just that you'll let it go if it's not relevant to the murder."

"Oh? So now you say it just *might* be relevant?"

"Oh, shut up! I need to get this right!"

"JJ?" Kitty tried to interrupt me, but I wasn't going to stop now. I wanted to tell this my way, figuring that I could do it best, so that Ron would know what he needed to know, and nothing more, keeping Carlos out of trouble.

"Okay. Here's the deal." I heard both Kitty and Ron draw in their breaths, as though about to speak, and I hurried on. "Carlos did something stupid. He admits it, and we know about it, and we're working it out. But it could get him fired if it became official, so we didn't want to tell you. But I see now that you do need to know. I just want you to promise that you won't let it go any further."

He didn't answer immediately. I'll give him that: he thought about it before he said anything.

"JJ, you know I can't promise anything," he said. "But," he added before I could turn and walk away, "I'll do my best. If it's truly unrelated to the murder, I'll keep it to myself if at all possible."

"I guess that'll have to do." With my agreement, Ron at last lowered his flashlight, providing a gentler, less cop-like illumination for us all. I blinked to try to clear my eyes of the after-glow that continued to blind me.

"So what is it?" he prompted. "Or do I ask Kitty to explain?"

"Oh, no, not me," Kitty said. "JJ will do just fine."

Forgetting I wanted to be the one to tell it so I could control the story, I decided it was just like Kitty to chicken out of the hard stuff.

I took a deep breath and got myself under control. "Last Wednesday Carlos took three boxes of ice cream bars from our freezer. For his kid's birthday party. That's all. No one saw him, no one knew anything about it until something someone said made me wonder, and Kitty and I went to ask." Given the hour and our obvious efforts at stealth, Ron would be an idiot not to know there was more to it than that. But it would have to do. "It has nothing to do with the murder."

"Except," he said with a sarcasm that stung the more for being deserved, "that a day later Letitia LeMoine's body was found in that same freezer."

"Yeah, but that was later."

"You have what, his word for that?"

"Independent corroboration," I told him. "And if you promise not to go hunting her up and giving her all sorts of ideas, I'll even tell you who."

"I've made all the promises I mean to."

"Then go soak your head." I turned and started for

my car. Before I'd gone two steps he grabbed my arm. The day before, his touch had turned my knees weak. Now it made me furious. "Let. Me. Go." I ground out each word, pulling away. He held on.

"JJ. Let me be clear. You two *will* stay out of this investigation. There is a killer on the loose. Until I know who, you keep no secrets. You focus on your PTA business, and I mean for real. You do not hide anything from me, and you do not run your own investigation. If necessary, I will lock you up to keep you safe." His voice rose on the last words, not quite to a shout, but close.

I felt the anger rising in me, a visceral reaction I could not control. I yanked my arm free. "Kitty can tell you whatever she wants. I have nothing further to say to you." I ran to my car, fumbled my keys into the ignition, and drove off. In the darkness, no one could see the tears streaming down my face.

I was halfway home before I realized I'd left Kitty in the clutches of the Law. I felt a stab of guilt, but I didn't go back. I couldn't face either one of them just now. Squinting through my tears, I kept driving. Kitty would be fine, not being cursed with my unerring talent for saying, doing, and feeling the wrong thing.

When I turned off the road into my driveway I realized that I was being followed. My heart just about stopped before I saw it was the police cruiser. Did Ron Karlson think he had more to say to me? He'd be in for a surprise, because I sure as mosquitoes in June had nothing to say to him.

The car stopped long just enough for Kitty to climb out, and sped off before I could wonder why Ron hadn't taken her home. I hadn't even gotten my seatbelt unfastened when Kitty opened the passenger door and hopped in.

175

"Did he get a call? Is that why he dropped you here? I can drive you home." I reached to turn the engine back on, but Kitty laid a hand on mine, stopping me. She studied me by the glow of the dashboard lights.

"JJ."

Against my will, I turned to look at her, forgetting there were tears on my cheeks.

"JJ, why did you run off?"

"What? What do you mean? He was coming over all bossy and insisting on knowing everything, like, like—" I couldn't finish the sentence, because I didn't know what the ending was.

"Like a police officer with a murderer on the loose and scared stiff a couple of civilians are going to get hurt?"

"Is that what he told you?"

"It's what I could see for myself. He *likes* you, JJ! He'd worry about you even it wasn't his job! Can't you see that?"

I ignored her. "What about Carlos?" I knew that Kitty was being reasonable. But I couldn't let go of my anger. It was all that was holding me up.

"He'll treat Carlos right. Can you really doubt that? But he's got a point. You know he does."

"I'll take you home now, Kitty," I said, disgusted with myself for being so hateful, and aware I was shoving away the only friend I had.

"Did Allen hit you?" Kitty's question took me so totally by surprise that I gaped at her like an idiot.

"Did Allen—good God, no!" But a bit of my mind was already at work on the question, because it made sense. It wasn't being warned off the case that had yanked my chain. It was something about the way Ron had grabbed me, and ordered me around. It wasn't that Allen had ever hit me, but he didn't need to. He'd had other ways to make it clear he thought I was inadequate, something I was only beginning to understand. And now I couldn't bear a man telling me what to do, no matter what his motives.

When Ron grabbed my arm and yelled at me, deep down I'd known, and hated the knowledge, that I still didn't have it right—and there was still a man telling me so. I wanted to explain to Kitty, but I didn't have the words. I tried anyway, because she had to understand why I was so angry. Ron might be just another man with a temper, but Kitty was my friend.

"Kitty, he, Ron, he sounded just like, like he knows everything and I'm an idiot who must be made to obey. Allen always gives orders that way, rather than talking things over."

"Heavens to Betsy!" Kitty's eyes flew wide open. "Allen does that? And you haven't killed him?"

"Please, Kitty. Don't make it a joke." I couldn't believe that small, pleading voice was my own.

Instantly contrite, she said, "I'm not. But you know, we all think of you as about the most self-confident and self-sufficient woman we know. Until you over-reacted to Ron that way, I couldn't imagine anyone would ever have the nerve to treat you badly, even knowing about Allen leaving you. Your reaction made me wonder, but I didn't believe it," she hesitated before finishing, "until I sat down here and saw your tears."

My tears were back, and I fought them. I hadn't let anyone see me cry in years. You can't be weak when you're raising a son alone and trying to find a place in a tight community, all the while holding out against an overbearing man.

"Hang it all, Kitty, I *like* Ron. But he had to go and prove he's just another bossy male who'll force us to do what he wants." Until I saw her face I didn't realize how much I'd given away. When I did, I reached for the ignition again. "I really need to take

177

you home and then get some sleep."

Kitty gave me a funny look. "Is that what you think?"

"That I need some sleep? Yes."

"That Ron's a bossy brute."

I had the car in motion now, so I didn't have to look at her. "Oh, hell, Kitty, I don't know. It just hit me all wrong. Yes, he acted like a bossy brute. I'm beginning to think it's what all men do."

"Crap."

She didn't seem to have anything more to say on the subject, and we drove the three miles to her house in silence. When I let her out at her door, Kitty leaned back into the car at the last minute and said, "I don't think so."

- 13 -

CHEERLEADERS AND TROUBLESOME HUSBANDS

Wednesday morning we let Sarah, Kitty's oldest, drive all the kids to school. It wasn't legal, because she'd only had her license a few months, but Sarah was a good driver, and Kitty and I needed time to plan. We also wanted to go to the bakery and fuel the creative fires. We'd need all the caffeine we could get.

Kitty, it turned out, wanted to talk about more than the Yearbook. "JJ, about last night," she began.

"What do we have left to do to finish the Yearbook on time?" I wasn't ready to talk about Ron, let alone Allen. When Brian had asked over breakfast what I'd been up to—he'd known I'd gone out, of course, and had seen the cars when we came back—I'd snapped at him. He looked hurt and didn't say any more, and I added guilt to the toxic mix of emotions brewing within. We still hadn't talked about Kat, either. I felt like I was failing Parenting 101.

To my relief, Kitty accepted my rejection of personal topics, and we discussed the Yearbook, which of course led to Letitia LeMoine.

"You know," I said around a mouthful of espresso brownie, "I've been wondering something. What did she live on? She didn't seem to have a job, and that car must've been a custom paint job." I'd never seen a lipstick-pink Bug on the lot, anyway.

Moira had been listening. "I heard she made out like a bandit in a divorce before moving here."

"That is not strictly true."

I swiveled to see who had spoken. It was Helen Arbuthnot, the head librarian.

"She inherited money when her husband died." Leave it to a librarian to get the facts straight. I looked at Kitty and raised my eyebrows, wondering if the husband had died of natural causes. I felt a surge of elation, and tracked it to its source: an increased probability that someone from the mainland had killed LeMoine. My pleasure was short-lived. How would a stranger have gotten her into the PTA's ice-cream freezer? We ran hard against that problem whenever we tried to think an outsider had done the crime.

Kitty and Moira were expressing their surprise, and I discovered one good use for the waitress: I didn't have to do any prying. Moira had already asked, "Who was he? How did you find out? Fancy!" while I was still thinking how to phrase the question.

Helen smiled, and I had a feeling she was laughing inside. "I'm a librarian. It's my job to find things out." She had also lived on Pismawallops for a long time, and knew better than to tell her secrets to Moira.

"Yeah, but how much did she get?" Moira was asking my next question for me. "I mean, was she rich, or would she have been around here looking for work next week?"

"I really couldn't say. She appeared to be quite comfortable." With that Helen touched her napkin to her lips, folded it, and laid it beside her empty cup. "I must be going. The library opens in a few minutes." She stood up.

I stopped her. "Have you told Chief Karlson about that?"

"But of course." She gave a public servant's smile and went out.

Well. About the only thing I hadn't learned was who had charge of that money now until Chantal came of age. And if she'd left a will. And who the dead husband had been. And if he'd had other relations who were unhappy that she'd inherited. Okay, the news had raised as many questions as it answered, but it was something. Maybe Helen could find out all the answers, but I thought I'd better let someone else do the asking.

Several customers came in, and Moira went to serve them.

"Well!" Kitty said. "I wonder what Ron makes of that."

I shrugged.

"Don't you want to ask him?" she persisted.

"I have nothing to say to Ron Karlson."

Kitty frowned. "Don't blame Ron for Allen's faults, JJ."

"Stop it, Kitty!" My anger surged out of control, and out of proportion. "Just leave me the blazes alone, will you?" The moment the words were out and I saw the hurt on Kitty's face I regretted them, but I couldn't take them back. I couldn't even apologize, or I'd burst into tears. I snapped the lid on my cup and stood up. "Let's go get to work."

We didn't speak on the drive to the school. Kitty was too hurt and angry, and I was too embarrassed. After I'd parked, as we were about to get out of the car, I touched her arm.

"I'm sorry," I muttered.

"I know," Kitty said. "But," she began, then

181

stopped. "I know," she repeated instead.

The worst of it was, she was right. I was holding onto my hurt like a shield to protect myself from my own feelings, and it couldn't last.

Meanwhile, we had work to do.

Wednesday must have been a good morning to cut classes, because we had more students helping than ever. Brian and Justin even came in during Second Period and offered to do the Track and Cross Country pages, probably because Brian was worried about me, given the way I'd snapped off his head at breakfast just for asking a reasonable question.

As a result of all the help, by noon I was feeling less hopeless, even as the brownie and coffee wore off. At lunch, six kids were hard at work, finishing layouts for the last six clubs. I was ready to kick back and relax, the job well in hand.

"Okay, JJ. You can start working on names, captions, all that. As soon as the kids finish with the pictures, they can do the same." Kitty jolted me from my complacency with a set of brisk instructions.

"What about you?" I sounded petulant, but I couldn't help myself. I'd been so happy, thinking we were nearly done.

"I," she said with a sigh that must have aged her three years, "am going to start checking that we have at least one picture of each student." She rooted around in the giant tote bag she'd started carrying around to keep the discs, class lists, drives, and anything else we might need all together in one place. We were still not taking any chances.

Kitty and I had talked it over. Maybe there wouldn't be any more trouble, either because whatever they wanted to destroy had been destroyed, or because everyone knew we were taking precautions.

"But who could have heard me telling you that I'd

take the stuff to the Chief on Monday?" It had been late. Who was left at the school at that hour?

"Let's see," Kitty had mused. "Track practice was just over, but I'm not sure about play rehearsals. And of course Annette and Elvis were still here."

"Now there's a likely pair," I'd said. "You know Elvis can't even figure out how to turn a computer on."

"Annette can," Kitty suggested. "But," she'd added more happily, "She would never delete the Yearbook files, because if it doesn't come out on time it might reflect badly on her. You know how she hates disorder and screw-ups."

We'd laughed, and gone back to wondering how many teachers and parents had been in the building when we'd quit working that day. At least Carlos had gone home long before then, I told myself. It was one more proof he wasn't the killer.

Now Kitty unearthed the class lists Annette had given her—with strict instructions to be sure every student was in the book twice—and pulled up her consolidated photo file. I dragged my mind back to the job at hand.

I started with the Chess Club. Since I knew most of those kids, filling in the names was easy, and writing the captions even enjoyable. I was, after all, supposed to be a writer. That's what I told people who asked what I did in the sort of tone that suggested "I'm a housewife" might not impress them.

But while I liked writing, I hadn't worked very hard at being a writer. I had a feeling that was about to change. With the divorce, I'd have to start earning some money, though Anne Kasper had assured me that courts still assigned alimony, and child-support was a given. But I hated the thought of being dependent on Allen, especially when he had proven himself such a jerk. And child-support would end when Brian graduated.

Another part of me wanted to take Allen for all he was worth. My two selves were in the middle of a glorious inner battle when an interruption reminded me what I was supposed to be doing.

"Ms. Mac, look at this." Kat's friend Carina was looking at a picture of what appeared to be large numbers of students at the beach. The Senior Clambake, I assumed.

"Look at what?" I asked, uncertain what might be at issue. It wasn't a very good picture.

"Tina. She's heading off into the dark with someone. I guess it's that jock from the football team she was so ga-ga over last year. She totally would not shut up about him. Do you think we ought to tell her mom she's doing that?" she added.

I smiled at Carina's innocence. "Probably not."

"But she could get in real trouble. You know, STDs and all that," she added with the wisdom of a child who has gotten an A in Health class.

"Good point. But I think it might make more sense for someone else to talk to Tina. Getting her in trouble with her mom might not help." I considered the picture some more. Tina did wear an air that suggested she had every expectation of getting laid. The boy was visible only as a dark form, already too far into the shadows of the trees to be identified. The thought of Brian and Kat kissing in the school halls came unbidden to my mind. Maybe I should do something. "Is there anyone Tina respects enough to listen to?"

Carina frowned, appealing to the other girls, who by this time were crowded around to study the picture.

"Well, maybe Ms. Day," Kat offered. "After all, she's the cheerleading coach. And she can throw Tina off the squad if she acts too slutty." I gave Kat a sharp look, but she seemed unaware of the direction my thoughts had taken and I relaxed a little. If she wasn't making any connections between Tina's behavior and her own, maybe I had less to worry about than I thought. Though I still needed to have that talk with Brian.

"Would she?" For some reason, I didn't want to throw the girl to the wolves.

"I don't think so. Ms. Day's pretty cool. She'll just make sure Tina's taking, you know, precautions. Besides, there's not much left of the year, and Tina's supposed to be graduating."

These girls were a lot more matter-of-fact about sex than we were in my day, though there was probably just as much sex going on back then. We just didn't talk about it so much. Kitty and I exchanged looks, and she shrugged with some of the same helplessness she'd expressed over our kids' embraces. I could see her point. Kids today had sex blasted at them so constantly it had practically become a meaningless concept.

I, on the other hand, had had no sex for. . . I pulled my mind back to the point. It didn't matter, because it sure as anything wasn't going to change anytime soon. Especially not with Ron "Butt Out of Police Business" Karlson. "I'll talk to Ms. Day," I said. "Unless you'd rather, Kitty?" After all, Kitty had girls. But she shook her head.

"You go ahead. I don't see any rush, though. I mean, this happened last fall. That's ancient history. Let's get the Yearbook out and then worry about Tina's morals."

I was less worried about Tina's morals than her health—and that of the boy, whoever he was. But Kitty was right. A few more days wouldn't matter one way or the other at this late date.

Kitty and I were just leaving the school when Ron

drove up. I kept walking toward my car, pretending I didn't see him, but he called out to us, so I had to stop. Kitty had already turned toward him, because she simply wouldn't see this my way.

"Can I talk to you two for a minute?" He asked us both, but kept his eyes on Kitty. By golly, Ron Karlson was ashamed to look at me. Or—I felt the blush starting up my neck with the thought—he assumed I would be embarrassed about my behavior the night before. But trying to make it easy on me would imply a degree of sensitivity that surely he had proven he lacked. As confused as the most lovesick teen, I looked at him. I would not let the man intimidate me, and that meant being able to meet his gaze, if it meant anything at all. I met it—and was annoyed to find no sign he was thinking of anything but business.

He led us away from the school, over toward the distant corner where we'd left my car. "I need to run something past you, get your opinion. Kitty, you're the closest thing I have to someone who understands the mind of a teen-aged girl."

Kitty laughed. "I don't think so."

"Hey, I didn't say you understand them completely, just that you come closer than I do, or my brilliant deputy. I mean, at least you have daughters."

She laughed again. "I'll grant you the daughters. That doesn't mean I understand them."

I wanted to say that, since I only had a son, I might as well go wait in the car. But I couldn't. If Ron was going to share anything about the case, well, I wasn't going to miss it. I also considered, for the most fleeting of moments, pointing out that he had warned us off. But he'd just say that asking our advice wasn't the same as letting us run our own investigation, which was all too true.

"And you two were teenaged girls once. The thing

is, I went over to the Mainland and talked to Chantal again."

"What did she say?"

"Same as before—she was out with a friend and doesn't want to rat on her. Doesn't know anything. But I was sort of fishing about their life in Seattle, since the police down there haven't come up with anything."

"Did she tell you anything about her stepfather?" Kitty asked.

"She doesn't know anything about him, his family, or how he and her mother got along, even though he only died two years ago, when she was certainly old enough to know what was going on. She supposes she gets to keep the money. Real loving kid."

"Do you think she has a reason for her attitude?"

"Maybe. I just wish I knew! Anyway, I also passed on the suggestion from Ms. Waverly that she come back to school here."

"How could she?" I forgot I wasn't speaking to him. "She can't stay in that place all alone, even if she gets to keep it."

"Ms. Waverly said to tell her she could stay with her. Awfully generous, I thought. Anyway, when I told Chantal, you'd have thought I was threatening her with torture or something."

"And?" Kitty prompted him to come to the point.

"Well? Doesn't that seem like an over-reaction?"

"For a high school girl offered the chance to stay with the principal? Especially one like Annette Waverly, who may be generous, but isn't, well, totally in tune with the teen-aged mind? No, I don't think it was an odd reaction at all, " Kitty said.

"So you think it was just that?" Ron asked. "She seemed almost frightened at the idea. And I'd have thought she'd want to get back to her own school and own friends."

Something was tickling at my mind. "Maybe," I suggested, "she doesn't much feel this is home. After all, she's just been going here this one year. Does she even have friends here?" I remembered what was bothering me, and forgot my grudge in my excitement. "Ms. Waverly offered her place to Chantal on Friday, too. When we found—you know." They nodded. "Anyway, Chantal's reaction was about like you describe. She seemed scared. But who wouldn't be? I mean, she'd just learned her only parent was dead."

"So she'd want to be with her family, wouldn't she?" Kitty supported me.

"I suppose," Ron admitted. "Though I didn't get the feeling there's any great love lost between that girl and her aunt. Her mom's aunt, really. I guess that's why I expected her to jump at the chance to come back. But you two don't think she would?"

"No," we chorused.

"Besides," Kitty added practically, "don't forget she's protecting whoever she was out with that evening—and I don't for a minute believe it was a girl-friend. Dollars to donuts she was with a boy, and they're scared he'll get in trouble."

Ron sighed. "You're probably right. I just hoped I could make something of it." He ran his fingers through his hair. "Lord knows I need some kind of break here. And I don't like her evasiveness."

"You think Chantal did it? Killed her own mother?" I wasn't as shocked as I should have been.

He shrugged, not looking at me. "She might have. You never know."

I remembered I was mad at him, and turned to walk to my car.

Kitty stayed to tell Ron what we had learned from Helen Arbuthnot that morning. I heard her saying, "Any idea how the stepdad died?" before I slammed the door.

When Kitty rejoined me, she gave me an exasperated look. "Geez, JJ, that wasn't very polite."

"Why should I be polite to him? I don't think it's worth it." I turned out of the parking lot onto the road, thinking about what we knew and what we needed to know. I couldn't see a way to find out where Letitia had gone the night she was killed. I did wonder. . . "Kitty, do you suppose there's anyone out there who knows for sure if she was Lucy Lemmon?" I also wondered how Ron had answered Kitty's question about Letitia's late husband, but I wouldn't ask.

"JJ," she looked right at me and she wasn't smiling. "You are an idiot."

"Indubitably," I conceded. "But do you think there is?"

Kitty's sigh rocked her to the toes. But her answer told me that this wasn't the first she'd thought about it.

"Lots of people. Maddy knows."

"What?"

"Madeleine Takahira," she enunciated. "Her youngest sister was in school with Lucy, when Lucy was in school at all."

"That doesn't prove Maddy knew."

Kitty sighed. "Yeah, but a couple months ago I heard them arguing, Maddy and Letitia. And Maddy got fed up with the superior act, and I heard her call the woman 'Lucy Lemmon.' I didn't put it all together until later, because I never knew Lucy, but when the gossip started going around. . ." she let the thought trail off.

"Why on earth didn't you say anything?" I stared at her, and Kitty made a nervous, fluttering gesture toward the road. I pulled my attention back to my driving, and the car back into the lane, while she answered.

189

"I didn't see that it made any difference. Even if she did come from here, she'd been gone for so long. I thought she should have a chance to make a new start."

"But you just kept quiet when she was so unspeakably condescending about her big city knowledge!" I exploded. "How on earth—why—oh, hell, Kitty, you know. Did you tell Ron about Maddy and her arguing?"

Kitty squirmed.

"You didn't!" I felt a surge of unholy vindication. "You sat in my kitchen scolding me for failing to mention that horrid scarf, and wanted to tell about Carlos, and all along you were hiding that! Katherine Padgett, you should be ashamed!"

"Actually, it's Katarina," she said. In response to my blank look, she added, "My name. After my Russian grandmother, not the English one." She returned to the subject at hand. "It was months ago, and anyway, why rat on Maddy? We both know she didn't kill anyone, so who could it hurt?" I guessed Maddy had not yet talked to Kitty about my tactless phone call. Maybe she wouldn't. Maddy is undoubtedly a great deal nicer than I am. And *did* we know Maddy was innocent? The books were okay, as far as they went, but the accusations had been made, and Maddy might have objected.

"It could hurt Maddy."

"What do you mean? Do you think it matters—about Letitia being Lucy, I mean?"

I shrugged. "How would I know? The Chief was interested, though." I didn't need to tell her that of course he'd be interested in anyone's fight with the dead woman. Curse the woman, anyway, for coming here and making a mess of things.

"Do you think it could get Maddy in trouble?" Kitty asked.

I gave it some thought. "Well, LeMoine was giving Maddy all kinds of grief—and Maddy knew something about her she wanted kept quiet. And now she's dead, and—hmm." I stopped, unable to figure out how it all related, or even what had happened to all my pronouns.

"That's just it. If it were Maddy who got killed, it would make sense. Ugh," she added, thinking about it. "You know what I mean. But this way?"

"Still, you know he's going to think our protecting her makes it more suspicious. And what about blackmail?"

"Well, yes, but really," Kitty waffled, "I mean, could you imagine Maddy, well, you know?"

It wasn't a very articulate argument, but yes, I did know. "No more than I could imagine her cooking the books. Which she didn't. But what will the Chief say?"

"Well, there you have it," Kitty pointed out. "That's why I didn't like to bring it up. The same reason," she added pointedly, "why you didn't tell him about Carlos and the ice cream."

I had told him about that, but I suspected that if I said so, Kitty would point out that I'd not done so until forced, so instead I said, "I think you ought to tell him." I hit the turn signal and slowed for her driveway.

"I suppose you're right."

I like that about Kitty, her ability to admit it when she's wrong. Then she went on, "I'll tell him, then, since I heard them. And since you can't, because you aren't speaking to him right now," she said sweetly as she got out.

"Oh, you are impossible," I said. She had me pegged and we both knew it. I just couldn't seem to stay mad at Ron. Especially not since he apparently wasn't holding any grudges against me. I drove home in a better mood.

The phone rang as I was getting out of the shower. Brian had very kindly agreed to run with me, as a sort of cool-off jog for him after track practice. I didn't much like his condescension, but at least it got me out for a run. I hadn't realized how much I needed my exercise until I didn't get it. And we'd talked at last, while we ran. That made it easier, somehow. Maybe it kept me from saying too much, since I was short of breath. We'd managed to set down some ground rules for his romance, without either of us losing our temper. I finished the run feeling better than I had in days, though we still needed to talk about how Brian was feeling about the divorce.

When the phone rang, I said a word I won't let Brian use, grabbed a towel and started for the door. A step later my smarter self kicked in. Let the answering machine get it. I had better things to do. Like blow-dry my hair so it would lie flat and not frighten small children.

I could hear the click and whirr of the answering machine as I went back into the bathroom, and my Mom's voice saying "Hello, dear," then the roar of our "ultra-quiet" vent fan drowned it out. Brian's shower hissed to a stop, and I started wondering what we'd have for dinner. A large part of any mother's life is spent thinking about what to have for dinner. No wonder so many of us become food-obsessed and even a bit padded.

By the time I got downstairs I had decided to boil up some pasta and root in the fridge for something to put on it. I had also decided once more to put off returning Mom's call.

I was filling the pasta pot when the phone rang again.

My "hello" may have been a little indistinct, as by

this time my mouth was full of dark chocolate, my drug of choice. I expected it to be Mom. She sometimes did that, calling right back to add something to her message or to see if I was just a little slow getting to the phone.

"Is that you finally, JJ?" The irritated voice was not that of my mother. It was the voice of the man who was trying to divorce me and take my son.

"Allen." I swallowed the last of the suddenly-bitter chocolate. "What do you want?"

"I want you to answer your phone occasionally! I've been calling and calling. You can't just avoid me forever, you know." Unfortunately, that seemed to be true.

"I've been busy. Did you try my cell?" There I was, trying to be conciliatory. Talking to Allen could so quickly reduce me to the old role, a role I despised. No wonder I'd lost it when Ron tried to be forceful and tell me what to do. Allen's voice cut through my thoughts.

"You didn't answer that either."

I reached for my purse and rummaged around until I found my phone. Sure enough, the battery was dead. I tried to remember when I'd last used it. It might have been dead for a couple of days. I wasn't very good about that stuff.

I dropped the cell back in my purse, and to keep myself from apologizing again, said, "You're talking to me now. What do you want? My lawyer is handling the divorce, if you haven't heard."

"Oh, I've heard, all right. She made it very clear. She also suggested that you might not want to talk to me. I couldn't believe that, so I called. I wanted you to know what that woman is doing."

"Exactly what I asked her to, it sounds to me. I told her I don't at all mind divorcing you, but I want Brian, and I don't much want to talk to you." My voice was sweet as corn syrup, and about as sincere. No way was I going to lose my temper with Allen and give him any leverage whatsoever. I'd beaten back my Inner Bitch, and I wasn't going to give him anything.

Allen began remonstrating, something about giving him a chance to know his own son, and I let the waves of sound wash over me as I stirred pasta into the boiling water and rummaged in the fridge, the phone tucked between my shoulder and my ear. Out of the corner of my eye I saw Brian enter the kitchen, and for his sake choked back the snide come-backs that were pushing hard to get out.

A few of Allen's nastier comments penetrated the shell I was constructing around myself: "not supporting you to lie around. . . If you think I'm going to pay. . . I can take everything, you know."

I realized with a shock that, for Allen, this was all about money. If he thought taking Brian would be the cheap solution, he was in for a surprise. Maybe. . . I cut off his venom and my speculations.

"I'm sorry, Allen. You need to discuss this with my lawyer. I have work to do, and I am paying her to handle all this." Paying her with his money, I hoped, but did not say, given the tenor of his rant. I hoped he'd be as nasty with her. Maybe I could even get sole custody. I felt a twinge of guilt at the thought. Would Brian want that?

Allen made one final attempt to get my attention, but I said, calmly but every bit as firmly as I would to a telemarketer, "I have to go now. Good bye." Then I hung up, with exaggerated gentleness because I felt like slamming the thing down hard enough to shatter.

Brian was watching me when I turned around. "Was that Dad?" I couldn't read his expression.

"Yes. I'm sorry, did you want to talk to him?"

He shrugged. "Not really. Did he want to talk to

me?"

"He wants to have you live with him, remember?"

Brian was too smart to fall for that evasion. Allen hadn't even asked about him, let alone asked to talk to him, and Brian's face told me he knew it. My heart broke for the hurt in my child's eyes. Hurt, and anger. I wasn't ready to face that.

"Pasta and mystery topping for dinner," I announced a bit too brightly. He gave me a wry smile. He knew what I was trying to do, and it wasn't working. That didn't mean he didn't appreciate it.

"Oh, boy. I love mystery topping. Well," he put on an exaggerated frown, playing along. "As long as the mystery topping doesn't have anything green and furry on it."

"No, no, it's okay. I threw out your fifth-grade science experiment last week."

We continued the witty repartee through dinner. I managed to cook up a pretty decent sauce for the pasta, and Brian, bless the boy, told me it was good. I'm not sure sometimes who's protecting whom in our relationship, though in this case he was probably using our lightness to hide his own feelings. It's weird to have your little kid suddenly—at least it seems sudden to me—almost an adult, kissing girls and noticing that you have needs too. That made me wonder which of my needs he'd been noticing, a direction I really, really couldn't afford to go.

I reined in my thoughts and asked him about track practice. That set him off in a new direction. We could both forget his hurt in his excitement about the track season. He'd grown four inches since his less-than-stellar freshman season, and the results still amazed us both. I relaxed as I felt our relationship settling into our comfortable old groove. Sometimes parenting a teen left me dizzy, as he shifted back and forth from child to adult.

After dinner Brian retreated to his room for his homework ritual. I retired to my computer to catch up on email, surf my favorite discount sites, and hunt for someone who wanted to hire a great writer and editor to telecommute. What I did not do was call Ron. Kitty had a decision to make and I wasn't going to make it for her.

At ten p.m. I gave up, turned off the computer, and went to bed.

I woke up Thursday with a tight hamstring, a headache, and a sense of foreboding. That might have been due to the headache, but it turned out to be spot on. Before the day was over, the painful hamstring was looking like the best part of it.

Anne Kasper, my lawyer, phoned before I'd even finished my first cup of coffee.

"Hi JJ. Sorry to call so early, but I couldn't reach you yesterday."

She couldn't reach me because I'd not been home from about eight a.m. to—by the time I'd finished my run—seven p.m., I realized. This life of mine looked all too much like holding a steady job.

"I'm sorry," I apologized automatically, then mentally kicked myself. I owed no one any apologies for being busy and hardworking. Still, Anne was doing me a favor, working for cheap. Comparatively cheap, anyway. "You should have tried me at the high school," I added. "I think I live there now."

"Oh, right. Kitty mentioned the Yearbook thing. You guys going to make your deadline?"

I figured that this chit-chat was costing money, even at my special rate, and gave the short answer. "Sure. What's up?"

"Allen is being, well, difficult." Anne was being diplomatic. Allen was being obnoxious.

"Why am I not surprised?"

"I would almost say he's being. . .vindictive. Like he's holding a grudge. Why?"

I had no idea. But she deserved the best answer I could find. "Well, I can only think of a couple of things, and I don't know how real they are. But for one, I think I didn't turn out to be who he thought he was getting when he married me."

"That happens often enough." She didn't have to point out that not every disappointed spouse made this much trouble.

"Unless he's on drugs or has been taken over by aliens, the only other thing I can think of is that there's another woman. Someone who wants him to get free of his obligations with as little expense as possible. Though he doesn't really need anyone pushing him that way. He likes to spend his money where it makes a splash. But the weird thing is him wanting Brian. I would think that having a teenaged son underfoot would complicate matters with a new young wife."

"Well, he's pushing for the earliest possible court date. I think he's hoping to get a judgment before this little problem at the school is cleared up."

I wondered what she would consider a "big problem," if our murder was just a little one. I didn't want to know. "That sounds like him. So what do we do?"

"Get all our ducks in order and pray that Chief Karlson solves the case. I could, of course, request a delay," she went on. "But I think we should go ahead. That will demonstrate confidence, and force him to come through on short notice, too. Barring a charge against you, I think we're good."

"If you're confident. I'll do whatever you think is best. Is there anything else you need from me?"

"Can you document Allen's visits, calls, et cetera, in the past year? If we are going to shoot for sole custody, we're going to need a strong demonstration

197

of his lack of interest in Brian's thoughts, feelings, or emotional well-being. For example, has he ever suggested Brian come spend a vacation with him? The whole summer, maybe?"

"Not to my knowledge." I had to hedge. It was possible he'd made such a suggestion to Brian, and the boy had kept it to himself.

"Did he come for Christmas this year?"

"For about four days."

"During that time did he take Brian anywhere special?"

She should know the answer to that by now.

"No. I think he spent pretty much the whole time on the phone."

We went on in that vein for some time. I offered to come in to her office, but she brushed the suggestion aside.

"I'd as soon just get through all this," she said. By which I took her to mean she had other clients coming in, clients who were paying full price. That was okay. I had a lot to do, too.

So I answered questions while fixing breakfast and harrying Brian through his morning routines and out the door when Sarah drove up. The kids were carpooling again, and I thought maybe we could keep this up even after we finished the unspeakable Yearbook. I ignored his questioning looks and raised eyebrows, putting him off with a whispered, "Later."

By the time Anne had finished with me, I was already late, and I almost forgot to mention Allen's phone call the night before. I summarized the conversation.

"Right," she said, pausing a moment, no doubt to make a note. "So he ignored instructions from your attorney and went ahead and contacted you. That could go either way. He can claim he wants to keep things friendly. But we can use it to point out his pattern of ignoring your wishes. Is there what you'd call a pattern?"

"I'd call it a life-long practice," I said, not caring if she knew I was bitter about it.

"Plus there's all that emphasis on money," she mused. "That's another red flag, though a little harder to prove." She was nice enough not to add "especially since you weren't paying attention when he was saying it." Instead, she said, "He's probably trying to soften you up for a low offer on child support or alimony."

When we finished, I glanced at the clock. I'd have to get my breakfast at the Have-A-Bite. I picked the phone back up and dialed Kitty, keys in hand.

"I'm on my way!" I hung up before she could ask questions.

- 14 -

WHO WOULD WANT TO FRAME ME?

"I can't believe what that SOB is trying to do," I ranted to Kitty over my coffee and, in lieu of a real breakfast, a two-pound cinnamon roll. Well, maybe not two pounds, but the Have-A-Bite made a cinnamon roll that could kill a person. I intended to enjoy every bite and go out with a smile.

Fortunately, Moira was too busy for gossip, and we huddled in as obviously private a conference as possible, emitting "bug off!" vibes that people seemed to be heeding.

"Why does Allen have it in for you?" Kitty asked.

I gave that some thought. "I don't know. Maybe he just wants a divorce without giving up anything, especially money, and what Allen wants, Allen figures he should get. I suppose he's found someone it would be expedient, or even just pleasant, to marry. Probably some trophy wife with blonde hair and only the right curves. I'm just an impediment that needs to be removed," I added with more bitterness than I'd intended.

"Oh, come now," Kitty protested. The problem with Kitty was, she could never believe people could be as nasty as they really were. So even though I'd told her all about Allen and his manipulations, she persisted in imagining he must be nicer than that. After all, he'd always seemed decent enough when she met him on his rare visits. He did have plenty of charm when he wanted. I'd certainly thought so once.

"Kitty, I am done being nice about this. You were the one who pointed out to me that my marriage was over long ago, remember? And that he'd been right to the edge of domestic violence, too. So now I'm saying you were right—and that I'm well off out of it. The man was inconsiderate when he put his job advancement above Brian's and my happiness. When he told me I couldn't do anything right he was out-and-out pond scum, and this whole thing proves it."

"I know he's pond scum," she protested. "But why does he want Brian all of a sudden after so long?" Maybe Kitty wasn't as naïve as I thought.

"Anne thinks he's softening me up for a no-cash settlement." I rubbed my temples, as though friction might improve brain function. "Maybe he figures I've done the hard part and now he wants a good-looking son to show off."

Kitty snorted, and I realized what I'd said. When we stopped laughing I said, "If Sunday was any indication, the hard part's just beginning, isn't it? Kitty, what are we going to do about Brian and Kat?"

"Nothing, at this point. They know the rules. But," she wasn't letting go of my other problem, not yet. "Unless Allen's an idiot, he can't think it's any kind of bargain to take on a teenaged kid who resents him."

"Kitty, even I have trouble believing it's *all* about money."

She sighed. "JJ, I have no idea what to think. I totally cannot imagine Mike doing anything like this."

I couldn't either. I put my cup down. "Forget Mr. Pond Scum. Let's get our plan together. What time does the Yearbook have to go in?" I considered licking the crumbs of frosting off the plate that had held my cinnamon roll, but decided against it. Moira was watching from the counter.

"We submit it electronically, so we don't have to race to the Post Office," Kitty told me. "But they absolutely have to have it by noon tomorrow."

"Or else what?" I like to know all the options.

"Or else we can choose between paying an extra thousand dollars or distributing it in the fall."

"Oh." There didn't seem to be much to add to that. "Well, then, what do we have to do to make the deadline?"

We spent the next half hour deep in discussion of the steps we'd need to take. I wanted to race off and just get started, but Kitty argued that we'd make better progress with a plan. A few of the other customers wandered in our direction, hoping for gossip, but we only had to raise our voices a bit and make comments about needing more volunteers, and they sheered off in a hurry. Just as well. At this point, new volunteers would be more trouble than they were worth.

While we talked, Kitty drew a rather neat chart of the process, with slots to assign every step of the job to one person or another. All that remained was to get over to the school and put the plan into action.

What with my phone call and our strategy meeting, by the time we got to the school it was Second Period. I expected the kids would have come and gone, and we'd have to go hunting to let them know we'd arrived. Instead, we found a room full of students who'd picked up where they'd left off the previous afternoon. Looking around at the kids bent industriously to their keyboards and monitors, I actually felt a little choked up. *Probably hormones*, I told myself.

I took a deep breath and hauled out Kitty's plan. Two of the clubs on my list were now finished, except the proof reading. I marked in the kids' names on the projects under way, and sat down to start proofing. That fell to me as a matter of course.

Kitty and Justin between them somehow convinced the people at the Orca Diner—the restaurant half of Island Arts where he worked—to bring over a large batch of their incredible vegetarian lasagna, so we kept working right through lunch. When I looked around the room about the time their after-lunch class should have been starting, I realized that all the kids who had been working all week were present. I grabbed a camera.

"Okay, everyone, time for a staff photo!"

"But most of us aren't even on the Yearbook staff," someone protested.

I snorted. "I say that anyone who's been slaving away on this thing all week is on the Yearbook Staff. And will be in the photo."

"What about the kids who were on staff all year but couldn't help this week?" That was Sarah, worried as ever about fairness. "Anyway, there's already a staff photo."

I sighed. "Okay, we'll have two photos. One for, um, photography staff, and one for editorial staff. Overlap is okay," I added before anyone could raise the objection. "Now, all of you cluster around one or two of the computers, and look this way. You too, Kitty. You're the Editor-in-Chief."

"Wait a minute, Mom. Let's use the self-timer and get you in here too."

Brian and Justin propped the camera atop a computer with the help of a couple of sweatshirts, and we all clustered around. The nice thing about using a digital camera was that we could see the closed eyes and funny expressions in the first six shots. The seventh, glory be, turned out pretty well. The only person who looked kind of weird was me. But everyone assured me I looked just like myself. I'd have preferred not to believe that, but we needed to get on with things, so I let the boys download the picture and put together a staff page for the very end of the Yearbook.

"What do we do about Ms. LeMoine?" Justin wanted to know.

"Is she in the other group picture?" I asked.

"Yeah. I just wondered, I mean, should we make some sort of comment or memorial or something? I mean, we never had a Yearbook advisor die in the middle of the year before."

"No shit." I couldn't help saying it. A couple of kids looked horrified, but most were smothering giggles. "Kitty? This is more up your alley."

They all knew what I meant. If you needed one of us to do what's kind and polite, you didn't look at me. You looked at Kitty.

She rose to the occasion, as I knew she would, and put together a tasteful, and not too mendacious, tribute to the late and not-so-very-lamented Letitia LeMoine. A photo of her, in soft focus, and her dates of birth and death, with the words "Rest in Peace, Ms. Letitia LeMoine" underneath. No exuberant and untruthful claims of how much we'd miss her, nor anything to suggest we were relieved to have her gone, however taken aback at the manner of her removal. She made no mention of murder. No need: I didn't think any kid who'd been at Orcaville High this year would ever forget.

In the midst of these reflections, Kitty's phone rang. She picked it up, said "Uh-huh," and handed it to me. I glanced at the caller ID and headed for the hall. I was not talking to Ron in front of Kitty and all the kids.

I was really glad I'd done that, because my day just got worse.

"JJ, I want to talk to you!" This was definitely Chief Karlson, not my friend, or possibly ex-friend, Ron. He brushed right past my greeting and polite inquiries into progress on the case, and barked at me like a Marine drill sergeant. Naturally, I reacted badly.

"What the hell? What is *wrong* with you?"

"I've been wondering the same thing about you," he growled, and followed up with a command to come down to the station. Then he hung up.

I stood and stared at the phone for a minute, before I pulled myself together and stuck my head into the computer lab to say in a reasonable approximation of my usual tone, "Kitty? I've got to run a quick errand." I devoutly hoped it would be quick, and that Ron would not be arresting me for murder—or for interference with a police investigation. "I'll be back as fast as I can."

Kitty looked at me with one eyebrow raised, and took the phone I was holding out to her. I shook my head and shrugged. She got the message, and didn't press me.

As I walked to my car I saw Annette Waverly watching me out the office window. I couldn't see her expression from that distance, but I raised a hand in a friendly wave. She didn't wave back. I shrugged. Probably the woman thought I should be sticking to the Yearbook, and she didn't like me leaving in the middle of the day. She'd dropped by the library to check up on us just often enough to tell me she hoped we were going to pull it off at whatever cost. Well, I wasn't going to go explain myself to her. My headache was back full force, and I could feel that sore hamstring with every step. I was also mad clean through at Ron Karlson.

The drive down to the police station was just long enough to give me time to stop being so mad and start worrying. What on earth had Ron so upset? I wasn't keeping any more secrets from him.

I was not in a good mood when I got to Ron. I had to make my way past the dispatcher, who must have been kin to Homer, because she was almost as bright and twice as nasty. After I had dropped everything to dash to the Station when called, the ditz wouldn't let me in until Ron yelled from his office that yes, he did want to see me, and right away. Then she gave me a knowing leer and stood aside. I couldn't tell if she was leering because she thought Ron and I had something going on, or because she figured he was about to arrest me. I ignored her and walked in, closing the door behind me in the face of her evident intention to eavesdrop.

"Good afternoon, Ron. What's up?" I had decided I shouldn't hold onto the anger I'd felt since Tuesday night. Instead, I was stubbornly friendly and polite, despite my irritation at the way he'd ordered me to come down to the station. Unfortunately, now he was glaring at me. "Good Lord, Ron, you're not still mad about Tuesday night, are you? You know damn well we were trying to do the right thing, whatever you may think of our approach."

"I didn't call you about that. I need to talk to you about *last* Tuesday. The day you and the rest of your PTA Board decided you had to 'do something' about Letitia LeMoine."

I gaped at him. He'd dragged me away from the Yearbook to discuss that? Our gripe session where we'd all admitted we couldn't work with the woman? I struggled to find something to say. Being me, I quickly found the wrong thing.

"So who'd you bully into telling you about that?"

"Why didn't you tell me yourself?" he countered.

Good question, that. "I really couldn't say. Probably because on the one hand, a lot has happened since then and I forgot. On the other hand, it's a little too coincidental, isn't it, all of us deciding she's got to go, and then someone kills her. I guess we must have 'done something' about her in a permanent way, huh?"

He was not amused. Mostly, he sounded tired. "JJ, I'm not accusing you of anything. But I am tired of playing games with you."

"Then don't!" I blurted. "Why don't you just tell me what you want from me?"

He didn't meet my eyes. Sitting at his desk, gaze fixed on his papers, he spoke without a trace of warmth. "First, I want confirmation that the meeting took place."

I chose to ignore his tone. "I wouldn't exactly call it a meeting. We all happened to be there, waiting for the bell, and started griping. By the time everyone had made it clear Letitia irritated the hell out of us, I knew we had to do something about her before she drove everyone off. She wasn't an official member of the Board, you know, just a very insistent volunteer. It's not easy to stop someone like that. I wanted Kitty to talk to her, to tell her straight out she was alienating people and causing a lot of anger and resentment."

"That's not exactly what it sounded like to the person who reported it," he said. "Did you maybe shout some?"

"I spoke vehemently. I was not shouting nor was I out of control."

He put his head in his hands. "JJ, once again, I am not accusing you. In fact, I'm hoping you can help me." He looked up again, and for the first time I met his eyes. Strange. He didn't look angry. He looked worried. "This is the second time someone has tried to point a finger at you."

"What do you mean?"

"First, the scarf. It might've been coincidence, but it does seem a bit suggestive that it was yours. I mean," he groped for a polite way to say it, and I took pity on him.

"You mean because everyone around knows that I don't suffer fools gladly?"

"That's one way of putting it," he muttered, not meeting my eye. Then, rallying, he said, "I know you didn't have the scarf. Kat told me about leaving it in the main office."

I shifted uncomfortably, recalling why she'd been in the office, and aware that I still hadn't figured out what I was going to do about that whole mess. This was becoming a less and less comfortable conversation. I reined in the impulse to take it in a new direction, and asked the salient question. "We don't know who put the scarf—where you found it. But presumably you know who told you about our, um, discussion?"

He shook his head. "That's just it. I don't. Tacy took the call." At my questioning look, he explained, "Tacy Hesse. The dispatcher. Also secretary, and everything else around the office. She's Homer's cousin," he added in what would have been a non sequitur if it hadn't explained so much. "She didn't know the voice, and the woman—that's all she could say, that it was a woman—didn't give a name. Just said that we should know that you'd been heard issuing threats against the dead woman. And she quoted that bit about doing something about her. Was that accurate?" he added.

I shrugged. "As far as I can remember. It sounds like me. But I didn't make any threats, I swear it." I reflected. "A woman? Kitty or Madeleine? I can't see it." Not even given that I'd gotten them both mad at me in the last couple of days.

"Neither can I," Ron admitted. "But—do you know yet about the PTA books? Could Maddy have been hiding something?"

I shook my head. "We'll never be able to prove there weren't records on our computer, but I've worked over the account book pretty thoroughly, and there's just no room for any theft."

"She says, and her family confirm it, that she isn't much with computers. And they were all together Thursday night, from about five on. And you need to stop playing detective, please." He did know about my questions to Maddy, but to my surprise, he didn't sound angry. I was beginning to realize that his anger hadn't been directed at me, at least not wholly. It had been at the whole nasty situation, and maybe, just maybe, he'd been upset that someone was trying to make it look like I'd committed murder.

I couldn't let it rest there. "Why are you so sure I didn't do it?" I'm not sure what I was hoping for. A declaration of love? Of unwavering faith in my innate goodness? I got something more blunt.

"In part because I can't think of a dumber way to handle the body if you killed her, and you're smarter than that. But mostly," he added before I could get a fat head, "because Brian is your witness that you were at home all evening. And he was on the phone to Kat enough to have her as a second witness, since you yelled three times for him to get off the phone and come eat dinner."

I was surprised how relieved I felt to find that, at last, I had a decent alibi, though I suppose a lawyer would argue that my son would lie for me, and his girlfriend back him up.

"How come I didn't know this?" I asked.

"You mean you weren't there yelling at him?"

"No, you're probably right about that, though I thought he was talking to Justin." I swallowed. There was too much I hadn't noticed. "I mean, how come you never told me you don't suspect me?"

He changed the subject. "So who do you think would be in a position to quote your, uh, decision about Ms. LeMoine, besides Mrs. Takahira, Kitty, and Carlos Hernandez?"

I shook my head, thinking. "I suspect I was kind of loud. Kitty kept trying to wriggle out from under her responsibility as President, and I got a bit worried. I'm not very good," I added, "at keeping an even temper and a calm tone."

That drew a laugh. Not a very good laugh, but he was making an effort and I appreciated it. "I might have known. So anyone walking by could have heard, and anyone who was feeling a bit of malice could have acted on it. Not," he added with a wicked grin that did strange things to that internal control I'd been exercising, "that anyone would have any reason for malice against a person with your tact and quiet modesty."

If I hadn't been so busy getting my visceral reaction to his grin under control, I would have taken offense at the implication that people might resent my blunt but incisive assessments. I was going to have to put some distance between this man and myself. I was not ready to feel this way.

A moment later, all signs of humor were gone, replaced by a grim look. "Which is why I wanted you to come down here. Someone has already tried to kill you."

"We don't know that for certain," I protested, remembering Kitty's reaction to the tale of the swerving driver. For that matter, I hadn't thought Ron had taken it seriously. What had changed his mind?

"Maybe, maybe not. Do you want to take a chance

on it? I don't."

I thought about Brian and didn't say anything.

"So tell me everything you remember about the car."

I shook my head. "That's just it. I can't tell one car from another, just that it was a four-door sedan. I couldn't even tell the color, because it was almost dark. And the light was out over the license plate, so I couldn't read that."

He sighed, though he couldn't have expected much else.

"So, twice suspicion has been pointed at you, and someone tried to run you down. I'm asking—I can't insist, but I'm asking, JJ—that you think about leaving the Island until I get this cleared up."

I stared at him. Leave the Island? Leave Kitty with the Yearbook mess? And what about Brian? Was I supposed to leave him behind for the murderer to stalk, or pull him out of school, or what?

"You're crazy. No way am I leaving. I *can't* leave."

He sighed. "Somehow, I thought you'd say that. But I had to try. I," he started to add something, then cleared his throat and, I was pretty sure, finished up somewhere other than he'd intended. "I'll do what I can to protect you, but promise me you'll be careful. Really careful, not the way you were the other night."

"I promise," I said unhesitatingly. I was neither stupid nor suicidal. I had no intention of being one of those horror-movie females who blithely enter the dark room where the monster was last seen.

"Okay." He didn't look convinced, but he dismissed me. "You get back to your Yearbook. I don't think you can get into much trouble in a room full of kids and computers."

It seemed a reasonable assumption at the time.

I left Ron's office with a lot on my mind. I couldn't figure out if we were still mad at each other. I should have been—I wasn't happy to have anyone grab me the way he had, and he really had been rude when he ordered me to come to the station—but it seemed less important now. Maybe he'd had good reason to be angry, and maybe he'd been frightened.

I was reeling from the suggestion that someone really was out to get me. I had been insisting that someone had tried to run me down on the road to Ron's house, but I'd met with so much skepticism that I'd come around to thinking I must've been mistaken. At worst, it was about getting the computer files, right? Except, we'd yet to see anything among the photos worse than an over-sexed cheerleader headed into the dark with a willing male.

Ron's obvious concern made the idea that someone wanted me out of the way seem too real. The trouble was, they were trying too hard. The attempt on my life made the efforts to frame me unconvincing. I couldn't be killer and victim both. Of course, I didn't have any proof of the near miss on the road. And why kill me? Because I was asking too many questions? Then why not kill Ron, who even I had to admit was much more likely to find the killer? I shuddered at the thought, suppressing an urge to cross myself, or spit over my shoulder—anything to ward off the evil of that idea.

Halfway back to the school, it occurred to me that I might be closer to an answer than I knew, and that was why the killer was after me. But if so, I couldn't see it. No, more likely the attempt to run me down was my imagination. And framing me was convenient because, face it, I wasn't not always tactful or even very nice, and everyone knew how I felt about Letitia LeMoine. Especially after my unfortunately audible comments the previous Tuesday.

I wondered again who might have called the police about that. I knew Annette had heard me, because she'd poked her head in to see what the yelling was about. Did she think I was the killer and rat me out to protect her school? Or was it one of the teachers? Patty Reilly or Ms. Day either one could have been there, and they knew I was nosey, and could have reason to want me out of the way. It could even have been Carlos or Fingal or one of the male teachers, pretending to be female. I wasn't convinced Tacy Hesse could tell the difference.

Maybe it wasn't even the same person tattling and trying to run me down, let alone committing murder. Maybe Tina was desperate to get those discs before Ms. Day found out she'd violated the cheerleader's code of conduct. She might have known enough to reformat the computers, making good and sure there wasn't any evidence about her. And maybe LeMoine had caught her at it and things had escalated. Or maybe that was improbable coincidence.

What if someone had reported me in all innocence, because they really believed I might have done killed LeMoine? I felt a chill at the idea anyone could believe that of me.

A honk brought me back to the job at hand. I swerved back into my own lane just in time, and the oncoming driver gave me the one-finger salute as he went by. After that, I quit trying to think and just drove.

- 15 -

KISS AND MAKE UP?

Nothing much had changed while I was away. Kitty looked up when I came in, but I shook my head and mouthed "later," and we got back to work. I set up a pattern: I'd edit a page, then spend a few minutes searching the photo files, looking for anything that might shed some light on the situation—or, at least, on someone's determination to get rid of those photos. I expected to find something a kid or kids had done that they wished hadn't been photographed, though with Facebook and all that they had a fat chance of keeping anything private.

The worst I found was a food-fight in the lunchroom, but however much those in charge of discipline might want to prevent such behavior, it was scarcely a secret, with what looked like twenty kids involved and all the rest looking on, and no doubt Tweeting photos.

Some time after five, with the boys in from track practice and my stomach letting me know I'd better think about dinner, I tackled one last page.

"I'll just proof this one and then we go home for dinner, okay boys? Why don't you make a start on your homework?" They ignored my suggestion, of course. Instead, Brian rummaged through my purse for edibles. He found an ancient granola bar and made a snide comment, but he ate it anyway.

Only Kitty and her daughters were left with us, and Kitty looked over at me, her eyes red and watery from hours spent staring into the glare of the monitor.

"I think it's going to take a couple more hours," she said, rubbing a hand across her face. "And we'd better do it tonight. Then we can do a final check in the morning and send it off."

I negotiated. "Let's eat and come back. I'm beat, and these boys need their dinner. Also time to do their homework."

"Yeah, me too, Mom," Sarah put in. Kat didn't say anything, just practiced her most pathetic look, with a side-long glance at Brian.

Kitty knew when she was beaten. "Okay, gang. We'll break for dinner. Anyone who is ready, willing, and able can meet back here at," she glanced at her watch, "half past seven."

From the looks of the kids, I suspected Kitty and I would be there by ourselves. At least that would give us a chance to talk.

On my way out, I stuck my head into the main office. Kitty had her own key, but I thought it would be polite to let the principal know we'd be there all evening. Through the open door, I could see her at her desk. She looked up and tried to smile when I gave her my message. This whole thing seemed to be taking a major toll on the woman. Despite the perfect makeup, she looked like she wasn't sleeping.

"Ah." She answered my announcement vaguely. "Yes. I'll be going soon. Mr. Fingal just left." I guessed she'd leave as soon as she'd made sure he hadn't screwed anything up, though she was too savvy to say so.

"We've nearly got the thing finished," I told her in

hopes of making her feel better.

She gave a sort of wave. "Okay, great. I'm so grateful to you two for taking care of the Yearbook," she added and made a show of turning back to her work. "I don't know what we'd do without you."

I felt an unaccustomed pang of pity for the woman. Perfectionism is a harsh mistress in this imperfect world. She looked tired, harried no doubt by this threat to her school and a fear of what might happen next. For the first time, it occurred to me that she, too, could wonder if she might be the next target. I wondered if Letitia LeMoine was killed for anything she in particular did—or just because she helped at the school? The thought that there could be someone out there with a grudge against school people, looking for revenge on anyone who came within reach, made me shiver.

"We're glad to help, Annette. And don't worry—we'll get this thing in on time."

"I knew I could count on you," she called as I disappeared out the door.

I had to trot to catch up with Brian, who as usual had snitched the keys from my bag while we packed up.

"I get to practice tonight, right?"

Oh, boy. Just what I needed: a driving lesson with a teenager. He must have read my thoughts in my face.

"Come on, Mom. I need more hours or I won't be able to take the test on my birthday." The set of his jaw said it wasn't worth arguing, because I would lose. Besides, he was right. His birthday was less than a month off, and he did need time behind the wheel. As tired and tense as I was, I wasn't sure I could cope, but that's what parenthood is about: doing the right thing for the kid even if you'd rather have a root canal. No one in her right mind actually wants to get in a car with a fifteen-year-old behind the wheel. But a good parent does it, again and again until he's more or less safe to turn loose on the road. A *really* good parent does it without crying or cringing.

I'm not that good a mom, but I let Brian drive, and only whimpered a little bit. He pretended not to notice, and I concluded we were back to being friends.

Once home, I moved into high gear, changing into more comfortable clothes, then trying to put a full day's housekeeping into about an hour while simultaneously preparing a tasty and nutritious dinner—or at least something better than microwaved mac and cheese.

Long before I was ready, but just in time to prevent me putting my feet up and refusing to move again, Kitty pulled up outside and blew her horn. I told Brian to get his homework done.

"And don't wait up for me. We might be late." I heard his laughter as I left, and joined in as I realized I sounded like a wayward teen myself.

In the witch-light of dusk the school was an eerie place. There were no cars in the parking lots, and I suppressed a little shiver of fear. A few lights glowed over doorways, emphasizing the abandoned look. At least it wasn't a dark and stormy night, just a dark one. As I'd predicted, none of the kids were with us. Given how much they'd been cutting class, I wasn't surprised to find they all had mountains of homework.

"Kat confessed," Kitty explained. "She and her friends made a deal with their teachers—they could cut class to work on the Yearbook, but they would do all the work, get notes from friends, and turn in daily summaries to prove they knew what they'd missed.

217

They're a little behind," she added unnecessarily.

"Geez. For every teacher?"

"Only math, history, and Spanish. They told Ms. Day," the cheerleading coach who was also the girls' PE teacher, "that they'd be sure to get plenty of exercise. Ms. Day," Kitty added, "is no idiot. She's not asking them to verify and she's not imagining they really will. She's just saying that to cover herself."

"That sounds awfully cynical for Kitty Padgett," I commented.

"No, not at all." Kitty looked thoughtful. "I thought she was being very nice and pretty smart."

"If she's so smart," I sniped, "how did she ever let Chantal become Captain of the cheer squad?"

Kitty glanced at me, then back at her computer. "But you know that, don't you?"

"You mean the part about how Fingal holds the final vote—and he told her that Chantal should have it? That she was clearly the best?"

"Well, she is good. At cheerleading."

"Yeah. You know how Ms. Day feels about Fingal?

"That he spends too much time watching the cheerleaders?"

I gave her a quick glance. We both remembered what Kat said about Elvis Fingal's wandering hands.

"Well, most men like to watch cheerleaders," I had to point out. "That's what they're for, as far as I can tell." We gave up and started to giggle.

Kitty tried to pretend she wasn't sniggering. "It's part of the Vice's job, JJ. Cheerleaders represent the school, and he's supposed to make sure they make us look good."

"I'll bet," I muttered. We both laughed some more, then Kitty sobered.

"Oh, come on. You don't really think he's doing anything, do you?"

I suppressed a shudder. "I'm not saying he's redefining the 'vice' in Vice Principal. But remember, Kat said he likes to look."

"To touch, too, if he gets a chance," Kitty recalled, a frown creasing her forehead.

"He gives me the creeps," I told her. So did the dark and silent school, though I wouldn't say so. I found myself wishing we had a night custodian. Anything so we wouldn't be there alone.

"He's okay," Kitty defended the vice-principal without conviction. "He's an Island boy."

"Huh." I didn't think much of her reasoning, but didn't want to get into an argument. Kitty is much too inclined to think anyone native to the Island is okay. The way I saw it, there were maybe four thousand people on the Island, half of them natives. Out of even a couple thousand people, there were bound to be some you didn't want hanging around your teenaged daughter. Elvis Fingal looked like one of them to me, but I didn't have daughter. I did know that he wasn't much of a Vice Principal.

Thinking that made me think about Annette Waverly. If Fingal was as bad as all that, was I being too hard on her? After all, she had to put up with him, and she had to cover the work he almost certainly didn't get done. I remembered her tired, harried look that afternoon.

"What do you think of Annette Waverly?" I asked Kitty.

"She's nice enough, I guess." Kitty didn't sound very enthusiastic, so I made an encouraging noise and she elaborated. "She doesn't seem very connected to the community."

"Is that your 'the best people come from the Island' mentality, or something more?"

Kitty gave that serious thought. "I think it's more. She's big on image, kind of a perfectionist," she echoed my earlier thought, "and she talks a good line about what's good for the school, but she doesn't know the students, and she hasn't been terribly helpful with our PTA, as you should know. And she shops off-Island."

That last was a sin even I condemned. Island businesses had a hard time of it, with a limited population base and few tourists. Still, selection in our stores was limited, and prices higher than elsewhere. I'd been known to shop on line, and I went to Costco whenever I was on the Mainland.

"You mean she doesn't patronize Island Arts and the drugstore?" I asked, just to be certain.

"I mean she doesn't even patronize the Pismawallops Market. She buys almost all her groceries off-Island, for Pete's sake."

"Well," I thought about it. "That may not be anti-social, but it sure as heck isn't fiscally sound. You'd have to pay a lot less for groceries to subsidize ferry fare." I laughed. "Should we be paying more attention to the school finances?"

Kitty laughed too. "Maybe. It just kind of feels like she's not really invested here. Like she wants things perfect so, I don't know, so she can get a better job somewhere else? I guess I just don't like her very much. She's, well, she's cold."

"She was thanking us profusely for our work this afternoon, though," I pointed out. "And not for the first time. I think somebody's gotten to her about treating her volunteers better. I don't think she said thank-you once last fall."

"Maybe she's learning. She's still young," Kitty added charitably. Ms. Waverly was younger than we were, to be sure, but I thought she was old enough to have learned tact if she was going to. Well, I was a fine one to judge her about that.

"Of course, the Yearbook is a PTA thing, but she's still the one under fire if it doesn't come out," I added.

After that we worked in silence for a long time. About half past ten I stretched, looked at my watch, groaned, and suggested we call it a night.

"How bad can it be?"

Kitty surveyed the files. "Maybe you're right. If the kids pitch in tomorrow morning, we can finish proofing the last half."

"We might want to cherry-pick our proof-readers," I suggested. "Sarah, Madison, Kat, but not I think Carina?" Kat's best friend was a lovely child, and talented in many respects. She just wasn't tops with grammar and spelling.

"Why don't we just pair the kids up—Carina knows a lot of the students, so she can make sure pictures are labeled correctly. Someone else can check the grammar and all."

"Works for me." I began saving and copying files. I was still putting everything on my thumb drive every night, more out of habit than anything. Kitty did the same.

We were on our way home before I remembered I hadn't told Kitty about my conversation with Ron that morning. Actually, Kitty remembered. I would have been happy to forget.

"What was that about this morning? Your sudden departure?"

"That. Oh. Well, it was Ron."

She knew that. "He was desperate to reach you? He apologized for Tuesday night and all is well?"

"Not exactly."

"What do you mean?"

"He didn't apologize, and I very much suspect all is not well. But," I took pity on her, "I don't think we'll bother fighting about that any more." I went on to explain what Ron had told me, that he believed someone was trying to make me look guilty. And that as a result he was now taking seriously the attempt on my life. I didn't mention his request that I leave the Island. It wasn't open for discussion or negotiation, because I was going nowhere, and I didn't want to risk another argument with Kitty, who might agree with him, especially once the Yearbook was done. We'd gotten over my recent blunders, and I didn't want to fight.

"They aren't doing a very good job of framing me, but there it is. We don't know if someone hopes he'll arrest me and I'll be removed, or if they are just throwing up smoke screens."

"Smoke screens?"

"You know, trying to divert attention away from themselves. Anything to confuse the issue. Whoever it is has a point," I insisted. "Ron is a good officer, but this is way beyond anything he's ever had to deal with, and he has to do it all himself. Adding leads to follow up and complicating things increases the chance that he'll never catch the killer. And," I added because if I didn't she would, "we've played right into their hands, because pointing a finger at me in particular confuses the issue, thanks to hormones." I wasn't ready to admit emotions.

Kitty was. "Do you really believe it's all just hormones?"

I stared out the window a minute before I answered. "Hormones are bad enough. Anything more I can't handle right now."

She didn't have any answer for that.

When Ron called me Friday morning, the first thing that flashed through my mind was that hormones were winning. The second, much more chilling thought was that he was calling on business. In his line of work, calls at odd hours are never good.

He rushed into his message as though he were afraid I might hang up before he got to the point. "JJ,

I forgot to tell you yesterday morning, but I found an envelope at the LeMoine house labeled "Yearbook." Looks like papers—I just glanced at them, but maybe a contract or something you need? Anyway, I thought you might want to pick it up."

I tried to sound grateful, because he was making amends of a sort. But as far as I knew we had everything we needed, and with the Yearbook within a gnat's eyelash of complete, it was too little, too late.

"Thanks. Can't you drop it by the school for us?" At least I wasn't grousing aloud about him not finding anything useful. I was really, really trying to keep matters friendly. After yesterday morning, I wasn't sure just what I felt. I knew that Ron's strong-arm approach Tuesday night had rubbed me very much the wrong way, but I hadn't yet decided if it was a deal breaker. Assuming there was any deal to break.

Ron was thinking about murder, not sex, and responded to my question, not my ruminations. "You'll have to come by the station and pick it up. I won't have time to drop it off."

His tone got my attention. "You're onto something?"

"No." He sighed. "Just more complications."

"Oh-oh. What now?" I kept my voice sympathetic, encouraging him to tell me his troubles. It worked.

"Chantal has gone missing," he said.

"What?!"

"I phoned this morning to arrange to come and ask more questions, and the aunt told me Chantal left yesterday afternoon and hasn't been home."

"Good lord!" I seemed to be short of intelligent responses.

"That's pretty much what I said, but the woman didn't seem too concerned. As though she expected something of the sort."

"You think she's protecting the girl from you?"

Another thought struck me. "Who is this aunt, anyway? Lucy Lemmon didn't have any sisters, did she? So this must be an aunt on her father's side? Or her step-father?" I had a thought. "Maybe she went to his family?"

"Chantal doesn't know who her father is. And I still can't learn anything about the step-father, except that he had money and left it all to Letitia LeMoine. As far as I can find, there are no other relatives." I could hear the sadness in his voice. "I think she's really a great-aunt."

"Huh." I thought for a while, with no discernable results. "So, what are you going to do?"

"Not sure. I'll start by talking to Miss Partridge—that's the aunt—then hunt up Chantal's friends. Whoever they are." He sounded discouraged.

My response probably didn't help any. "I'm not sure she has any. I know more about her rivals."

"Oh?"

He sounded interested, so I rambled on. "Well, there's Tina Ainsley, the former Captain of the cheer squad. I heard she's been complaining that Chantal was stealing her boyfriend as well as her job."

"Who's the boyfriend?" Ron was paying attention now. I was sorry to disappoint him.

"No idea. No one seems to know, and the general opinion is that he's an off-Island boy. Unless," I added, "it's the football player who's been mooning over Tina. Kevin somebody or other; I could look it up. But my understanding is that Tina dumped him, not vice-versa, so he's not likely to be the one Chantal 'stole.' Some of the kids think Chantal made him up, but it seems unnecessary. A girl like that is bound to have a boyfriend."

"Huh. I think I'd better come by after all. Maybe take copies of some photos, if you have any of these kids. Maybe Miss Partridge will have seen someone."

"Of course. We have pictures of all the kids." I sighed, remembering just how much work had gone into making sure of that. I remembered the photo Carina had found. Maybe Ron could make more out of it than we could. He could try, anyway. "There's one that might help, though I doubt it."

"Can you elaborate, JJ?" I could hear his patience, which is never a good sign.

"A picture. Tina and some boy. Suggestion is she's been up to, well, you know," I finished lamely. Talking to Ron about sex was just a little too much for me.

"Who?"

"I don't know who. The girls didn't know."

"The girls?"

"Kitty's girls, and their friends. They don't know Tina that well. Or Chantal, either. And of course," I added, "the photo is from the Clambake last fall, so I don't even know if this is the same guy. Tina strikes me as the kind for whom boyfriends have kind of a short shelf life." And Chantal, I didn't need to add, was another of the same sort.

"Huh." Silence while Ron thought about this. "I'd better see those pictures, and find someone who knows Tina better, as well as Chantal. No one could have a secret boyfriend in a school the size of ours, let alone two girls with the same boy."

He had a point. Even in bigger schools, girls like Tina flaunted their conquests and everyone knew who they were. So who was she seeing that she didn't want to talk about? Or could she actually care if people knew she was having sex? Given the casual attitudes of Kat and Carina—girls I believed to be more sweet and innocent than otherwise—toward sex, I very much doubted it. Maybe she was trying to hide him from Chantal. That seemed like a more logical conclusion, leaving only the question of whether it was now Tina or Chantal who had the unknown male on a lead.

"I'm just getting breakfast." I glanced at the clock. "I can meet you at the school in thirty minutes." Brian was going to hate me; he was still in the shower. Well, he could either eat his breakfast in the car, or gel his hair in the boys' bathroom once we got there. His choice. I heard the shower shut off, and shouted up the stairs.

"Brian! Move your hindquarters! We need to meet Chief Karlson at the school in half an hour!"

He thundered down the stairs, wearing nothing but a towel. "What's up?"

"Chief Karlson wants to see some stuff from the PTA," I extemporized. "I told him we could meet him at school in thirty minutes."

He glanced at the clock. "Mom! That's, like, an hour early for school! I can't get ready that fast!"

I looked at the clock, too. "It's twenty minutes earlier than usual. You can do your hair when we get there."

He gave me The Look, the one teenagers go to special secret classes to learn so they can shrivel parents who say stupid things. "I'll eat in the car," he growled, and thundered back up the stairs to perform the mystic rites that nowadays boys, as well as girls, must perform before going out in public.

Ron was waiting when we pulled into the school parking lot, leaning on his car in just about the spot where I'd first seen him as a person, not just a cop. I shook off the memory. This was too serious. A girl's life might be at stake. Maybe more than one, I thought, considering Tina's presumed extra-curricular activities as well as Chantal's disappearance. In any case, I doubted Ron wanted me that way, not now that he knew what sort of person I was.

Brian bounded off to wherever the kids hung out before school, leaving behind a dirty cereal bowl and an empty milk carton. At least since he was eating I'd gotten to drive.

"It could be unrelated, you know," Ron greeted me. "Something personal. Or medical," he suggested.

"You mean she's off for an abortion, or she's got the clap?" I couldn't help it. Being blunt—not to say crude—made him blush and made me feel like I was in control of the conversation. "Either way, we need to figure out who her friends are, if any. Especially boys."

"I presume that's where the pictures come in?" Ron had regained his equilibrium.

"Yeah. I'm pretty sure we don't have anything of Chantal and any boyfriends, but we can look, and there's a photo of Tina with someone—maybe the boyfriend she accused Chantal of trying to steal?"

"*If* we can identify him, and *if* he is now Chantal's boyfriend, then maybe I can find out *if* he knows anything." Ron shook his head. "Fat chance."

I knew what he meant. Lots of girls wouldn't tell their boyfriends if they got knocked up, and we were only making wild guesses about why Chantal had disappeared anyway. Though I supposed she could have run off with her boyfriend.

"Any boys missing?"

Ron had already thought of this. "None reported. I'll have to wait and see if anyone's ditching school today."

Stepping closer, Ron touched my arm. I looked at him, and saw the man, not the cop.

"Uh, JJ? The other night. . . I, well," he floundered. I didn't help him out, just looked at him and wondered. He took a deep breath.

"I'm sorry, okay?"

Feeling perverse, and enjoying the effect on him, I still didn't answer. I heard him sigh as we went in, and felt an evil sort of satisfaction. I had some of my power back. But in the back of my mind I knew he had changed everything again. Yesterday, he'd been too worried and full of business to apologize, and I'd been too upset to care. Now he was remembering, and I couldn't help liking the fact that he didn't let it slide. But a part of me didn't want to forgive and forget. Life was simpler with no men in it, and anger was an easy emotion to understand.

Ron unlocked the library with a master key I was surprised the Principal had allowed him to have. More likely he'd had it since the previous principal, who'd been pretty relaxed about security. It occurred to me to wonder if Annette Waverly had made any effort to recover all those keys. She'd never asked Kitty or me for our key.

We were standing side by side, staring at the computer while the screen went from black to a series of meaningless flashes and symbols, and I was excruciatingly aware of Ron's body next to mine. He shifted, to put a little space between us, I thought. Instead, he put his arm around me and pulled us together. I turned to say something in protest, and couldn't speak because he was kissing me.

My knees went weak. No one had kissed me like that for years. I responded so completely that, had he known, he could have done anything he wanted with me right there and then. Instead, he broke off the kiss, put me aside, and reached out to double-click the photo icon on the now-ready computer.

"Ron." My voice squeaked, and he squeezed me. His arm was still around me, and with great reluctance I removed it. I cleared my throat and tried again. "Ron? I can't do that."

He kept his eyes on the computer. "You most certainly can, and very well, too." Only then did he turn and look at me. I'd never have believed the mild Ron Karlson could leer like that.

I glared at him.

"What? Are you still mad? I'm sorry I got rough the other night, but dammit, you scared the spit out of me, heading in there with no forethought and no back-up. And if you're mad about what I just did," he paused and looked at me until I blushed, "I'm not apologizing. I've wanted to do it for a long time, but opportunities have been scarce."

"Fine, then." It wasn't a gracious acknowledgement of his apology or my culpability. But it was all he was getting. "But it doesn't matter anyway, because it doesn't matter what I feel or want, because my lawyer warned me—no men in my life until after the custody hearing."

He stepped a little farther away. I avoided looking at him.

"That bad?"

"That bad. Allen's fighting dirty, and he's already proved he's a jerk. Don't think he wouldn't use anything he can get. Moral turpitude and a bad example and who knows what else." I had a sudden vision of Brian and Kat and wondered who was a bad influence on whom, but didn't think it would help to bring that up, either with Ron or a judge.

I wasn't sure I was making sense, but he seemed to understand and turned his attention to the computer. I couldn't believe it. How could he shift just like that from seduction to detection? My own breathing was still ragged, and I was experiencing sensations I'd almost forgotten. Wonderful in their place, but this was definitely not the place. I clamped on a mental chastity belt and turned my attention to the computer.

My hand on the mouse only shook a little, so I was able to pull up the correct picture on the second try.

Ron peered at the screen.

"The girl's clear enough, but the guy could be pretty much anyone, couldn't he?"

I had to agree. The photo wasn't going to help us ID the boyfriend. "Maybe they show up together in some others, too. Or maybe we can find one of Chantal with someone. I haven't personally looked at all the pictures."

"You'll have to do the searching. Go ahead and print this one for me, though. Maybe it'll tell someone something. And a couple of Chantal; I doubt her aunt has any pictures of her, and we'll need some if there's to be a search. I have to go across and talk to the woman, anyway. Do you think you can hunt up any good photos for me?"

And still finish the Yearbook by noon? No way. So of course I nodded. "No problem. Come by when you get back and I'll show you what I have." At least by then the Yearbook would be done and sent, one way or another.

He turned and walked away, careful not to touch me. I wanted him to touch me. I could not believe how much I wanted him to touch me. At the same time I wanted nothing to do with him. And I wanted to keep Brian, so Ron would just have to keep his distance for now, whatever I decided about him in the end. I'd gone a long time without any, I could go another month or so. Maybe by then I'd know what I really wanted. And maybe pigs would fly.

- 16 -

WAITING AND WAFFLING

Kitty came in a few minutes after Ron left. I'd phoned her cell before leaving home, knowing that unlike me, she would actually check her voice mail. "I got your message and came as soon as I could get the kids ready. What did Ron want?"

"Chantal has gone missing. Ron wants us to figure out who her friends are—boyfriend, especially, if there is one. Maybe it's Tina's mystery man? If Chantal really was stealing him, the way Tina complained she was, she might be with him."

"That picture was from last fall, you know. That's decades in teen-dating time."

"I know that, but we have to start somewhere. And he wants us to ask around and find someone who knows about Tina and her boyfriend. Or boyfriends."

"Chief Karlson has been away from high school for a long time, hasn't he?"

"Well, a little longer than I have."

"Long enough."

"For what?"

"To forget that you can't ask questions like that and not set everyone talking. I thought he didn't

231

want us involved. Now he tells you to start asking questions all over the school?"

"Good point." I gave it some thought, remembering the warning he'd given me the previous day, but seemed to have forgotten this morning. I was the one someone was trying to kill, but he needed a break in this case. "Let's start with the pictures, and keep quiet for now. We're checking them all anyway, so between us we'll see everything. Maybe we can find another of her with the boy. Then we could get one of the other cheerleaders in and pretend we need an ID—see if she says they're a couple or what."

"Weak." Kitty had lost much of her meekness in the last week. She was starting to sound more like Kat. Or like me, God forbid. "But it'll do, I guess." Unless she thought of something better, which she probably would.

"Anyway, the kids'll be in soon, so we'd better get started." She turned to her computer, the one next to mine, and moved a manila envelope off the keys. "What's this?"

"That? Oh, Ron brought that. He found it at the LeMoine house. Looks like paperwork for the Yearbook, but we've got all we need." I didn't want to admit that circumstances had made me forget all about it.

"I see. And what else happened this morning? You look a little, well," she scanned me with a knowing eye. "You look flustered."

"I'm worried about Chantal." I pulled the shreds of my dignity around me and dared her to push.

Too bad for me, she took the dare. "Oh?"

I suspected her kids knew that tone and that arched eyebrow, which perfectly conveyed she didn't believe a word I said.

"Are you sure there wasn't any other distraction? You two alone here," she added just in case I didn't get it. Or didn't realize she got it.

To my relief, several of the kids charged in at that moment, and we leapt into the thick of the remaining work, with three and a half hours to go until deadline.

"Hi Mom, hi Ms. Mac." Kat bubbled over with appalling energy. "We're ready to get to work."

"Right." Kitty looked them over. "Everyone got permission to be here?"

Not that anyone would say so if she didn't, but we had to ask. Everyone nodded. "Okay." Kitty scanned the group again. There seemed to be some new faces. "Those of you who've been here know the drill. Take a section from the second half and start proofing. Pair up—you're checking IDs and grammar, spelling, the lot. You," she pointed to a boy who seemed to be with Sarah and Melissa. I didn't know the boy's name, but recognized him in a vague way, though he'd not been helping us before this. "You in any clubs or sports?"

The boy answered, "I play football, Mrs. Padgett." His tone suggested he was astonished she didn't know that.

"Good," she answered, consulting the complicated chart she'd developed to track our progress. "We need someone to proof the football and cheerleader pages."

He hadn't seemed terribly enthusiastic, but perked up when she mentioned the cheerleaders. I made a mental note to engage him in a discussion of the merits and morals of the same. Kitty directed him to a computer and made a note on her chart. "What's your name?"

"Kevin. Kevin Olsen."

Kitty wrote that down. "Right. Thanks for coming to help out. Brian?" My son had come in while I was distracted. "You work with Kevin, okay?" Without giving him a chance to suggest he wanted to work with Kat instead, she turned to Maddy's daughter, who had come in right behind Brian. "Hi, Madison. I wondered if you'd be joining us."

"I had a test, but it's over and I can work all morning. Has anyone proofed the Honor Society, Mrs. P?"

She studied her chart. "Nope. Nor Spanish Club. You're in that, too, aren't you?"

The girl nodded. Madison Takahira is as smart as her mother is dim. Well, that's not fair, because Maddy isn't dumb. She just stinks at math and was weak enough to let us bully her into taking a job she wasn't equipped to do.

"Okay," Kitty said. "You take this computer and work on captions for the Honor Society pictures. I think they've all been put together okay, but you also check to be sure all the pictures really are Honor Society, and that the names are correct. When you finish that you can move on to Spanish Club and do the same thing there."

"Got it." Madison sat down at the computer like she knew what she was doing. I figured she did. She and Sarah, Kitty's oldest, are good buddies, but while Sarah has been struggling to figure out who she is, or wants to be, Madison just seems to know. I envied the girl, being more like Sarah, myself—in terms of being confused by life. Sarah is nowhere near as bitchy as I am. Anyway, Madison was just what we needed: a quiet, hard-working kid.

A quiet, hard working kid with a chip on her shoulder, as it turned out.

We'd been working for some time when Madison swung around. "Mrs. P? I don't want this picture in here."

Kitty and I both came over to look, wondering what made her sound so angry.

It was a picture of the Honor Society students setting up for a party, with Letitia LeMoine front and center hanging a garland.

"What's wrong with it?" Kitty could probably guess as well as I could, but the question was automatic. We didn't want to make changes at this late date, not if we could help it.

"I don't want that woman in it." The girl's voice was calm, but there was no give to her. "She as good as accused my mom of stealing, which is total bull."

"We all know that, and no one is blaming your mom for anything."

"So what?" I'd never heard Madison sound so teenaged.

"So Mrs. LeMoine is dead. She did some annoying things, but she is dead, and she was part of the school this year. I don't think we can make her go away just like that."

"She didn't even belong at that party. Her kid sure as hell—uh, heck—wasn't in Honor Society."

Madison had a point. I started to say so, but she wasn't done.

"And even dead she's messing up our lives. Chief Karlson was out at our place asking all sorts of questions, like he thinks Mom killed her."

"I don't think he really thinks that," I tried to console her. "But he has to question everyone. He's quizzed Kitty and me enough, that's for sure." At least she didn't seem to know that I'd tried to question her mom, too, or she wouldn't be speaking to me.

"Mom's been upset for days, and she's worried that no one will believe her or trust her. And that scares her, because she and Dad are trying to refinance the house."

That explained a lot.

"No one believes she did anything wrong, Madison. I hope you can convince her of that." I didn't think Maddy would listen to me about it just now.

Madison relaxed a little. "Well, maybe. But I still want to find a different picture."

I looked at Kitty, who shrugged. "Go ahead." She showed Madison how to access the scrap heap—the file of pictures we hadn't used. "They aren't sorted. Happy hunting. You have ten minutes." Even that was stretching the time we had available.

I was having trouble keeping my mind on my job, thinking about the missing girl. Who were Chantal's friends, anyway? Who was the boy she was out with the night her mother was killed? Assuming, of course, that it was a boy. What else would it be, though? Unless she'd killed her own mother and Justin had seen her moving the body. Could Chantal even have lifted her mother in and out of a car and into the freezer? Letitia LeMoine was a pretty good-sized woman, while Chantal was more shapely than fit. No, she'd been up to something, and I wondered with whom. What boy would be in such danger—or such a danger to her—over being found out, that it would be worth lying to the police? Police who were just trying to find out who killed her mother. Of course, it was just possible that she and her boyfriend had removed an interfering parent, in which case it was no wonder Chantal wanted to keep him under wraps.

"Hey, girls," I blurted. "Who's Chantal's boy-friend? I assume she *has* a boyfriend." So much for discretion. I could tell by Kitty's look she thought I'd lost my mind. Maybe I had.

Madison, Melissa and Carina turned around to look at me.

"Oh, she has one, all right," Madison assured me. "She was bragging in the girls' bathroom just a couple of weeks ago, about how her boyfriend knew his way around better than most of the bumbling bumpkins here, or some such. So we concluded he's not an

Islander."

"But you didn't ask?"

"Hell, no—sorry, Ms. Mac. No, we didn't want to give her the satisfaction."

I looked at the other girls. They shrugged. "I guess Madison's right," Melissa said. "I've never seen her with anyone."

"Which is a bit odd, when you think about it," Carina suggested. "I mean, I really don't think Chantal is the modest type, you know?"

I knew. "Huh. So, someone from the Mainland like you say. Or," I had another thought, "do you suppose she didn't really have anyone and was putting on a show?"

"Well, anything's *possible*." I could tell Madison didn't believe it. How could a girl like Chantal be without male companionship for nearly a whole school year? She'd have to fight them off with a club.

Kat spoke. "Maybe she was dating someone older. Someone who could get in trouble for, what's that thing they call it when the girl isn't of age and the guy is?"

"Statutory rape?" I suggested. That was a new idea, though it shouldn't have been, given what I knew about the girl.

"Yeah. That."

"Isn't she seventeen? Or do you have to be eighteen?"

Melissa's question sparked a debate over whether Chantal was, in fact, seventeen, and if she was, how old you had to be to have sex with an adult. I listened without comment. Something was percolating in the back of my brain, but I couldn't force it out.

Just to help things along, I asked, "What about Tina Ainsley? Who's the boy she went off into the dark with at the Clambake?"

None of them knew that, either, though somehow

they'd all heard about the photo. Gotta love a small school. So why didn't any of these kids know the boys?

Kevin didn't know, either, so whoever he was, he wasn't boasting among the guys. Or, as the girls had suggested, he wasn't a student, at least not at our school.

"But, man, you know," Kevin said, "I really liked her. I was bummed when Tina turned me down for the Christmas dance, you know." He looked genuinely glum. "She told me she wasn't going, that she doesn't play with little boys." His indignation would have been funny if it were not so chilling. Just who was Tina shagging? Kat's suggestion was looking more likely by the minute.

The idea in the back of my mind had nearly taken form when Kitty recalled us all to the job at hand.

"Alright, crew, we've got less than two hours until I have to email this to the publisher. So let's get going!" We obediently turned our attention back to proofing. We even had Kevin, the football player, partner with Kat to figure out if we had photos of everyone, since he and Brian had finished checking the football players and cheerleaders. Kitty'd been about halfway through the list, but now she, Brian, and Justin were reading the instructions for submitting the whole thing to the publisher.

A few minutes after Kitty had chased us all back to our tasks, Madison looked up.

"Come take a look at this, Ms. Mac," she called. I crossed the room to study the picture she had up on her monitor.

"Do you think he's putting the moves on her?"

I bent closer to see what she was talking about. I didn't spot it at first. The picture, a crowd shot of an assembly of some sort, was busy and showed no one very well, which was no doubt why it had ended up in the discard file. I followed Madison's pointing finger to a pair of figures at the back of the crowd. The Vice Principal and. . . Chantal LeMoine? He had his hand on her shoulder in a way that could have meant nothing, or could have been a possessive gesture. I remembered again what Kat had said at Sunday's dinner.

"Is that Chantal?"

Madison nodded. "You bet. And Mr. Fingal hanging onto her like, like—I don't know, it just doesn't look right."

I looked at her. "Do you have reason to think he'd do that—put the moves, as you say, on one of the girls?" I wanted to know if Kat had been exaggerating.

Madison didn't hesitate. "For sure." In response to my sharp look, she added, "Oh, not me. But there's talk. . . a lot of the girls say he's, like, flirty. Mostly," she dropped her voice even more and turned pink, "with the ones who are, you know." She gestured, outlining a bosom much larger than her own, or mine. One like Chantal's. Or Tina's.

We looked at the photo again and our disgusted shudders hit simultaneously. I couldn't imagine anything nastier than Elvis Fingal flirting, let alone touching me, and I would have thought that the girls would all feel the same way. I squinted more closely at the picture.

"He might have been getting her attention, about to tell her to move or something," I suggested, trying to think it out.

"He might've been," Madison agreed. "Or he might have been up to something else. Look, Ms. Mac, you've been asking about Chantal's boyfriend?"

I kept my expression neutral. "Yeah?"

She looked pained. "So, I'm just thinking it might have something to do—you know. Like, maybe she

239

was, um, seeing Mr. Fingal?"

It wasn't the most articulate comment, but I got what the girl was driving at. If Elvis Fingal was having sex with a student, even one who was over legal age—and if Tina was legal, Chantal almost certainly was not—it would not go over well. Reason enough for her to keep it a secret. Or for him to put pressure on her to keep it a secret.

At this point I discovered that the other students had been listening in. Kat said, as though reading my mind, "What if he's the 'boyfriend' Tina complained Chantal stole from her?" The girls gagged dramatically, unable to imagine not one, but two girls actually wanting Mr. Fingal, but Kitty and I looked at each other. There are other reasons for sex besides physical attraction, and Chantal was well-trained by her mother's example to look for the route to power. I recalled Chantal's horror at the thought of returning to the Island, and her determination to protect her boyfriend. And now she was missing. By her choice? I didn't like where my thoughts were taking me.

While we had been talking, Brian had been fiddling with the manila envelope I had left by his computer, looking for more info on how to submit the Yearbook.

"Oh, gross!"

Brian held up a photo, printed on the same paper as the Yearbook info, which is why I hadn't noticed it. I couldn't see what it was, with everyone pushing in to look and jostling Brian.

"Give me that." Snatching the whole sheaf of papers from a Brian too surprised to resist, I saw it was a photo of the Spring Spirit Masquerade dance.

The girl was Chantal, though so heavily made up as to be nearly unrecognizable. She was dressed in a costume that did not meet the decency rules I recalled. Zorro stood with his arm around her—and one hand cupping a barely-covered breast. He wore a mask, of course.

"Who?" It's possible I squeaked the question.

Kitty knew. "Fingal."

A chorus of confirmation rose from the kids as I flipped through the rest of the papers. There were perhaps a dozen photos, all printed the same way—from a home printer on cheap copy paper. They were from various events through the winter, and in each shot Fingal had an arm around a girl. Tina and Chantal showed up most often. I wondered why the hell Ron hadn't looked at them. I mean, here was his answer about Chantal's lover, and a huge reason for her to disappear.

I had chilling thought. These photos might have been—*must* have been—responsible for Letitia LeMoine's death. Had she taken them, or had someone sent them to her? She must have confronted Fingal. Whoever took the pictures, she'd printed them out, and she had gone to Fingal with her accusations. Maybe she'd threatened him. The conclusion was obvious. But she hadn't taken the pictures with her when they met, and he'd only known they must be on the computers.

"I'd better call Ron," I told Kitty in a low voice

She nodded. "Outside." She raised an eyebrow at the kids, and said more loudly, "Okay, everyone, back to work. We've only got ninety minutes!"

I walked out toward the parking lot, pulling my cell phone from my purse. I pushed the power button and stared blankly as the phone stared back just as blankly. Thinking back, I remembered it had died two days before, and I'd never plugged it in.

I could have gone back and borrowed Kitty's phone. But the office was closer, and I figured I could ask for a moment's privacy. Ms. Peabody wouldn't object. Annette might be there, but I knew I'd have to tell her soon anyway. I'd just make damn sure Elvis Fingal wasn't in his office.

He wasn't, and neither was Annette. The secretary stepped out, and I looked up the number for the sheriff's office and dialed. Standing at the desk in the office, I kept an eye out for passing students while the phone on the other end rang three times before someone picked up.

"Pismawallops Police. Deputy Roller speaking."

Damn. I wasn't about to start explaining to Homer Roller, the human error.

"Can you put me through to Chief Karlson?"

"No ma'am. He's on a case."

Well, of course he was. And so was I, and I needed to talk to him right away. "Where's Tacy?" Maybe the dispatcher could help, though she was no bargain either. Look at the trouble she'd gotten me into yesterday.

"She's out today."

Double damn. "Well, then I need to talk to the Chief. He has a cell phone, doesn't he, Homer?" I remembered Ron had gone to the Mainland to try to find Chantal.

"Yes, ma'am, but I can't give that number out."

Either he hadn't recognized my voice, or Homer didn't realize that Ron might actually want to talk to me. In fact, Ron had given me his cell number. It was right there on the note pad next to my phone at home. Vowing I'd learn to program my phone—assuming I could remember to keep it charged—I tried the direct approach.

"Homer, this is JJ MacGregor. I have important information that I need to get to Chief Karlson right away. So give me the blasted number, curse you." Oops.

"Gosh, Ms. MacGregor, I can't do that. Really."

I ground my teeth. I wanted to cuss him out for an armpit-scratching idiot who might be costing a girl her life. Instead, I took a deep breath and spoke calmly, because I did not want to explain all this to him. "If you won't give me his cell number, would you please contact him immediately and ask him to call me?" I gave my number. "And may I stress again that this is extremely important, and related to his case?"

"Well then, ma'am, I suspect you ought to tell me about it."

"And I disagree. This goes to Ron and he decides who else needs to know." That was a mistake, using his first name. Homer was dumb, but not dumb enough to miss that, even if he didn't know exactly what to make of it. I could hear the leer in his voice when he spoke again.

"Well, now, *Ron* isn't available, so you'll just have to wait, won't you?"

"Will you just give him the dad-blasted message?" Then I schlepped to my car, about a quarter mile away at the end of the parking lot, passing Ms. Waverly on my way out of the office. Digging the charger out of the mess in the glove compartment, I headed back to the computer lab, fuming.

Kitty raised an eyebrow when I came in and plugged in my phone. "Did you reach him?"

I matched her low tone, so the kids wouldn't hear. "No. I got that idiot Homer, and he wouldn't put me through, wouldn't give me his number, anything. All I could do was leave a message and hope."

"You didn't tell him what we suspect?"

"No way. He's about as intelligent and discreet as the *Weekly World News*. I'm not telling that pea-brain anything."

"My thoughts exactly," Kitty admitted. "I hate to speak poorly of anyone," she began, and I interrupt-

Rebecca M. Douglass

ed.

"But it's hard to avoid it with Homer Roller. Know what, Kitty?" I added. "You need to get in touch with your Inner Bitch. All this sweetness and politeness might addle your brains."

Her laugh drew the attention of the kids at the other computers, so we got ourselves under control and got back to work. It seemed kind of callous to keep plugging away at the Yearbook, but I didn't know what else to do.

I couldn't sit still. After a few minutes, I whispered to Kitty, "I ought to at least find out if Fingal is at work today. Somewhere we can keep an eye on him while we wait for Ron. And I think we should show those pictures to Annette. She needs to know she's been nursing a viper to her bosom. As it were."

"You know," Kitty whispered back, "I never before realized what a truly disgusting expression that is. Yeah, you go find out, and let her know. There's no way she can ignore this."

Before I could more than nod, Annette Waverly herself came in. "Good work, everyone!" Her stenciled-on smile evaporated when she turned to me. "Chief Karlson is on the phone for you. You can take it in the Teachers' Room." She kept her voice low so only Kitty and I heard, I hoped.

I grabbed the envelope Kitty shoved toward me, muttered something I hoped the students would take as a good excuse for leaving again, and bolted for the door.

Annette turned, apparently to in a hurry to get back to her office, leaving me alone as I picked up the phone with a neutral greeting.

"What have you found, Ms. MacGregor?"

That was Ron, so businesslike I knew someone was listening. At least Homer had passed on my message.

244

I told Ron everything.

He gave a low whistle when I finished. "That's hard to believe." I chose to take that as astonishment, not skepticism.

"Right. Well, it looks like Fingal has been having fun with both Tina and Chantal, if that helps you any."

He didn't rise to my bait, but gave me instructions—and his cell number—as though I were an employee, which I had no doubt was what he wanted whoever he was with to think. "Right. Please make sure where he is, and tell Ms. Waverly all this. She needs to know at once so she can take appropriate steps to protect the students. Then get back to your work." I figured he meant the Yearbook, but wouldn't say that aloud. "And don't do anything else until I get there. There was a pause while he looked at his watch and did some mental calculations. "I'll catch the eleven-fifteen ferry, and be there just after noon."

I hung up, torn between amusement and irritation, and went in search of the principal.

She was in her office, looking oddly flushed. Maybe the work was getting to be too much for her.

I walked in without waiting for an invitation, and closed the door behind myself.

"Ms. Waverly, you need to see these pictures."

"What? Have some of the students taken indecent photos?" Her tone matched the curled lip, somewhere between a sneer and a snarl at the thought of students taking such liberties.

I stepped closer to the desk. "After a fashion. But it's who's in them that matters." I spread the half-dozen pictures on her desk. She bent over to look at them and recoiled as if she'd been struck.

"Good Lord!"

"Exactly." I risked another look at the photos, all

of which showed Fingal in various degrees of contact with Tina Ainsley, Chantal LeMoine, and a few other girls. "Clearly, we have a problem."

"That is Elvis, isn't it?" She sounded as though she had no hope it wasn't.

"Yes. He's at work today?"

"He was, until about a quarter hour ago. He complained of a severe headache and I sent him home. So that should be okay. The man," she added, forgetting his larger sins in the smaller, "is of little use in any case."

"Well, those girls seem to have found him of some use." She seemed to have trouble seeing the main issue, and I was having trouble bringing myself to point it out. She would be so upset.

My comment seemed to set off a struggle in her. Finally, sounding about half strangled, as though she didn't want let it out, she said, "Tina Ainsley left just before Elvis did. She was sick and needed to go home. You don't suppose—and he just left—could they be, you know?" She couldn't seem to finish a thought, but I didn't need for her to. I could finish it myself, and in fact took it a lot further, to see that Tina was in danger of losing more than her virtue, which I was pretty sure was already history. Ancient history.

At last Annette reached the inevitable decision. "Someone needs to go after her. And him."

"Chief Karlson's coming on the 11:15, and I need to get back to the Yearbook." Then, instead of leaving while the leaving was good, I had to say it. "You'll have to do something about it."

She gave me an appraising look. "I am going to go to Elvis's house and confront him. And if he is there with that little huss—that girl, I will put a stop to it. That is not acceptable at Orcaville High. We cannot have such a thing getting out."

It wasn't acceptable anywhere, but I didn't see any

need to belabor that point. It seemed like she had
missed the important part, the part about murder, and
I wasn't sure what to do. I was still debating that
when she spoke again.

"I'm just a little concerned that they may not have
gone to his house, but to hers. Not likely, but it does
worry me. Can't you go there, JJ? Just run over and
make sure? Perhaps this is all an unnecessary worry,
and we can keep it quiet."

"I don't think so." I could see I had to be explicit.
"He probably killed Letitia LeMoine to cover what he
was doing. We found these pictures at her house."
Annette reached for the pictures again, but I had
already tucked them back into the envelope, and
didn't hand it over. Ron wanted them, and I wanted
to give them to him.

She turned paler. "She kept—" she started to say,
then, "we still have to do something to protect Tina.
You *must* make sure she's not at her house."

"I can't!" My head whirled. I wanted nothing to
do with confronting a killer, but there was Tina, who
was only a stupid kid. And we had to get the Yearbook done in the next hour. And, if the vice principal
didn't know we were after him, I had no desire to
interrupt Elvis Fingal *in flagrante delicto* with a cheerleader. Not to mention the murder thing.

"Please! Just think what this could do to the school
if it got out," Annette begged.

In the end I caved in, as I knew I would. I couldn't
risk a child's life, even one who had such bad judgment.

"This is undoubtedly the most outrageous thing
I've ever done for this school," I told her. "You owe
me. Big time. And I'll just check her house and
phone to tell you if she's there or not. Then I come
back and finish the Yearbook, and we wait for Chief
Karlson."

She opened her mouth as though about to argue, then shut it with a snap. "Right. Let's go then."

Outside the office I turned down the hall toward the library. I thought I heard Annette coming out after me, headed for the door to the staff parking lot. I hurried around the corner before she could call out and ask why I wasn't rushing to my car. But I wasn't going anywhere without telling Kitty and making sure she could deal with the Yearbook. Besides, I'd

Errata:

p. 248. Final line missing; should read:

need my phone.

- 17 -

RIDING TO THE RESCUE: I MIGHT BE AN IDIOT

"You're doing what?" Kitty had obeyed my whispered demand that she come out into the hall to talk. Now I stood there with my cell phone and charger in one hand, my purse in the other, and tried to explain to Kitty why I had to leave her in the lurch

"I have to. What if he's planning to hold that girl hostage, or kill her before she can tell what they've been doing? We can't wait."

Kitty sighed. "Yes, I can see that. You're right. We're just about done here anyway, and I can handle the rest even if you don't get right back. But is it safe? What if he is the killer? And you know what Ron is going to say about this." I did.

"One thing bothers me," I admitted. "Annette still seems more concerned about the school's image than she is about what Fingal's done. It's like she can't even process the real danger. God knows what stupid thing she might do."

"I believe you." Kitty turned back toward the door. "And we *don't* want a lot of gossip, so let's start by keeping this from the kids. If we can," she added, remembering who'd found the pictures.

I wondered if it was a student who'd taken the pictures in the first place, and I thought about what might be the consequences, what had already been the consequences, and felt sick.

I left Kitty and trotted back down the hall toward the main entrance and the student parking lot, where I'd left my car. There was no sign of Annette Waverly. No doubt she was well on her way to Fingal's house, ready to read him the riot act. I stepped it up to a trot as I headed yet again for the distant corner where I had parked next a scruffy alder, which was now dripping large splats and wet leaves onto my windshield.

Once in the car I plugged in the cell phone and then backed out of my parking place. Then I concentrated on driving. Maybe I got a little anxious, too, thinking about what Fingal might do, because I accelerated until I felt an adrenaline rush. After all, here I was, riding to the rescue of a foolish teen-ager, saving her from whatever over-her-head mess she'd gotten into with a predatory man. Maybe I'd find Chantal, too. Ron would appreciate that.

I'd been ramping up my coffee consumption all week, and was starting to feel the effects. My hands were shaking, half from excitement, half from caffeine. I clutched the steering wheel tighter to steady them, and sped up some more.

I cruised up to the Ainsley's house, craning my neck to see if I could spot Fingal's car or any evidence that all was not well. I didn't see anything, but if he was there, most likely he'd have pulled around behind the house, rather than advertise his presence. I pulled up, and swore when I realized that I should have been a little less obvious myself. If he was in there, I'd just given myself away. I sat a moment, thinking. Then I put the car back in gear and drove the rough drive around to the back. There was no sign of Fingal's car there either, nor of any other vehicle. I relaxed some, but I had to be sure.

Climbing the back steps, I hammered on the kitchen door for a minute, and tried the knob.

The door wasn't locked. For just a moment I hesitated, uncertain about my next step. But I thought of Elvis Fingal and the girls and went in. Waiting for Ron would be safer, but where did that leave Tina? Though I was sure now there was no one in the house, I opened the door.

Inside, I paused. I couldn't hear any sounds, but what did that prove?

"Tina? Tina! Are you here?" No one answered my shout. There had been no sick girl, no headache for the Vice Principal, just a neatly planned rendezvous. I felt sick to my stomach as I headed back to my car.

I had to turn on the ignition to get enough power to my cell phone to make the call, but eventually I reached the principal.

"Annette? It's JJ. Tina's not at her house. I'm headed back to the school now." I thought I should be very firm, and very clear what I would and would not do. This was a job for the police.

She had other ideas. Before I could hang up, she said, "JJ! You must come at once!"

"Why?" I really didn't want to try to apprehend a killer.

"Because he just took Tina off in his car, and I don't know what to do." Her voice had risen to a near-wail, and my heart sank. If he'd seen Annette and guessed we were on to him, who knew what he might do. We couldn't afford to wait for Ron.

I sighed, trying to think. "Follow them. Try not to

let him see you. Call when you know where he's taken her."

"But what if he's going to do something awful?!"

He had already done something awful, both murder and statutory rape. It didn't seem the time to remind Annette, and it wouldn't do any good to put her in danger too.

"Where does he seem to be going?"

"I'm not—oh!"

"What?"

"I think he's going to the LeMoine's house. Oh, JJ, this can't be good!"

I had to agree. Stifling the part of myself that was screaming to back off and play it safe, I said, "I'm on my way. Call me if they end up going anywhere else."

She agreed to that and I hung up without waiting to see if she had more to say.

She didn't call back, and as I neared the LeMoine house, I paused in the road. I didn't want to just drive up and charge in. If Fingal knew we were on to him, he might panic and do something irreversible. I drove past the house, slowing only a little as I craned my neck to see if there was anything to see. No sign of Fingal's car; that would have been too easy. But a car I took to be Annette Waverly's was parked smack dab in front. I couldn't be sure, but it looked familiar, and who else would park there just then? I cursed her for being so obvious.

I saw no sign of Annette. Should I call Kitty and tell her where I was? What good would that do? She had to finish that Yearbook, and I didn't want her coming and risking herself, too. I tried again to reach Ron, hoping against hope he'd caught an earlier ferry and could come let me off the hook. His voice mail picked up on the first ring, and I glanced at my watch. He was probably on the boat now.

I shook myself. I was procrastinating, trying to tamp down my fears, or hoping that everything would be over before I got there. What a dreadful hope! The realization of what that would mean spurred me into action at last. I locked the car and trotted down the road toward the house, the cavalry charging to the rescue. *Or Custer riding to his last stand*, whispered a little voice in my head, a voice that stopped me in my tracks.

This was insane. One of two things was happening in there. Either Fingal and Tina were having an assignation, in which case he would be very upset to be interrupted—and he clearly wasn't quite sane, if he'd killed Letitia LeMoine. Or he had decided he needed to get rid of the girl, before she turned him in. He might even have both girls. And what was Annette doing? Did she even realize yet the danger she might be walking into? She was so concerned with the reputation of the school, she couldn't seem to grasp that lives were at risk. It was that which decided me to go in, rather than waiting for the police.

I compromised. Trotting back to the car and my not-so-portable cell phone, I dialed Kitty's number. Not waiting for her to find a private place, I blurted out what I was up to and what I was thinking.

"Maybe I'm crazy, but this feels bad. Really bad. But I can't wait, either. Annette's already gone in."

Kitty gasped. "You should wait for Ron. But—I don't know, JJ!" Her voice rose on the last words. "There's Tina, too. Just—oh, be careful! Someone will be there as soon as possible."

I hung up, feeling intensely grateful. Even if "someone" was only Kitty, I felt less alone. I could sneak in, and try to find out if Annette, or Tina, needed rescuing, but remain hidden until back-up arrived.

I reached for the door and my phone rang. I snatched it up. "Hello?"

"Hi, sweetheart, I finally caught you!"

I groaned, but silently. "Hi Mom. Look, this isn't a good time. I'm late for something. I'll call you back later, okay?"

"Well, of course, dear." I could hear her disappointment, but Mom knew I wouldn't say it if I didn't mean it. "I'll call tomorrow."

"Love you, Mom!" I hung up, and thought for a moment. It was going to be fun telling her about all this. If I survived. That turned my thoughts to self-defense. A discouraging rummage in my car turned up nothing more weapon-like than the paperback in my purse, so I started for the house again, uncomfortably conscious that I was unarmed.

There was no question of approaching the house without being seen. LeMoine hadn't done much to keep the blackberries pruned since she moved in, but the previous owners had, and there was still a wide stretch of open yard all around, and an impenetrable wall of stickers beyond. All I could do was march up to the door and walk in.

After a moment's reflection, I decided to march up to the back door rather than the front. It felt less blatant, and in any case, I wanted to be sure I was in the right place this time, though Annette Waverly's empty car left little room for doubt. I wished that she had more common sense.

As soon as I rounded the corner of the house I saw a car I was pretty sure was Fingal's. This was it. My heart pounding, I stepped up to the kitchen door.

I didn't knock. If what I believed was true, I needed any element of surprise there might be remaining to me. Even so, going in was probably the stupidest thing I had ever done. I knew that, but I opened the door anyway.

The big kitchen was empty, and when I paused to listen, I couldn't hear anything. That might have been because my heart was pounding so hard it drowned out all other sounds. Fingal and Waverly had to be in here somewhere, with or without Tina. Maybe Annette had been clever enough to sneak in and wait for me before confronting the man. I only wished she had waited outside. I never told her to go in!

I stepped through the doorway from the kitchen, expecting a dining room. Whatever the room had once been, it was a living room now, and a great deal dimmer than the kitchen. With all the blinds drawn I could hope I hadn't been observed approaching, but I also couldn't see a thing, since the gray overcast outside offered little light to push past the blinds.

I took a step into the room and waited for my eyes to adjust. When they did, there he was, sitting on the sofa as though he lived there. Elvis Fingal, all alone, just sitting there. For a moment I thought he was asleep—or dead—but he turned to look at me. I took another step into the room, without getting too close to him, though he looked harmless and relaxed. I was puzzled. He should have been in the middle of a giant brawl with Annette Waverly, or up in bed with Tina. I felt a cold chill. Could he have killed them both, and be sitting there so calmly?

"Okay, Fingal. Where's Tina? And Chantal?" No point in beating around the bush. I wanted him to know we knew about him. Then I added, "and where's Ms. Waverly?"

He ignored my questions. "What are you doing here? This isn't your house."

I almost laughed. "It's not yours, either, Fingal."

"I've been expecting you, you know," he added. "I knew Annette would tell you I'd left. I knew you'd follow to save poor little Tina."

I'd already figured he'd used Annette and her devotion to running a school with no hint of scandal, as well as my tendency to race in where angels fear to tread. It didn't matter. I would take Tina and leave. I could turn him in later. If Annette didn't show, I'd leave her, too. The girl mattered most.

"I'll just take Tina and be going. Chief Karlson will be along for you soon." I devoutly hoped that was true.

He laughed. He actually laughed his smarmy little chuckle, and I heard him say, "I don't think so," just before lights and pain exploded in my head, and I pitched on my face.

When the world wobbled back into something like focus I was sitting in a kitchen chair. An attempt to move revealed that I was, in fact, tied to the chair. My brain was still fuzzy, but I knew I was in trouble. It was only a few loops of twine around my arms, but it was strong twine and the chair a heavy, solid piece—blast LeMoine, why couldn't she have had some crap from the discount stores that maybe I could have broken? Not only that, but my head still spun, as though I might pass out again at any moment. Or puke. I tore my mind away from that thought.

I groaned, partly because my head hurt, but mostly because I'd been such an idiot. Any fan of murder mysteries or old movies could have told me what would happen, charging in there by myself that way. I'd known it myself, and vowed to stay hidden, and then I'd done this. What had gone wrong?

I struggled to remember. I'd gotten carried away, envisioning myself as a white knight riding to the rescue of the clueless women. Now I was the clueless woman in need of rescue, and no help to Annette or Tina at all. In front of me I could see the kitchen sink, and noticed dirty dishes piled high and spilling over. The week since Letitia LeMoine was killed and Chantal fled to the mainland had not improved their appearance. Or their smell. I fought another wave of nausea.

I turned my head a bit, carefully so that it wouldn't fall off, and located Elvis Fingal. He stood just inside the kitchen door, looking at me as though confused by my presence. Why should he be confused? Hadn't he knocked me on the head and tied me up? No, that wasn't right. I'd been looking at him when something hit me. What the hell was going on here?

"What the hell is going on here?" I repeated the question aloud.

Fingal glanced behind him, back through the doorway to the living area, as though hoping for an answer. I could believe that. I mean, Elvis Fingal was not a good advertisement for the overall IQ of Islanders, though he came in a cut above Homer Roller. In any case, as my head cleared, I was getting a pretty clear idea of what was going on, though I still didn't know who had hit me. What I really wanted to know was what was going to happen next. I figured Elvis didn't know, and might be open to suggestions.

"You'll have to let me go, you know."

Elvis looked behind him again before answering. I didn't much like what he said when he did answer.

"I, uh, you know, don't think we can ought to do that, you know."

Even aside from the sheer awful destruction of the English language, the implications of his statement made my head spin again.

"Why not?" I kept my voice reasonable, no small feat under the circumstances. "You can't keep me here forever, you know." Of course, that was the problem he was trying to solve, and some solutions might not be to my liking. I rushed on. "The police are on their way. They should be here any minute," I lied. Or maybe, just maybe, it wasn't a lie. I had no idea what time it was. Maybe Ron had caught an earlier boat. Maybe Kitty would think of something.

Maybe I'd been unconscious for an hour and the ferry had landed. "I think you'll be better off if you turn me loose before the police get here." If Kitty came, would she just end up in the same trouble I was in?

Elvis took a step or two into the room. I chose to interpret that as a good sign and continued.

"I just came to be sure Tina was okay. And Annette. I guess maybe you have that in hand, so if you'll untie me, I'll just be on my way." I knew things were way beyond that, but hoped I could convince this idiot he had made a mistake he could walk away from. "I won't hold it against you, Elvis—it wasn't you who hit me on the head."

I was making an impression on him. I knew I was. The glances over his shoulder had become more frequent and less assured. I took a breath and prepared to drive home my argument, hurrying before whoever hit me on the head came back. I opened my mouth, and nothing came out, because one thought drove out everything else. If Elvis hadn't hit me, and I remained confident he had been in front of me at the time, then either Tina had—or Annette had. I swore under my breath. Had one or the other of the idiots I'd been rushing to save been on the other side all along?

I figured Tina was the likely culprit. She probably didn't want to be saved from her lover, and presumably didn't realize he was a murderer.

I took a deep breath and started in on Elvis once more, more urgently for fear of who might interfere. "So come on, let me go, and everyone's happy."

This time, he shrugged what looked to me like a "why not?" shrug, and I began to congratulate myself on my powers of persuasion.

He had taken several more steps toward me when a voice spoke from the doorway.

"I think we'll just stay as we are for now."

I craned my neck regardless of pain in order to see the speaker. I knew that voice.

"*Annette*?" I was confused. Had she hit me? If so, my ideas of what I was doing here needed revising. I was not here to rescue Tina, who maybe wasn't even here. Nor, clearly, was I here to rescue Annette Waverly, whatever I might have thought when I came in. That joke was on me, and I didn't much care for the punch line. Knowledge of exactly why I was there hit me like a fist in the gut, and my vision blurred again for a moment as I fought another wave of nausea.

When I could see and think again, Annette had moved into the room. Now I could see her without craning my neck, which was a small improvement in an intolerable situation. My head ached so badly I feared I might vomit, and every movement cost me.

"Well, JJ. You should have minded your own business," she told me in her most stern Principal voice.

Something inside me burst loose. After all, she had lured me here. I hadn't even wanted to come. She'd practically forced me. "Let me go, you festering bit of anal retention!" As I added a few less pleasant epithets, I realized where I'd seen her car before, her car that had looked oddly familiar when I'd parked behind it. I'd seen it on my road at dusk. A lot of things clicked into place for me, now that it was too late.

Elvis looked shocked. "Tsk." Really. He actually "tsked" at me. "Such language. I do hope you aren't teaching your son to talk like that."

Both of us looked at him like he was a blithering idiot. Which he was.

"No, JJ, we will not let you go. I do not wish for anything scandalous to happen in my school. I think you will have a little accident." To my horror, she pulled a gun out of her purse. It was a tiny, pearl-handled cliché that probably couldn't shoot straight for more than a few yards. That didn't matter, because she was only a few feet away. The woman was insane. She had to be, to think that another murder would improve matters.

I wondered for a moment if it would help to go ahead and throw up. Or if I was going to have a choice in the matter, the way my stomach churned and my head spun. Fear that I would disgrace myself lent force to anger, and I fought to control my response. Screaming at them wouldn't help, and neither would puking on myself.

Or would it? Screaming, not puking. My conscious mind finally caught what my subconscious had been aware of for a while. A car had driven past. Now I heard the faint rattle of a doorknob. Could it be Ron, coming to my rescue? What was needed was a distraction, something to make sure no one else heard what I was hearing. A little warning about the gun would be in order, too. I chose hysterical shouts. By this time, hysteria came naturally, and a string of profanity with it. I had no idea I could cuss like that.

I made sure I was loud and clear about the word "gun," and the rest came without thought, given how frightened and angry I was. I had never before in my life used the f-word so many times in one sentence.

As I'd hoped, the total release of my bitchiest, most foul-mouthed self startled Waverly. She stared at me for a moment as though thinking she hadn't heard correctly. Then she spoke two words.

"Shut up."

I don't think I would have been so frightened if she had shouted, but her frozen voice sent chills down my spine. I had goaded her, and she had only grown colder. This was a woman who really could kill me. That seemed to be the meaning of her next words.

"You cannot judge me. You are a vile woman and you will not stop me." She emphasized the words "will not" just a bit, and raised her gun. Then she hesitated.

Out of the corner of my eye I saw Fingal staring at us with his mouth hanging open, and I knew something: Annette Waverly had killed Letitia LeMoine.

"You!" I gasped. "You killed her, not Fingal, the poor deluded idiot." I'd forgotten for the moment what he really was.

She interrupted me. "And you, Elvis. You betrayed me." The calm cracked, just a little, and I grasped at the break in her armor. Anything she did or said that didn't involve shooting me was good, even getting her angry at Fingal. Worst case, I'd settle for her shooting him instead of me.

"What did he do to you, Annette?" I had to keep her talking, but my effort was unneeded. She went on as though I wasn't there, her attention centered on the whimpering Fingal.

"Chasing around with those little girls. You lied to me! You, you," the crack grew wider, her voice shaking now. "You swore I was the only one you loved!"

I nearly dropped dead with the shock, saving her the trouble of shooting me. Annette Waverly and Elvis Fingal??

The good news was that the gun was no longer pointed at me. The bad news was, it was aimed at Fingal, who stared at it as though he couldn't understand what was happening.

"Don't shoot me," he pled. Maybe he understood enough. And he'd be no loss to the world if she did shoot him. But I'm an idiot, and couldn't just watch murder done, despite my preference for shooting him rather than me.

Her hand moved a little, and I said the first thing that came to mind, hoping to distract her. "Why, Annette? Why kill her? Murder is *not* good for schools."

261

She didn't even glance at me, just went on talking to Fingal. "I killed that woman to protect you. I didn't believe her! I had to shut her up before she ruined my school and got you in trouble, and you went like an idiot and put her in the *ice cream freezer*." Her voice rose on the last words. Funny, that seemed to bother her almost as much as it did me.

He flapped a hand as though he could brush away her bullets, and tried to defend himself. "I, I couldn't—I had to—" but she wasn't listening.

"And now it turns out she was telling the truth, and you really were assaulting little girls right and left. So now I'm going to kill you, you bastard, you unspeakable idiot!" Little flecks of spit flew from her contorted mouth as she tightened her grip on the gun. Fingal still seemed frozen in place. I wanted to scream at him to run for it, but didn't dare draw her attention back to myself. I wasn't dumb enough to think that she wouldn't shoot me when she'd finished him.

I was still staring when the gun went off with a surprisingly loud noise for such a little weapon. Fingal screamed, and maybe I did too. Waverly swiveled at once to cover me.

I closed my eyes as the gun swung toward me. I didn't have the nerve to look down the barrel and wait to be shot. I closed my eyes and tried to find the words that would stop a madwoman, and knew that they didn't exist. *I'm sorry, Brian.*

I counted three heartbeats—somehow, it seemed important to know, as though I would ever have the chance to put the information to use—before I heard something more.

Not a shot.

A shout.

"Drop it, Waverly!"

My eyes flew open, in time to see her fist convulse

on the trigger. The bullet came so close I could feel the heat. It must have frightened me out of my wits, because I would have sworn I heard two shots.

At the same instant, a tall, lean form launched itself from the doorway, knocked the madwoman sprawling, and grabbed the gun. Another blur came right behind, tripping over Fingal where he had fallen. I had to stop counting heartbeats, because I was pretty sure my heart had stopped beating. Terrified for all of us, I tried to launch myself into the melee, and landed on my face with the heavy chair atop me.

It didn't matter, because there was someone sitting on Annette Waverly, and she no longer had a gun.

I blinked. The star tackle was Brian. *Brian.* I started to shake, realizing what could have happened to him. He looked at me from his perch on the principal's back, opened his mouth, looked some more, and shut it. Smart boy.

I turned my head very slowly, because the nausea was back, and because it wasn't easy to turn, given I was face down on the floor with a chair on top of me. A pale Kitty knelt by Elvis Fingal, gamely applying pressure to a wound high on his right side. A part of my mind registered that he must be alive. I gave a sort of a groan, and Kitty turned to me.

"You okay, JJ?"

"Urgh." I cleared my throat and tried again. "Think so."

Kitty looked from me to Fingal's wound, then at Brian sitting on a stunned but not subdued Annette Waverly. She wiped her right hand on Elvis's shirt and rummaged in her pocket, pulling out a tiny Swiss Army knife. She kept her left hand pressed tight against the oozing wound, and after a moment I understood that I had to help.

I crawled closer, dragging my chair like a hermit crab in its shell, struggling to maneuver myself into position to open the knife blade. I couldn't do it. I didn't seem to have that much coordination. My fingers were going numb. Finally Kitty pushed the knife into my hand, and I managed to hold it while she opened the blade. Then she took it back and cut my right hand free. Handing me the knife again, she returned to her first aid efforts. I could finish cutting myself loose, if I didn't shake so much I bled to death instead. No one said anything through the whole process. We were all in a sort of shock.

Untangled from the chair at last, I struggled to my feet, still shaking, and looked around the kitchen. After a moment's thought, I used the knife to cut the drawstrings from the window blinds. Using the nylon strands, I helped Brian tie Annette Waverly's hands behind her back before he pulled her to her feet and dumping her on my recently-vacated chair. She recovered during the process, enough to speak. We ignored her curses and the lump forming where she'd struck her head on the floor under the force of Brian's tackle. It was slightly larger than the one on my forehead, from where I'd fallen when I was hit, and much smaller than the one on the back of my head where she hit me. I told her to shut up.

She didn't like it. The language that poured from her raised my eyebrows. Hadn't she just reprimanded me for a few conventional cusswords?

Brian, to my delight, contrived to look bored. "Really, Ms. Waverly. That sort of thing just indicates a paucity of vocabulary, you know."

He winked at me. "Our school principal used to tell kids that when she heard them cussing." He then proceeded to stuff a dishtowel in her mouth.

If my laughter was a little hysterical, neither he nor Kitty was tactless enough to notice. Anyway, Kitty had more important worries.

"JJ? We'd better get an ambulance for this one."

"Maybe we should let him die. Then we'd have her on murder for sure," I suggested, and was closer to meaning it than I liked to admit. She might be a killer, but Elvis Fingal was a pedophile, and her accomplice, and letting him die didn't seem so unreasonable. That would clear up the problem without dragging the girls into it. I fought off the temptation, and was looking for Kitty's cell phone when a voice spoke in the doorway.

"Well, now. Looks like you have everything under control, and you didn't even wait for me."

Ron. I melted with relief at the sight of him. A moment later, I boiled over with the rage that comes after fear.

"Where the hell were you when we needed you? Because you weren't here Brian had to take on that madwoman with her gun. My son," I added, in case Ron had somehow forgotten who Brian was.

He ignored me, working quickly to improvise a bandage that would provide pressure on Fingal's wound and free Kitty, who stepped to the sink to wash up.

"'S'okay, Mom," Brian muttered. "We had a gun too."

"You *what*?!" I have never allowed guns in my house, and he knows it. By this time I was pretty much in hysterics, but Kitty did her best anyway. She cut me off before I could get any farther than, "I ought to kill you."

"It was the starter's gun from the track team, and I used it, not Brian." Kitty no doubt meant for her tone to be soothing, but her own excitement sabotaged the effort. "Brian just thought of it."

"I'll bet he did," I began. Kitty stuck a hand over my mouth before I could say more. Later I would no doubt thank her. At the moment, I had to restrain the urge to bite.

"The EMTs will be here in a minute," Ron reported, having finished his first aid and radioed for help. I ignored him.

"C'mon, Mom," Brian tried his hand at soothing me. "It worked, didn't it? I remembered Mr. Ammon saying even the blanks spat out a wad that could hurt at close range. So we snuck up real close and—" He faltered and turned pale. When he snuck up close, he'd been just in time to see his principal about to shoot his mother. No wonder the poor boy was pale, and no wonder he'd attacked without hesitation. There was only one thing to say, and I said it.

"Thank you, Brian." Then I burst into tears.

They were all over me at once, Kitty hugging my shoulders while Brian patted me as one would a frightened puppy. Ron, on the other hand, began an examination that almost, but not quite, put an end to my hysterics.

I was just becoming aware of pain—more pain, besides the pain in my head—when Ron, touching my arm, exclaimed, "Good God! She's been shot!" and I gave a sort of a sigh and passed out. Again.

- 18 -

ALL OVER BUT THE SHOUTING?

I wasn't out for even a minute. Kitty had time to get a damp cloth to mop my brow, but Ron and Brian were still hovering helplessly when my eyes opened again. They'd lifted me up onto a chair, which might not have been the best plan. I raised my head, fought to regain equilibrium, and lost. I threw up. On Ron's shoes.

The rest of our business took forever—bandaging my arm where Annette's bullet had creased me, telling my story, and trying to get some sense out of our captive. The only thing I didn't mention was that I'd been hit on the head, because they'd scream "concussion" and haul me off to the hospital, and I didn't want to go. I sort of let them think she'd gotten the drop on me with her little pistol. They thought the bruise on my face was from diving over with my chair.

The ambulance came and took Elvis away to the hospital on the mainland. "He'll live," was the laconic evaluation by the EMT. I still wasn't sure that was a good thing.

Waverly had clammed up. She had even stopped complaining about her bruises, since my guardian angels had pointed out she had done much more damage to me than they had to her. Kitty hadn't even shot her, as it turned out. The claims of potential injury from the starter's pistol were much over-rated.

None of that mattered. Ron had more than enough for an arrest, for assault and attempted murder on both Fingal and me. It would take more work to get her on killing Letitia LeMoine, but I'd heard her confess it, and no doubt her lover would rat her out, once he came to and discovered the trouble he was in.

Ron finally let Brian and Kitty take me home, after one last check to make sure I really was okay. I had to slap his hand away a couple of times when the check got too thorough.

"Though I think," he said for about the tenth time, "that you ought to at least swing by the health clinic."

"No." I was firm. My tetanus shot was up to date, and the nurses couldn't have bandaged the wound any better than Brian had, proudly putting to use what he'd learned in his health-class first-aid unit. In any case, the graze was scarcely deeper than the scratches the blackberries had inflicted on me a few days earlier. I told myself I'd go if I got any blurred vision or other disquieting symptoms, and continued to keep quiet about the concussion.

Once in the car with Brian and Kitty, I finally could ask what I most wanted to know.

"How on earth did you two end up there just in the nick of time? How did you know to come armed, for that matter?"

They exchanged glances, something I couldn't quite read.

"Well, there was your phone call, for starters," Kitty said. "That made me pretty uneasy, especially since I thought Ron was still in the ferry line."

I nodded, and Brian took up the narrative. "I heard her say something about Tina, and it made me curious, so I asked. Well, and I could hear a lot of what you said. You know how cell phones are. Good thing, though," he added. "She said you and Ms. Waverly had gone off because Mr. Fingal had taken Tina away and you were pretty sure he was the killer. But Tina was in class when I left, and Mr. Fingal was in the lunchroom at break. Tina's in my math class," he explained.

I raised both eyebrows. "What's a Senior doing in Sophomore math?" I started to ask, and dropped it. Tina was long on looks, not brains.

"When he told me that, I just about died." Kitty took up the narrative. "We knew we had to come after you, though we still weren't sure if it was Annette or Elvis, or both, trying to trap you. But we knew it was a set-up, and someone had lied, and you didn't know it. And you didn't answer your phone."

"It was dead," I admitted. "I had to leave it plugged into the car." I had to ask. "Just how did you get that gun?"

Brian and Kitty exchanged guilty looks. "Well," Brian tried, "we didn't like to charge in there unarmed."

I couldn't argue with that logic, given how my attack had worked out. Though a weapon would have changed little in my case.

"I thought of baseball bats," Kitty said, "and that made Brian think of the starter's gun. So we just ran off to the gym, and I'm afraid I broke a lock getting at it. They do keep stuff like that locked up, you know."

"Glad to hear it," I said.

"Well, but I was getting desperate, so I went ahead and broke in. Ron can write me up for it later."

It seemed unlikely he'd worry too much about it.

"When we came out of the gym," Kitty continued, "we just drove like crazy to the house. But when we got there we weren't sure what to do. We didn't want to just drive right up and park by the door, you know."

"Same as me," I confirmed. "I parked down the road and walked back."

"I know. We saw your car. In fact, we parked right by it," Kitty said. "And we saw her car in front of the house, which seemed strange." Waverly hadn't tried to hide. I had assumed she hadn't thought of it, but Kitty and Brian were more suspicious.

Brian took up the story again. "We figured we'd better sneak up, since we didn't know what might be happening." He thought again about what had been happening. I could tell, because he got very pale and stopped talking. Kitty had to finish for him.

"The front door wasn't locked, and we couldn't see anything through the windows, so we snuck in, and we heard you yelling."

"I didn't even know you could use that word as an adverb," Brian said.

Kitty tried to scowl at us both, but we were giggling. "I don't think you should use that sort of language around the kids."

"Did the job, didn't it?"

We all laughed, then Kitty said with no trace of humor, "If your intention was to warn us of the gun, it sure did."

"It was. I heard you, and I didn't want anyone coming in not knowing she had a gun. And I wanted to get her to talk, so Ron—I thought it was him— would know who was there and which side she was on." Besides, if she was talking she wasn't shooting. I decided not to say that aloud.

"Well, I wasn't all that surprised," Kitty said. "I mean, maybe Elvis had tricked her, but it just seemed too neat. And maybe," she for once broke her rule about not running down Islanders, "maybe it was a bit too clever for him to have figured out on his own."

"So Ms. Waverly, the total stickler for everything being done according to THE RULES, killed Ms. LeMoine?" Brian wanted to know. I could hear the capitals in his voice, and knew what he meant. "And why'd she try to kill Mr. Fingal? Weren't they in it together?"

"I think it was that obsession with rules that got her in trouble," I said. "I think she was so determined there would be no scandal about Fingal and the girls that she lost all perspective. Ms. Waverly must have killed Letitia when she accused Fingal of—" I broke off with a glance at Brian. "Waverly needed to shut her up. Then she decided she'd have to kill Fingal. And m-me." I stuttered a bit, remembering how close she'd come to doing it.

"To keep him quiet," Kitty guessed. She didn't mention me, either out of consideration for my feelings or Brian's.

"Well, that and because she was one angry lover."

"What?!"

I'd thought I would enjoy the revelation, but I didn't. "They were lovers. She was royally peeved to find out Letitia wasn't lying or mistaken. Her man really was screwing cheerleaders on the side." Saying it made me feel sick again.

Kitty stopped the car in the middle of the road so she could turn and stare at me. "Annette Waverly was Elvis Fingal's lover?"

"Gross," was Brian's addition.

"Yes, and yes," I agreed. "A jealous and deadly lover, as it turned out. But she didn't believe it— about the girls, I mean—until I showed her the pictures." I was starting to understand more. "That's when she set this up." I stopped. If I hadn't shown her the proof. . . what? Would she even have been caught?

"The pictures, right," Kitty said. "Well, you know

the rest. We charged in and there you were."

I started to shake. I knew where I'd have been if they'd arrived even a few seconds later. Brian wrapped an arm around me and held tight as Kitty made the turn into my driveway.

"It's okay, Mom. It's all over."

Of course, it wasn't all over. Once we were inside and I was drinking the very sweet tea Kitty insisted on making for me, we had to talk it to death. We were in the middle of speculation on how Ron had gotten there so soon when it hit me.

"Oh my God!" I sat up suddenly, slopping tea on-to my shirtfront, and looked at the clock. It was after two. "The Yearbook! Kitty, we've missed the dead-line!"

She smiled. "No, we haven't. At least," she lost the smile and started rummaging for her cell phone, "I don't think so."

While I puzzled over what the heck she meant, Kitty checked her messages and texts.

"We made it! I told Justin to have Mr. Ammon ap-prove the final draft—we had to have someone's signature—and he texted to say he sent it off at 11:55."

Five whole minutes to spare. Not bad. I looked at Brian.

He shrugged. "We put Justin and Sarah in charge, told them to finish up the little stuff, and to send it in if we weren't back."

"I was going to have Justin send it anyway," Kitty said. "I'm no good at that stuff."

I took another sip of my tea. "Kitty, I hate sweet tea. But," I added in a hurry, seeing her face, "I guess it's good for me, right? Under the circumstances? Thanks for making it." I had another thought. "Who's running the school?"

"Mrs. Peabody?" Brian guessed. "As usual." We

all laughed a bit longer and harder than this deserved, letting some of our relief out the easy way. We were still chortling when the phone rang. I started to get up, but Kitty waved me back and answered it.

"MacGregor residence," she said in a crisp, businesslike tone. I expected her to hand the phone over to me. To be honest, I thought it would be Ron, calling to make sure we were all okay, or to chew us all out for putting ourselves in danger. Instead, Kitty stiffened. "Mr. Davis, this is not a—" A burst of noise could be heard interrupting her, and she tried without success to complete her sentence.

Before I could move to take the phone and try to deal with my not-soon-enough-to-be ex, Brian stood up and reached for the receiver. "Give it to me." Without waiting to listen to his father, he said, "Dad, this is not a good time. You can call our lawyer if you need something. Otherwise, you can leave us alone, just the way we asked. Goodbye." His tone remained respectful throughout, but he didn't pause for any response, just said his piece in his steady voice, which had changed in the last few months to a mostly consistent baritone, and hung up. Kitty and I looked at him in admiration, and he blushed as he sat down.

"I figured he might get the message a little better if it came from me," he explained. With a glance at the clock, he added, "Justin's going to be wetting his pants, wondering what the heck this was all about. I need my homework, too, so can I have him come over, Mom? School just let out, so there's no point in me going back to class."

Just like that, he returned things to normal. I couldn't tell if he did it deliberately, or if he was just being a teenager, with a teen's priorities, but inside of two minutes, he had put my almost-ex-husband in his place and declared an end to weirdness. I got up and gave him a big hug.

"Today, Brian my dear, you have my permission to do damn near anything you please. Tell Justin I'll feed you guys the best dinner in my freezer."

He laughed, brushed me off the way teen boys do when their moms hug them in front of witnesses, and headed for the door. He stopped once and turned, opened his mouth as if about to say something, then ran upstairs without saying it.

Kitty and I exchanged glances, shrugs, and smiles. Kids.

"I'd better move," Kitty said. "Sarah was supposed to collect Mikey from the grade school and be in charge until I get home, but I took the car, so I'd better go pick them up. Anyway, they won't do their homework without me to nag them."

"It's Friday, Kitty. No one's doing homework. That was just Brian's excuse to get Justin over here so they can talk it all over." I wondered if Sarah knew what was going on. Kitty's next words suggested she did not, but of course, that wouldn't last long.

"Well, I'd still better pick them up, and get home before the kids—or Mike—get wind of what went on. I don't want them thinking I've been killed or something. In fact," she added dubiously, "I think I'd better come up with a good explanation for charging off like that."

"You were honor bound to rescue your idiot friend," I told her. I touched her arm, and now I wasn't joking. "Look, I know what I did was stupid. I just couldn't make it real, I guess, so I went ahead without thinking."

She shook her head. "And thanks to the sense of responsibility you pretend not to have, you were beautifully manipulated by Annette. She knew you'd have to do something if you thought she and Tina were in danger. That's who you are. That woman is nuts," she added, "but she's not stupid."

Remembering the face behind the little gun, I had to agree. In fact, it gave me the shakes all over again, so that Kitty didn't want to leave. I finally got her out the door by promising to call if I needed help. I was hoping for a different kind of help, and let the divorce judges think what they would.

Ron didn't call. He simply showed up—driving my car, which had been left at the LeMoine house when Kitty and Brian drove me home—right ahead of Justin. Brian must have been watching out the window, and he assessed the situation in a hurry. By the time Ron was at the door, Brian was thundering down the stairs. He greeted the Chief politely, and gave my shoulders a careful squeeze.

"Justin and I are going to the school, okay? I left my backpack and everything there." Justin wasn't supposed to drive other kids around yet, his license being far too new, but Ron and I both ignored this. They left with our blessings, Brian no doubt telling Justin all about it, and I was alone in the house with Ron Karlson.

For a minute we looked at each other without speaking. In point of fact, after my first glad rejoicing that Ron had come to offer comfort, I remembered that he was just as likely to skin me alive—metaphorically speaking, of course—for going off alone on my investigations and nearly getting myself killed. Worse, he'd be right, though I still wasn't sure what I should have done. In any case, I didn't want him to chew me out right now. He could do that later, if he felt he had to. I could feel tears forming just from thinking about it.

If that moment was a test, Ron passed it with flying colors, because the first words out of his mouth were, "Thank God you're okay!" He followed them up with another inspection to make sure.

275

"No more dizziness?" He couldn't help looking at his shoes, which appeared damp, but clean enough.

I blushed, then found myself laughing and crying and squirming a bit, as his inspection proved very thorough indeed. Some small part of my brain was trying to put the brakes on, and that part won, after a fashion: my hysterics became sufficiently pronounced that Ron was forced to haul me into the kitchen and start in on the tea again. While I drank, I finally managed to say something coherent.

"Um, I'm sorry about your shoes."

"Least of my worries. Sorry I was late for the show."

"You got there. The ferry must have been on time for once."

"The Harbor Patrol brought me. Right after you hung up," he explained, "I started thinking, and I didn't like what I came up with. I couldn't ring you back," he added, reminding me of my dead phone, "so I decided to come, as fast as possible. You see, I found out who Chantal's father is."

I set my cup down hard, slopping tea on myself for the second time in an hour. "Who? How does that relate, anyway?"

"It relates because her father is Elvis Fingal."

I gave him my sternest mom-look. We sat on opposite ends of the U-shaped window seat, the table between us. "You are absolutely making that up."

"Scout's honor." He held his hand up in the three-fingered boyscout salute. "His very first year teaching," he explained cryptically. "Her aunt knew, but she wouldn't say anything until a lucky guess put me onto it."

I felt a wave of nausea as the implications washed over me, and sternly fought it back. I'd had enough of that. "So Chantal—so he—with his own daughter!"

Ron looked a bit sick, too. "Miss Partridge says he

never knew. When Lucy found she was pregnant, she ran off to this same aunt, her mother's sister. She—Lucy, that is—refused to tell on him. Said she loved him, didn't want to get him in trouble, all that. I don't think Miss Partridge is quite as bright as she might be, because she let the girl get away with it. Just like she was going to let Chantal go into hiding instead of telling me what she knew."

"So Letitia—Lucy—once loved Fingal. But when she found out what he was doing to her daughter—to *his* daughter—" I began, then stopped, feeling sick.

"Yeah. It was too much even for her. Put that together with what Ms. Waverly told you back there, and you get the picture, however ugly." He grimaced.

"Good God," I said, staggered by the realization. "I wonder. . . he left after just a year or two here, you know, and only came back last year. Maybe he had good reason to leave his last job."

"I don't know, but I'll be in touch with the schools where he worked." There was no sign now of Ron the friendly guy. He was all cop, and a cop who had just seen a little too much of the world. We both knew there must have been other girls over the years. There always were, with men like that. "So," he said, "like you, I thought Fingal had set up both you and Ms. Waverly."

He didn't say anything more about my adventure. I took it as forgiveness.

"Has either of them talked?"

"Fingal's still unconscious."

"He hid the body," I remembered.

"Waverly's not talking, so we may have to wait for him to come around so we can sort it all out. But Tina Ainsley has made a statement, with a little encouragement. She'd been pretty peeved about Fingal taking up with Chantal over the winter, starting right

277

Rebecca M. Douglass

from the beginning of the year, when he made her Captain of the Cheerleaders." He shook his head. "I guess the man had been carrying on with Tina for the better part of a year, and along comes Chantal and he falls for her in an instant, starts in to give her anything she wants, so he can be the big powerful sugar-daddy."

"And it worked. And her mother played right into his hands, because she was pushing for Chantal all the time, too."

He nodded. "Just a mom who wanted her girl to have all the advantages she didn't. She was probably fool enough to think that what she had with Elvis Fingal was unique. Maybe she even thought he helped Chantal because he'd realized she was his kid. When LeMoine found out the truth she must've been as angry at herself as at him."

We sank into silence, each lost in our own thoughts, until I glanced up and caught Ron looking at me in a way I didn't think had anything to do with solving murders. I opened my mouth to say something—anything that might distract him—but he held up a hand.

"Don't. I'm just enjoying seeing you alive and well."

I nodded. That seemed safe and reasonable. But he wasn't done.

"I was married once, JJ. Did you know that?"

I nodded again. I knew it, though Ron had been single as long as I'd been on the Island. I'd never even heard of him paying attention to anyone in particular.

"We had almost ten years, wonderful years. Then she was gone, just like that. She went out fishing in our little boat, and the weather turned nasty. They think she ran out of gas. The Coast Guard found the boat, but never her. I thought I would never look at a woman again." He forced a laugh. "And when I did, she turned out to be married. Remember what I told you, JJ? About assuming you and Allen had gotten a divorce long ago?"

I remembered.

"That was a lie. I looked you up. I don't suppose you remember how we cleared up the traffic jam at Homecoming last year?"

Didn't I? I didn't know where this was going, but I most certainly remembered that night. It was the first time I'd been aware of Ron Karlson as a human being, not just a uniform.

"It wasn't that long ago."

"I went home afterwards and checked you out." He had the grace to blush. "It was unethical of me, but I wanted to know everything about you. And if you were still married to the man who brought you here and left you, since he wasn't around much."

"And you found I was," I said. Even to me I sounded too cool, too calm.

He glanced up at me, hesitated, and went on. "Yeah. I didn't know what to think, after that, since he never seemed to be here. But every time I turned around, there you were." He slid off his seat and came to crouch beside me. "And then you told me you were finally getting that divorce and I could hardly stand it. I even managed to make myself think you were sending out signals."

I wasn't sure what to say to that. I had been, but did I want to admit it? He didn't give me a chance to answer. His right hand was on my leg, the left holding onto the back of the seat just behind my head.

"I knew I was falling for you, but I didn't know just how badly until I heard those gunshots this afternoon. I was sure I'd come too late—and I'd lost you the worst way." He took a deep, ragged breath. "But I haven't lost you, and I don't intend to." His hand began to wander up my sweatshirt, and I found it hard to breathe. All my resolutions and promises to Anne Kasper were swept away by sheer, physical need.

I'd like to claim that what stopped me was a sense of justice, because Ron was on his knees pouring out his heart to me, declaring something that sounded an awful lot like love, and all I could think about was sex. But it wasn't my finer feelings that stopped me. It was the telephone.

At the first ring, Ron jumped back, and I stood up, automatically moving to answer the call.

"Hello?"

It was Anne Kasper, asking me to come by in the morning to go over some issues about the divorce. There couldn't have been a more effective reality check short of a cold shower. She must have noticed something funny about my voice, because she asked about three times if I was okay. By the time I convinced her I was fine (I was, depending on what you meant by "okay"), my mind was at least partly back in control, and I didn't go back to where Ron stood waiting. The reminder about the divorce took the edge off, you might say.

I had no idea how long we might have stood there, separated by six feet of faded linoleum and my unresolved life, if Ron's phone hadn't rung in its turn.

He muttered something that sounded an awful lot like a cuss word, and fished the device from his pocket. I stepped into the living room to give him some privacy, aware that it was business, and not wanting him to give himself away. A minute later he followed me, and if he was still thinking about seduction, or even love, he did a great job of covering it up. The cop was back on duty.

"That was the Mainland calling. They've found Chantal, and Fingal's regained consciousness.

They've generously offered to allow me to be present when they question them. Very kind, as it's my case," he added with just a touch of sarcasm. He started for the door, then turned back after a couple of steps. I waited for him to say something about us, something I wouldn't know how to answer. Instead, he asked, "Could you drive me back to my car? I left it at the LeMoine house."

I nodded, glancing at my watch, and heard myself saying, "You just missed the 3:45 ferry, and there's not another until five o'clock. So what's the rush?" Given I'd just resolved—for about the tenth time—to keep my distance, I couldn't believe I was saying this.

"I'll take the launch." The Pismawallops Police had a launch big enough to get him to the mainland safely, if not comfortably. "I left my prowl car on the other side, anyway." He had another thought. "Are you okay to drive? Your arm doesn't hurt too bad?"

I hadn't felt dizzy for at least an hour, and my arm was fine. I could drive that far. I took a deep breath and pasted on a confident smile, shoving all thoughts of sex or romance back into the dark hole from which they'd escaped.

"Let's go, then."

We completed the five-minute drive without talking, and I was feeling more in control of myself every minute. I could handle this stuff, keep us both under control until I knew what I was doing—and until the divorce was final.

I pulled up next to Ron's rusty green Bronco, which still blocked the principal's car. She wouldn't be needing it anytime soon. He hesitated before getting out.

"Are you going to be okay? Get those boys to come back home, okay? Damn, I don't want to leave you alone right now!"

"I'll be fine. Get going, and give me a call when

you know something."

He ran a hand through his hair, the dark—and the not-so-dark in places—curls springing back into place in its wake. Then he grinned a feral grin and kissed me. It wasn't any quick peck, either, but a serious promise. He was gone before my vision cleared.

-19 -

NOW FOR THE HARD PART

We didn't hear from Ron until late the next morning. But when we did, it was worth the wait. Kitty had come over for morning coffee, and to check that I was really okay. She made such a fuss I almost sent her away, but thought better of it. It made her feel better, and she deserved whatever she wanted, for saving my life. Besides, she'd brought muffins and espresso brownies from the Have-A-Bite. We were still licking up the last pastry crumbs when the cruiser pulled into the drive. Brian must have seen it, too, because he thundered down the stairs in time to join us at the kitchen table. The sun was even making an effort to shine, turning my kitchen nook into the cozy spot it was meant to be.

"So. Tell all," I commanded, pouring Ron a cup of coffee. He looked like he'd been up all night.

"Well, first off, Annette Waverly denies the whole thing, and that may make prosecution difficult, since it will end up being her word against Fingal's. I think she's crazy as a whole flock of loons, but she hides it well. I've had to piece together what happened from Chantal, and Fingal, who's going to be fine."

"I'm so happy to hear that." My dry response startled a laugh from Kitty.

Ron spun us a tale it must have taken a lot of patience to worm out of Chantal. I couldn't see that girl talking comfortably to him about what had gone on, though I assumed she did want her mother's killer punished. She'd hidden to protect Elvis Fingal when Ron started asking awkward questions, but had eventually decided, in the first glimmer of intelligence I'd seen from her, that he didn't deserve protection. She'd been scared and confused and it was hard for her to see what she should do.

Letitia LeMoine had gone to the school on Thursday night to pick up Chantal from cheerleading practice, and had apparently gone to the office to confront Fingal. Chantal had seen her arrive, since she'd been very late in any case. Then instead of coming to the gym where the girl was waiting, LeMoine had gone inside, leaving Chantal to wait some more.

"Chantal just shrugged when I asked why her mom was so late. I got the impression the girl considered herself lucky to get picked up at all," Ron said. "Anyway, after she'd waited a while, she went to the office to see if her mother was still in there and try to hurry her up."

"And heard her arguing with Elvis and Annette?" Kitty asked.

"No, she says she looked in the window in time to hear Waverly order Fingal to get rid of the body and clean up the mess. Chantal says she was as cool and calm as if she was telling him to fill in the attendance reports or something. Then she—Waverly—went back into her office and closed the door."

Brian looked sick. "So Chantal just left? Didn't call the police, didn't even try to save her?" He sounded appalled, as though he knew he would rescue his mother. As he in fact had done.

"She says she sort of freaked out, and all she could think of was to get out of there. She had her own keys to the car, so she just took off and drove home. My guess is she had some idea what might have started the fight," Ron said drily.

Kitty shuddered. "It must have been awful for her, coming to school the next day and pretending everything was okay."

"She didn't know what to do. And she was terrified that if she did anything odd, Waverly and Fingal would figure out she'd seen them, and kill her too, which shows she's not totally stupid. She thought she'd just carry on for a while like nothing had happened. I don't think she realized at first that taking her mother's car would give away that she had been at school when her mother was killed, much less that if she'd known nothing, she might be expected to report her mother missing. But when Annette offered her a place to stay, she got scared. It made sense, for her to go to the only relative she knew, and going off-Island made her feel safer."

"So I assume she had no idea about her father?" I certainly hoped it was true.

"Nope. In fact, she got sick when I told her. Which," Ron added with a grimace that suggested maybe he'd had a little too much of people barfing on his shoes, "seemed like a healthy response."

"No shit!" Brian still couldn't get over it.

"Watch your language," I said automatically, but I was thinking about something else. "Does Fingal know? That Chantal is his daughter?"

"He does now. They finally let me at him early this morning and I sprung it on him. I think that's why he's talking. I think he was shocked to find he'd been—well, with his own daughter."

"Didn't he recognize Lucy?" I found it easier to use the name I'd never known her by. Lucy Lemmon was a hypothetical person, unlike Letitia LeMoine, whom I'd so disliked and now had to pity.

"Again, he says not. But I'm not so sure I believe

285

that. I guess he really never did know he'd gotten Lucy pregnant, and even if he ever did the math to see Chantal was the right age, he probably figured he was just one of many. Maybe he was, or maybe *she* was one of many and he didn't even remember."

I shuddered at the image of Elvis Fingal as Don Juan. He must've had something, but I sure as mosquitoes in June couldn't see it. "And he was Annette Waverly's lover too."

"Right. That's what kept her from killing him right off the bat. She loved him, or at least he says so, and he says she didn't believe Ms. LeMoine. Only later—when she saw the photos—she changed her mind." Ron stopped. We'd already been there. If Elvis Fingal had died, I'd have felt like an accessory to the murder. Not a happy thought, however disgusting an alleged human being he was. And yet, if I hadn't shown her, and she hadn't acted as she did, we might never have had any evidence against her at all, might not have even discovered she was involved.

"So what did he have to say about the murder?"

"That all he did was hide the body."

"That's all, huh?" This whole conversation was making me wish I hadn't eaten the pastries. I looked at Kitty, and she looked a little green, too. It made me feel better, and I took a deep breath to steady myself.

Ron had gone on. "Fingal says that when Ms. LeMoine started yelling at him, Ms. Waverly just picked up the scarf from the Lost and Found, and pulled it tight around her neck. Just like that." Ron gave a little twist of his hand to demonstrate, and I had to look away. "He seemed sort of stuck on that, how she just strangled the woman, no discussion, no nothing. Just did it."

"Why on earth," Kitty started to ask.

"She wanted no scandal. That's what she kept saying yesterday," I reminded her.

"But she must be crazy," Brian protested. "I mean, she thought she could cover up murder more easily than, than, the other?"

I had a more pressing question. "How the heck did the body end up in the freezer?"

Ron shook his head. "Fingal says she just ordered him to get rid of the body and went back into her office. He was going to take it to his car—he's not so dumb as all that. He figured he could dump it off a dock somewhere in the middle of the night. But he thought he heard Carlos coming, and panicked. The lunchroom was nearest, so he dragged her in there, and the freezer just sort of suggested itself."

"Carlos never said anything about staying late," Kitty started to say, then realized, "Oh! It was Chantal, of course, not Carlos."

"You'll be interested to know," Ron added, "that Fingal says Ms. Waverly messed with your computers, trying to destroy any other scandalous photos. So on some level she must have believed LeMoine, however much she denied it. He also admits he made the call to the station, hoping to get you in trouble before you learned too much. And I found about twenty boxes of ice cream bars in Fingal's freezer. Guess he couldn't bear to throw them out."

I had to ask. "Why on earth didn't he come back later and take care of the body, rather than leaving it and keeping the ice cream?"

"Because he was too scared. Once he was away from the school, he couldn't bring himself to come back. Of course, he didn't exactly say that, but I think it's a safe guess. Yet he never thought that the ice cream could give him away."

I shook my head. "What a bunch of stupid people," I said, before realizing how condescending that sounded. To my relief, Ron laughed.

"You could say that. But it's all a mess. Chantal

didn't actually see the murder, after all—just Fingal dragging away the body. Waverly says he must have killed the woman, because she went home at five, as usual. And that's all she'll say. Since she lives alone, there's no one to confirm or deny it. Though I've yet to see what she'll say when Chantal testifies that she was there."

"What about the little matter of attempted murder yesterday?"

"She says her actions were misinterpreted."

That seemed laughable. How could you "misinterpret" the bullet holes in Fingal and me? No one laughed.

We all sat for a while, thinking about just what it did mean. I would have asked if he knew who took the photos that had blown it all open, but Ron had fallen asleep, his head still resting on his hand. I never did learn that.

"Better take him upstairs and put him to bed," Kitty suggested.

"No way!" I glared at her. "Do not even tempt me!" Then I glanced at Brian and felt myself blushing. He appeared to be trying to smother a laugh.

"Oh, go ahead, Mom, I won't tell."

"Brian, this is a small town. Someone would tell." I shook my head. "No, you take him home, Kitty. I'm getting untangled from one man before I get tangled up with another." An unfortunate choice of phrasing, I realized as Brian's laugh escaped. I rolled my eyes at him.

"Oh, grow up."

Kitty giggled, so I directed the same comment at her.

Ron woke up enough to walk to Kitty's car, and mutter some thanks for the coffee. I patted his shoulder, and told him I'd see him at the trial.

Kitty drove him away, and I went back into the

house. Ron Karlson could wait. I'd solved his murder for him, and now I had my own business to resolve.

"Come on, Brian. Let's get cleaned up. We go see Ms. Kasper in an hour."

"We?"

"We." I put an arm around his shoulders, a not-quite-uncomfortable stretch. "I'm not going into battle without you at my side this time."

The phone rang. Brian answered and handed it to me. "It's Grandma."

I looked at the phone, took a deep breath, and reached for it. "Hi Mom. Sorry I haven't called. It's been kind of a hectic week."

About the author

Rebecca M. Douglass was raised on an Island in Puget Sound only a little bigger than Pismawallops. She now lives and writes in the San Francisco Bay Area, and can be found on-line at www.ninjalibrarian.com and on Facebook as The Ninja Librarian. Her books include the tall tales for all ages, *The Ninja Librarian* and *Return to Skunk Corners*.

Made in the USA
San Bernardino, CA
23 March 2014